the plum plum pickers

a novel

by Raymond Barrio

Canfield Colophon Books

A Department of Harper & Row, Publishers, Inc.

THE PLUM PLUM PICKERS

Dedication

this book is affectionately dedicated to
my wife Yolanda and our four little chicanos

FOREWORD

Raymond Barrio's "The Plum Plum Pickers" should cause a stir all along the Monterey Peninsula and a storm in Santa Clara County for the way in which the horrendous living conditions of the prune pickers are pictured.

The Santa Clara writer tells the story of Manuel and Lupe Gutierrez, Mexican migrants, and their children.

As he recounts the drama of their lives he alternates their story with hard-hitting shots at the "agricombines" that import the chicanos, oppress them, and defend themselves against the organizing pressures and aspirations of the Mexican and Indian-Mexican farmhands.

You meet a cast of characters like Turner, the company owner; Morales, the Spanish-speaking stooge-overseer; and Quill, the general manager of the Western Grande fruit plantation, as the figures come into conflict with a phalanx of migrant fruit pickers imported from Texas.

The story is at its best when it depicts the migrants in all their human warmth, victimization, and desperate yearning for better living.

Barrio, who knows his county and its inhabitants better than the sheriff, limns his fruit pickers against the beautiful mountainous background, the big Bay, and the California skies.

All the more wretched therefore is their denial in the congested camp conditions where they are consigned to live in squalid cubicles.

This picture of social conditions is a reminder of the earlier school of social and proletarian literature, but once more it seems valid and necessary.

There are millions of Spanish-speaking people in the United States, and many of these exist on the migrant-unemployed-disadvantaged level.

Barrio's novel speaks in a substantial way to that interest.

There are some beautiful scenes as the chicanos toil in the orchards, try to make do in their squalid camp lives, dream of better days to come, and look to the Mexican and Aztec heroes of the past for inspiration, so as to get on and above the level that they are now condemned to.

The novel is strongest when it pictures a mass of people unknown to their better-living neighbors in the expensive communities of the San Francisco Bay Area.

Seasonally these fruit pickers come into the news, then they are dropped out of it. Barrio gives us the year-around picture.

Human beings shouldn't have to live in the denied way we have consigned these dreamy, hardworking, hardliving, beautiful people to do.

— Earl Conrad

(—Author of numerous novels, as well as books on civil rights, such as his recent "The Invention of the Negro. ")

1

Bang bang. Crash.

A bonging garbage can lid, if that's what it was, came sailing out of California's blackest sky, and smashed a garage door to splinters. Morton J. Quill, his blubbery majesty, jumped a double somersault in his bunker. How about that. Now that didn't belong in the dream. He'd been driving his own hearse around carefully as usual, listening closely as usual, to all the underworld noises infiltrating his tender sleep. It was good that the crash came along when it did.

He pulled the covers back. He hesitated. He got up, breathing heavily, waddled to the door, opened it, and stared out at the insolent darkness. He stood there, testing his prescient powers, as though foreshadowing his own death, as though plums could be prevented from ripening relentlessly, as though the very skies would fall.

"What's your hurry, Quill?" grated a low voice, snapping him to the end of his tether. "It's only me, man. Pepe." It was indeed Pepe. Pepe Delgado, champion prune picker. Short, smart, and rotund like himself, materializing out of nature's blackest air. "Whatsa matter, el miserable pal?"

Quill, "I didn't hear you."

Pepe, "I sure had one bat of a good night I mean it." Meaning, drinking or wenching.

1

Quill, "You heard the crash."

Pepe, "That what it was. Man, it sounded like a cannon firing. Probably woke the whole camp up."

No, it didn't wake the whole camp, said Quill. Still, there was no use peering any longer into the offending darkness. "It was some idiot. Broke my window too."

Pepe whistled phew. "Eh what, amigo? Again? Like last time?" Crossing himself. "Madre de dios. The devil you say."

"It's getting to be a big lousy joke if you ask me." Quill felt immensely grateful for Pepe's oozing unctuousness even though he knew it was put on.

"I know, I know. Say, I got it. Call the cops."

"Ha."

"You must be right again, amigo. Sure, probably just what they want."

"It's signed 'Joaquin M.' this time. Stupid."

"You got to be kidding." Pepe whistled pheew softly again. "Joaquin Murrieta." Trilling the r hard rrrrrrrrrrr Spanish style. "The Metsican Robin Hood, eh. The terror of the gringos." He whistled pheeeeeew once more, long, low, fey, and mournful.

"But I don't believe it, Pepe. I don't believe a Mexican is doing it."

"You don't." Then, "Why not, pal?"

"It's too stupid."

"Yeah. You told me. Say, isn't there good and bad in nearly everybody. Sure. I'm always saying that. Say, why don't you try taking iodine? Bad Metsican, good Metsican, si si. Same for Gringo, Spinach, Kraut, Fang, Nit, anybody. Got it?"

Got -- "NO!" snapped Quill.

Pepe, thinking again of his woman as was his wont -- not necessarily his wife -- evidently felt he'd helped Mr. Quill enough and vanished in search of some sleeping prune pickers for his terrific crew. Mr. Quill remained rooted there in misery in the night light, his solid, forbidding martyrdom lying heavily upon the land like a giant gaseous burp.

Yeh. Yeh. Sure, it could have been a dog tossing a garbage can lid. A flying saucer. Sure sure. Or a cat. Oh yes. But not likely. Since he was such a peaceful man, why did they pick on him to take..... Mr. Turner's punishment? Why not ..... Mr. Turner himself? Taking in another deep breath by dawn's weary light, Mr. Quill shuddered. Slowly he took hold of his blubbery self once more. The Western Grande Compound.....

The Western Grande Compound, the pickers' paradise, the migrants' home away from home, his own proven domain, was also Mr. Quill's own private gravy land train. He was trying

2

to learn, and perfectly willing to let it be his undoing. Mr.
Turner's guidance was truly a godsend. Right at this moment,
however; right now, with the weather piling up, he found he
couldn't prognosticate right. Would they or would they not
pick prunes, all the prunes, and nothing but the prunes, those
pious and pretentious prune pickers? The slim pencil flash-
light trembled in his fingers as it unraveled the crudely drawn
words on the crumpled paper:

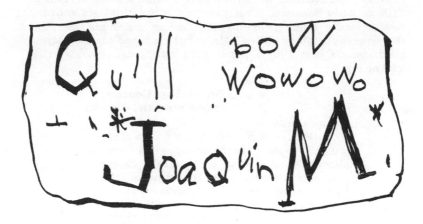

There it was. An accusation. In black and white. Very
crude. Tasteless. Slander. Ah yes. He knew -- suddenly a
sharp bite nicked his hip. Something -- bit him. Bit! Hadn't
had enough food -- a flea? -- he'd -- goddem mutts, sons a
bitching sure -- mark his words -- creaking garbage can lids,
empty beers, loose pits too, prune pits. Pretty smart for
prune picking country all right. Maybe hmmmmm. The paper
headline kept right on, big and black:

10,000 Migrants Leave Texas Behind for
Santa Clara County Annual Prune Pilgrimage

-- a hoked-up temporary emergency every year, a nightmare
in migration, a pilgrimage to help the gods get plumper. Well
if they didn't pick prunes, they'd have to eat dirt. Quill noticed,
not entirely to his surprise, that a new element had intruded
itself in Texas this year: the commendable and incredible in-
trigues of that brave Texas Ranger, Captain McAllee, the
tongueless wonder who never uttered a blasphemy, not a word,
and his brave band of real tough Rangers who silently slapped
hell out of Mexican celery strikers, tapping their skulls,
smacking hamburgers out of their mouths, banging them in

3

jail, stifling their protests, and cowering the judges. Ataboy Mac! That sure was the way to do it right. Cheers for the alligators, the new vigilantes. The grand old western days were closing in again, best wishes, hey, just like Mr. Turner liked to sigh.

Maybe pickers weren't smart as they used to be, nor so smart as Mr. Turner. But smart or sour they sure knew how to pick. Strike, eh. Signing the note Joaquin M. was one big mistake. At other times it was either Santa's Nose or Pancho Villa or Luis Bananaz. Pretty funny. In the dim light growing lighter by the minute, turning the flue up under his bitter pot of yesterday's gluey coffee, Mr. Quill focused his remaining good eye on yesterday's paper still sitting on the offending wicker chair:

Drawbridge Courier
May Sixteenth

Condemnation

(P.A.)--Some dwellings are no more than one-car garages occupied by families, according to Sunnyvale's Community Development Director in his preliminary report, preparatory to instituting condemnation proceedings.

Mr. Frederick Y. Turner, the highly respected bean grower and owner of the Western Grande Compound in question.....

Funny. Mr. Turner never cared for beans. He stayed with cots, grapes, cobbler, prunes, and cherries.

According to the order, building code violations include exposed wiring that could endanger lives, faulty or non-existent plumbing, lack of hot running water, termites and foundation inadequacies. One of the fifteen buildings, noted the Building Inspector, is an outdoor communal toilet for all the families as.....

What in hades did they want them to do. Crap outside. Die. Great scott, what the devil was wrong with a few leaky pipes. Those deranged inspectors. Just because they had running water. Blind. No heart. Yap yap yapping. They really did not care. Weren't these migrants much better off precisely because of Mr. Turner's limitless benevolence. The Western

4

Grande was only slightly weathered. House. Lean-to. Walls. Roof. A place to roost and cook and slap their tortillas around in was a godsend to most of the riffraff coming by here from Texas. And after all, thought Mr. Quill, innocently reversing himself every time the logic of the matter got too much for him, weren't these workers human beings too. Mr. Turner often said, and he was often absolutely right, that dogooders did all the world's total harm. Except Mrs. Turner; of course Jean Turner sure did a lot of good.

With a momentary thrill, Mr. Quill realized that the laundry might be aired on TV later in the day from San Jose or even on the evening news. Memories stabbed his chest, stimulating, in their turn, other sharper pains. He wished he could apply for a new heart at the Stanford Hospital. But wouldn't they just laugh at him? Hurriedly he tried thinking of other things. He had nothing, absolutely nothing to show for the miserable, rotten, stupid, empty life he was leading.

Well, whatever had been out there hugging the darkness was gone now. The Western Grande was slowly coming awake again, all set to rip another beautiful day to shreds. All the families were in various stages of wakeful destruction. A baby bawled. A pot banged. A candle sagged. A rectangle of yellow light shone spectacularly out of a black wall, signalling the start of a new campaign of terror. To think of it -- wanting to tear these beautiful handbuilt redwood huts down. Whatever for. For the love of God. Where would they go. A nasty trick, serving Mr. Turner with a thirty-day notice to demolish the "ghastly" buildings just because of some outmoded "alleged" building code violations, just when he was gunning for, or rather grooming himself for -- Mayor of Drawbridge.

The thrust was so patently political.

Mr. Turner, however, as everyone said, was one very shrewd cookie. No cowardly city council anywhere was going to pop any papers on him. Nossir. Where would the scum go. They couldn't very well camp in the garbage dumps. What was the good of raising good, fat, healthy, plump prune trees next to the garbage pits if you didn't also raise enough prune prickers? And they sure had some good pickers. Manuel Gutierrez in Cabin No. 9 was a good one; slow but efficient; never complained; always hungry; never caused trouble; his wife Lupe helped out too, although their tots often got in the way. Too many kids. Wasn't that the poor for you though. And wasn't it good for them to go out into all that fresh natural air and free sunshine, though.

Mr. Quill backed away from the shattered window.

He felt sick, shocked, stabbed.

The high-arched white wicker chair his grandmother made him take in a fit of pique stood there, silently accusing him.

He felt for his lumpy, greasy robe. Sleep was gone. A twinge of pain shot clear through his chest again. He rubbed the flea bite fiercely, getting indescribable relief from the insanity of the unbearable itch.

Now the sky was coated with dark handsome overlays of grays, all clear. A motorcycle ripped across the compound's enclosure, cut around Cabin No. 12, and vanished behind the Hangman's Tree. Mr. Quill satisfied himself that old Black Bart, the straw dummy, was still dangling from its giant limb in the cool night air. The prunes were ripening fast all right and maybe -- just maybe -- Mr. Turner might flip and give him his raise. What if there weren't enough prune pickers this season though. The camp wasn't even full. Would they get in in time from Texas. They were all bbbbbbastards.

Except Mrs. Ferguson. She was a first-class -- Phyllis Ferguson in No. 5, the cabin he called The Wheel of Fortune was obviously much too saucy a woman for her countless lovers.

"I've got to have it," gulped Quill to her the day before, referring, he thought, to the rent. She'd once threatened to move out, pure bluff, but succeeded in neatly scaring the few wits he had out of him

"Have what?" Mrs. Ferguson pried her luscious eyes wide in phantom innocence. So easy for her. It was practically impossible for him to choose between her honeymelon breasts and that small white patch of inner thigh she kept exercising by rubbing her leg against her robe.

"Never mind --"

(The story of the jewelry having come from San Francisco's most exclusive story was such an obvious lie; he always suspected that she had been a rather smart jewel thief, or a compulsive kleptomaniac from the very start, only to suddenly give up and turn to welfare and easygoing prostituting.)

"You're nuts," she said.

"I know just what you are inferring," he warned.

"You're sure? You do? You do know?"

"Yes. I Do Know."

"Then perhaps you'd better be more careful."

"Just what do you mean by that?"

"Just be more careful, sweetie."

He broke his visual contact, dropped his eyes, and wandered. He was at such a distinct disadvantage with her. She liked sleeping with anybody, pay or no, and yet -- there was no place to grab her by. Slippery. She was flip or sarcastic by turns. She was fat and blousy, cheerful and sousy, when she was up and sober. Two cockroaches in every coffee cup. Three to a pot. And the toast smoking briskly. What kind of monkey business would it be like living with her? A merry

6

widow without means, with the heart of a senseless girl --
"We prune pickers got to hang together," she'd lie. "Screw
'em all!" she'd shriek. He couldn't give up fantasying about
her, nor could he forgive her. The only sweetness he'd
ever wanted in all his life, as he'd never tasted any other,
and yet she both repelled and fascinated him, a truly crushing state of internal affairs. His insides bubbled.

2

In his rage, beside himself with bitterness, frustration,
and impotence, Mr. Quill often sat staring long and hard at
Mr. Turner's tintyped image fastened to the wall of his room
-- the Compound's office wall by day -- as though trying to
unravel the enigma of his worthlessness.

"I will fix you good, sir, if it's the last thing," he would
mutter, "I ever do."

It was, and he did.

3

When Lupe Gutierrez heard the crashing glass, her first wish was that they were breaking up the Golden Cork bar again. Good God, she prayed -- ay dios, dios.

She stumbled sleepily to the window, shaking the cobwebs from her mind, unable to make anything out at first. A dark shadow sped through the compound yard. She had to hold herself together. Manuel, Manuel, she whispered; he had to get up anyway. She hated to wake him. Who was that running like that for? And where were they running to? Or from?

She saw a dark hulk standing in Mr. Quill's doorway, and then another. She recognized Pepe Delgado talking to Mr. Quill. They were probably discussing plans to tear down the shacks after all. Their homes. That was it. They were already starting. She was ready to start crying. After all this time. Moving, always moving. From Guadalajara to Monterrey to Reynosa, then across the border to Laredo and then that hijo of a maldito malcriado hijo de la gran puta Texas Rangerr in Rio Grande City -- and now here, Santa Clara. Moving, moving, always moving. A big jump. She'd heard that that's what gypsies were like, and she didn't like it, not one bit. She? A gypsy?

An invisible motorcycle made a tremendous burst across the compound yard, cutting into her dark thoughts, and disap-

8

peared into the orchard behind the big hangman's oak, followed
a few minutes later, in the growing daylight, by a perfect stick
of six soldiers, no, wait, they were police, wearing crash
helmets with night sticks, waving in unison as in a night frieze,
as in a stark Greek tragedy.

The baby cried.

Lupe sighed. Crazy world. She shrugged her tired shoulders,
and turned the ghastly overhead bulb on.   Manuel, pobre hombre, poor man, was still profoundly asleep.   She would have to
wake him. What news she had to tell him. What a jolt that was
going to be. A Hell's Angel, and she crossed herself hard, for
she was sure that was what it was, or whatever it was, it had
to be the devil himself at play, could have roared right through
their shack and Manuel would not even have awakened.

> Ando borracho
> ando tomando
> el destino cambió mi suerte....

-- for when I'm drunk, moaned the girl on the radio singing
softly, I go around drinking, and fate has changed my luck....
The coffee pot bubbled merrily, joining contrapunta to the singer's romantic warbling.

> Yo -- yo, que tanto
> lloré por tus besos....

I -- I, who cried so much for your kisses --

> Yo -- yo, que siempre
> te hablé sin mentiras....

I -- I, who always spoke to you without lying, humming along,
Lupe pushed some strands of her hair back, holding Cati in
the crook of her arm, frying chile with eggs, pungent and
strong and good and healthy and noisily filling the air. Turning
around, looking back behind her, the one light globe piercing
her eye, she saw her little Manuelito wake up and climb upon
his father's sleepy head.   Then little Mariquita followed suit.
Lupe smiled.   A silent struggle ensued.   Soon Manuel sat up,
roughing their two little heads.   "Qué -- ah, qué pasó, cora-
zón?" He wanted to know what the matter was, my heart.

What was the matter?

Nothing.

Lupe, almost in tears, and the day not yet begun, held her
tongue. This rickety stove was what was the matter. This
stupid bare splintered wooden floor was what was the matter.
This one simple room was the matter. This lack of privacy

was also the matter. This having to walk down to the public
bathroom, sharing it with fifteen other families, was the mat-
ter. Those skimpy curtains were the matter too. And no hot
water was the matter. The children --
"Nada. " No, nothing, my heart. . . .
He heard some commotion outside. "Probably Ramiro and
his hot motorcycle, " he chuckled.
"Ramiro has a motorcycle?"
"Well, he says he was going to get one. "
"He says, he says. You and your cousin. "
"Aghhh, " sighed Manuel, as though explaining everything.
"Anyway, does it make much difference? He has no family at
least. Let him have his fun. He should enjoy himself. "
And we shouldn't. Lupe thought it but did not say it. Manuel
stood barewaisted and shaved at the tin basin next to the stove,
with the water brought in from the night before and heated on
the stove, the noise of his splashing mingling with the frying
chile. The children pulled his trouser legs, imitating his shav-
ing motions, as Lupe changed Cati's diaper on the cot. Cati
screamed out in rage, kicking her tiny legs furiously.
They ate their breakfast on the narrow crowded unpainted
wooden table in silence. Manuel, silent most of the time anyway, was by nature of a quiet disposition, which was just fine
for Lupe as she liked so to rant on and on. Except now. Now
she wanted to be quiet too. So many things were bothering her
all at once. The time the Texas Rangers arrested Manuel for
walking with the pickets, when she was too speechless to talk,
when the Ranger threatened to arrest her and take her children
from her, still frightened her, like a living nightmare. Afterwards, Manuel planned their move away from Texas, anywhere,
when he saw the children hungry. To try to find a little better
way, a less bitter way to live and to work and to find a little
joy. Lupe didn't want that to ever happen again. She prayed
it would never happen again. She would be good, she would be
quiet, please, dear dios, she would complain no more; at
least she didn't have the police to worry about here in Santa
Clara; she felt confident with them, and was confident they were
at least impartial, and for that alone she was grateful.
Serafina Delgado could make all the fun of her Pepe she
wanted to; half her children were already grown tall. She
could laugh and relax. But right now, with Manuel gone off to
the apricots or wherever Roberto Morales' gang was taking
him, that vicious Roberto, to pick the Della Sierra apricots
in Sunnyvale, Lupe just didn't feel like talking to anyone. She
felt in fact a little dizzy. A little? A lot. Ay dios, she hoped
she wasn't pregnant. That would be all she needed. She had
not been drinking, so that wasn't the cause. She leaned over

10

the cracked, chipped, badly mottled mildewed sink and pushed a loose hair back, looking into the raw new herringbone sky, and she found the only thing she really felt like doing was kicking their only broken chair. A thick, shiny, dark brown cockroach the size of a small mouse scudded past her toe with great confidence. She almost threw up. She had to get a good grip on herself. What in God's name was one more cockroach? It looked so much like a big ambulating red kidney bean. She couldn't help herself. She couldn't be pregnant. She just couldn't be. No, no, dear God, dios mio. She looked up through the smudge in the window at the gray sky, at all those gaunt silent plum trees outside, and prayed silently herself. She couldn't help pitying herself. The world seemed like a fury and all the gringos therein intent on lying and stealing and having their special fun and everything they wanted in huge carload lots, wholesale, special. And and and here and she couldn't even get herself a new dress. Not even a cheap dress. She wouldn't even be able to make one, with baby Cati taking all her time. She was trapped. Would she rob a stage? She didn't know what she'd do. Maybe they wanted her to become a cheap prostitute, like Phyllis Ferguson, who seemed so happy at her profession, making so many men happy, and so much easy money. Well, if she did it, she'd be a good one. She knew how.

But -- she couldn't.

She kept on dressing. Would any of her dreams ever come true? No? Would she get a new dress? No? Ever? Never? When hair grew on trees, perhaps. When would that be, Manuel, dear God, ay dios mio, Manuel out there, dios, dios dios, picking all those tender cots, everybody and Roberto's crew, picking like filching idiots in the hot maniacal sun to the limit all summer long, storing away like squirrels for the hungry fall hunger and the starveling winter, those long cold days, and for the nice rich people like the Turners, picking apricots, picking berries, picking pickles, picking luscious pears, picking prickly pears too, picking prunes, picking peaches, picking poison, picking grapes, stooping over to pick ripe tomatoes too, Ponderosa and those meaty tomatoes . Maybe they really did want her to become a prostitute. Maybe that was all there was to it. Mother, prostitute, and wife. Ay dios.

Into all those thrice-blessed crops poured the intense rays of God's own California golden sun, which should have pleased her some, and the fine sugary fragrances, which should have given her some small delight. Instead little creases of strain worried and pinched her, registering their annoyance on her usually calm, plump face.

She sat pensive for a long time, studying her little brown

11

ceramic statuette of la Virgen de Guadalupe, her namesake, and Mexico's greatest mother, a young, loving, smiling, peaceful, warm, life-loving madonna, so sweet and serene, so lost, so unperturbed, half in dim yellow light, half lost to subdued shadows, next to the torn window curtain casting its shadow against the rugged textured grain of the wall planks.

Hanging the diapers cold in the nippy morning air. The sun glinting gold in her face. Screeching bands of urchins from neighboring shacks in the compound. Flipping about like loose little Indian gods inside the Western Grande's enclosure. Yelling, hooting, hog calling. Hey, you pig! Manuelito, already a wise traveler at six, couldn't be enticed outdoors. Baby Cati at last lay asleep. Relieved, Lupe realized she'd awakened too early that morning. Baby Cati, that wiggly fat Mayan statuette, that entrancing beauty in miniature, lay comfortable and warm in her own private world, her orange-crate crib, cuddled in, breathing sweetly, beneath the lace-like shredded curtains, guarded over by her virgin. Manuelito lay back on the lumpy sofa, his little eyes closed, sniveling, shivering, moaning with a slight fever. Could it be the devil's own fever? Devil Mountains, and summertide, dios mio, what might not a summery fever bring. Mariquita, four and a half, sniffled and pulled her mother's thin dress. Lupe dried her hands on her apron and stuffed a radish in the child's mouth to quiet her, hardly listening to the radio's tinny blurb from San Jose:

> ah, summer is heah at last!
> warm lush fragrant beautiful
> summer!
> have you done your
> summer shopping yet?

The summer that was so full of idiotic impulses thrust itself forcefully upon Lupe's gentle fellow farm-folk. She could almost taste it. She could forgive almost everything that could be forgiven, even the sin of extravagance. All around Drawbridge, up and down Santa Clara County's unflappable peninsular towns, Sunnyvale and Mountain View, Palo Alto and Los Altos, Santa Clara and San Jose, practically anything that could be disgorged by the summer gods was disgorged. The sun beamed proudly down with its incredibly potent rays, fully meriting worship as man's most powerful god, from across incredible distances already being spanned by intrepid spacemen, stirring the seeds, pulling up the sap, energizing the green chlorophyll of countless billions of leaves. The whole trick, which Lupe hadn't yet been able to figure out, was how first to get ahold of some magic money, and then hire somebody to do all the stupid work. The springtime cornucopia of plenty was bursting and aching once again right on schedule, to turn anything out, anything anyone wanted or could ever want. Delightful riches everywhere in stores were for everybody, for ordinary orchard owners, for simple farm folk, for common growers, for truck drivers, for pleasant professors, for sincere citizens, for efficient processors, for supermarketeers, charge checkers, inspectors, generals, governmental agricultural bureaucrats, cockroaches, rats, not to mention forty million thrifty American housewives. For everybody, fortunately, forever, thanks be to God, except -- for the fruit pickers.

Lupe listened.

She listened to the cicadas and to the worshiping branches, praying that her Manuel, lost out there somewhere in those lush vast early morning orchards, picking fruit, wouldn't dare get into another fight.

At times she indulged in lush dreams of Guadalajara.

At times her inner tensions were unbearable.

At times she relieved her formless yearnings by visions of enormous mansions and sweeping closecropped green lawns.

Her strange inner mirages had a nasty tendency of twisting, changing shapes, and finally disappearing.

She couldn't have a clean dream.

Mr. Quill, no mirage, sat there, plump and contented, the general manager of the Western Grande, out in front of his country store, living it up, nibbling on goose liver, munching popped corn, draining beer cans, dispensing ice cream, dreaming he was alive. Not much help there. What was Miami like ? Should they have gambled on Florida instead? She'd heard it was even worse. So here they were, stuck in California. Forever. Manuel, having to hitch a ride again with Alberto's crew, causing Silvestre to grumble, to get to the tomato paste patch in time, or to the apricot line, or whatever it was they had to pick that day. Manuel's own used car refused even to cough. And he had no money for repairs. Troubles always came doubles. Manuel had no license either. Another trouble. She could have smashed the window into flying shards in that insolent sun. She could have knocked the wind out of her dreams to let the evening breezes in, the sweet air she remembered painfully from her yesterday's girlhood in Salpinango, near Guadalajara. It had been so sweet; now life was so complicated. She didn't go back because -- because they couldn't. How could they? She could easily knock the dirty grease stained window out with a cup, and build at least half a cathedral of dreams with memories. But they didn't have even half a brick to call their own.

Four of Manuel's compañeros, Alberto, Silvestre, Jesus and Santiago -- four galloping fruit pickers from Rio Grande

City in south Texas -- traveled all over the country summers together, picking oranges down south, the lemons, melons, squash, the beans and walnuts for the gringo gueros chingados sponging off humanity in this permanent disease called California, the newest of most modern tortures, offering many fineries before your dangling tongue and never, never letting you sip. Those four traveling caballeros shared cottage No. 12, jestingly christened the Bar-Noon Saloon by Mr. Quill. Two of them unmarried, the other two with families back in their Texas home. They traveled all over the western world picking crops together, from Texas to Idaho, Arizona to Fresno, to Oregon and back, high roads and low roads, made no difference, 99 or 101, laughing, pushing on. Lupe didn't really mind them, they were so funny, making her laugh, making Manuel laugh, she liked that, Manuel was so serious, and they were countrymen. The one thing they did which as a woman she did not like she could do little about: she didn't like their dragging Manuel to the Golden Cork cantina across the boulevard on El Camino Real for their Saturday night hijinks. To dine on beer. Manuel could drink up a whole day's pay in one night. Though most of their big debts were once again nearly paid up, they were still in debt to Mr. Quill and Mr. Turner for the unpaid part of last winter's food and lodging.

Manuel, he worked very hard and he could find work where others gave up. He certainly did work hard. Certainly he had a right to a little distraction. But didn't she also? Of course she did. Fighting to keep a tear from spurting out, Lupe squashed the sponge in her dripping fist. The dishes took an unmerciful beating that morning.

Plump plum trees filled the fertile land for miles around. Hundreds, thousands of plump prune-making plum trees in neat rows all the same size and all the same height, all pruned exactly the same way. Her own hunger, the babies' food, their very survival depended on the wellbeing of those thousands of prune trees. Without them, without their fruit, they could.... do worse. Fruit and vegetable picking and stooping over meant backbreaking, backstraining work, with only very little energy for laughter left over. Sweat and grime and flies and dirt and stink and latrines and pain and endless aches and fear and tired nights were always the most certain pay of all. Mr. Turner owned many of the cherry orchards too. Was there nothing he did not own? The cherries were already ripe. They went fast. The apricots would soon be under way. The prunes would be next, and the walnuts would come in later in the fall, all marching endlessly down the rows, picking, plucking, gathering, filling, boxing, crating. How could there be so much cultivated fruit? How could one single man own so much? The honied huns, fat little yellowglow ping pong apricots had to be

14

gathered before they too fell splat, before they puddled into apricot mud on the ground for ants and earwigs to reincarnate themselves into still more useless ants and earwigs, varmints of the earth, something just a little lower than the fruit pickers themselves.

Lupe dipped her head forward, hunched, leaning on the sink. She studied her scuffed shoes. ... her worn, misshapen, and scotchtaped shoes. She thought of her only other pair, the high heels that hurt so when she walked in them, as she was not used to them, and she thought of how some ladies owned as many as three and even four pairs of shoes. What would it feel like to own her own home? Or just a little square plot of earth just to plant her tiny avocado tree in? A dream. Yes. A fool. Tonta. Si. A crazy dream. Un sueño loco. Ay dios dios. Just looking at the hundreds of boxy new houses hedging in all the flat land of the valley all the way up to San Francisco, fifty teeming miles of rich, happy growth, knocking down the orchards, made her sick.

This was paradise, they all said.

4

"Pepe!"

"Eh? Ah!" Pepe's corpulence stood out against the brilliant shadows, way out in the farthest corner of Mr. Turner's favorite prune orchard. "Mande, mi corazon!"

In the Mexican lexicon -- "What is thy wish, my heart?" -- the heart and the fruit and the pulp and the juice and the food and the seed and the spit and the joy are all naturally intertwined, all mixed in with a great deal of art and pride and without shame.

Serafina called. "Desgraciado!"

"Who? Me? Yo?"

"Sin verguenza!"

"But why should I be ashamed?"

"Because you are neither fulfilling your fat destiny nor the bare buckets enough, you enormous pendejo." Serafina, her patience strained, had difficulty controlling her ire.

Pepe was not easily intimidated. "Do not worry, vieja. Margarita will do my share."

"Ah --" Serafina slapped the air with her hand and bent down to the tiresome, monotonous task of gathering the plump plums fallen to the sweet ground like light purple manna from the heavens, looking light like bluepurple circular rugs under each tree. The cool air, shaded from the burning sun, filtered sweetly through the branches. Truly, Margarita was doing her share and more. Slim, quick, serious, a thorough mystery to her mother, the seventeen-year-old was also a pride. Truly Pepe was most certainly not doing his rightful share. He was truly loafing. He complained about it. That's what they always said, eh, those gringo hijos de la chingada with the blind blue eyes. The question of being with shame -verguenza- or without shame -sin verguenza- was not altogether academic. It would take a strong man all day to gather in a ton of prunes, forty boxes weighing fifty pounds each, to earn perhaps fifteen dollars. That was how a whole family, gathering plums on their knees together, helped fatten the family larder. True, Margarita also had her own destiny to work out, but in the meantime there was a little matter of filial respect which she wasn't altogether insensitive to. Too bad the same couldn't be said of her brother Danny.

A policeman, coming into the trees, politely inquired where Ramiro was. Ramiro who? responded Serafina. Ramiro Sanchez, snorted Pepe. Margarita looked up, startled, opened her mouth, then shut it again. He is Manuel Gutierrez's cousin, offered Serafina, shutting Pepe up. Where can we find him? inquired the law politely. Serafina shrugged her shoulders, lifted her palms, smiled, and said, Quien sabe? They wanted to know. Well, well. Mr. Quill had admitted him to the outermost shack, an unused tool shed, but after that first day, he was never to be found again. Young fellow, shock of thick black hair. He was a cat driver. He was also a prune picker, a hoer, grazer, ridger, weeder, insecticider, irrigator, and pruner. He could go anywhere, this Ramiro Sanchez. He could do anything. Why do you want him? asked Serafina. Just talk to him, they said, and left. Soon after his arrival he was in the Golden Cork bar when Danny, Margarita's brother, was in danger of getting beat up, and Ramiro spirited him out of the way. Margarita was furious with herself for spoiling Danny shamelessly, another shamelessness loosed upon a craven world, another excess love, for Danny would surely end up in serious trouble some day.

"Why did those men want to hit you?" she wanted to know.
"God, I don't know, sis."
"They must have had some cause."
"God, there were these three other chicanos there and, well God, sis, you wouldn't get it."
"What were you doing in the bar?"
"God, do I have to tell you everything?"
"You were probably buying cigarettes in the machine."
"That's your line."
"Because they wouldn't dare serve you a drink."
"You seem to know it all."

16

"I see."

She saw. What was important was to let Danny keep his budding machismo intact, his budding manhood, like the young bull he was, without getting himself killed. She would find out soon enough. Her papa, though strict, when in the mood, would often spout out what was on his mind.

"That's what they always say, eh, corazon, those diablos with the blue eyes? Eh? That we chicanos like to loaf? Well you can bet your lace boots I love to loaf." Pepe loved to loaf all right, all year, if he could. He was the best walking, talking, loving example of the perfect mañana man. "Y por que no? And what the devil is so wrong with that? I use my brains instead." A logic not easily dislodged. But Danny's anger had been aroused and as long as Danny remained angry, Margarita feared for his safety. The unspoken contract between them let her go just so far in judging or advising him. She would, by mere instinct, by her mere presence, help guide him safely through the dangerous, treacherous shoals of young manhood. In old Mexico, she well knew, the mortality among young hot bloods ran high, and the blood ran swift. Under certain circumstances remaining alive was more important than pride. Often it was merely a question of timing, giving him enough of a chance to cool off.

Now they were having to concentrate all their energies on the harvests, for temper was another luxury none of them could really afford. When the fruit was ripest, when the fruit was most luscious, the picker was the one who paid most of all -- for being last, lowest, and least on the human scale.

Pepe, a good friend of Manuel's, tried hard to hold back his resentment. Ramiro Sanchez, Manuel's cousin, had no sooner arrived in their midst than he accused Pepe of dishonestly creaming off some of his crew's earnings. Which was not exactly the most tactful way of breaking into a new social grouping.

At the Golden Cork, that Saturday night, Pepe sat back by himself, nursing his resentment privately, watching the others, Silvestre and Alberto, Manuel and Jesus, laughing and joking among themselves.

"How did you get the fuzz off your back, Ramiro?"

"It was so easy."

"You got a goddem rabbit's foot."

"I didn't do nothing, hermano."

"Let's tip up another beer here, hermanos."

Ramiro smiled. Why not? Within the dark interior of the Golden Cork the smoke slowly swirled and intermingled, garish red bulbs mixed with blue, making evenglows everywhere, every night Saturday night, evengloss, the happiest nights of the year, when work was temporarily forgotten, when happi-

17

ness was a foaming glass of suds, when bosses and snots and chiselers and pennypinchers and pinchi cabrones and when box after box after stupid box of stupider apricots were stuffed away for gross consumption. Overhead, the thick chiseled beams ran the length of the ceiling, black against white. Lengths of chartreuse, mauve, and charcoal gray crepe criss-crossed back and forth across the beams from front to back. The return of the natives, redskins turned south, Aztec to Tenochtitlan, and now coming back north again to Santa Clara. It was all carefully worked out, the destiny of the race. Very clear, the babble of voices. Very fortunate, the escape from ancient tribute. Very cunning, the confrontation of modern ir-ritations, all leading to the cultural death of a whole people. Splotched and tassled cloth posters, tacked to the walls, de-picting bullheaded toros in various upward thrusts, necks taut, horns out, blood glistening from the banderilla wounds, showed signs of great age. Blood, the universal cleanser. Blood, the Aztecs' sacrificial offering, from freshly palpitating hearts. Blood -- but who wanted blood any more? Who? Who?

Zeke Jonson, a great luminous mechanic who occupied shack No. 6 of the Western Grande, pushed the cantina door open with a slight roll of his heavy shoulders, and lumbered in. Another silent bull of a man until provoked. He propped himself against the bar, slowly raised his idiot finger, picked up the sweating bartender's fast beer serve, knocked it off with one long gulp, then looked around. Pepe was still sitting alone, grimly deter-mined to down another night. Silvestre, still trying to catch Ramiro in a lie, looked around too. The others, Jesus, Manuel, wily Alberto, sat around smiling their friendly acquiescence that all was all right with the world. It was sure one big nice wonderful world all right, the best possible.

"Hey."

Silence.

"You."

A bar silence, when someone commands Hey You, usually turns sour.

"Hey, I said," said Zeke, rolling his heavy silvery gut up to Silvestre's table. Silvestre, usually happy-go-lucky, equ-ally heavy-set, scowled and turned his head away.

Ramiro Sanchez, born in south Texas of Morelian campesi-nos from Michoacan, had already invested all the dream life he'd ever want. What he wanted now was to live, to really live. He'd invested a good portion of his twenty-four years making steady progress toward sweetening the condition and circumstances of his birth: born Mexican by descent, and an American citizen by birth had caused him to end up here among the prune pickers of Santa Clara County with an insolent idea that this wasn't exactly the most ideal existence available to

18

him out of all human misery.

He had time.

He figured he had time to spare to make things hot for -- well, things couldn't get much hotter than in Texas. "That jail in Brownsville sure is mighty warm." Chow not too bad either. Free frijoles. Hey. Meaning: he got lumps on his head only if he glared back at the Rangers. Mexicans were very welcome in south Texas as long as they stayed in their place, kept their mouths shut, picked all the celery they could, and never complained. How else could the ranch owners, those great humanitarians, and fat growers get fatter otherwise?

He had just -- a weird circumstance. Here, now in San Jose, he'd just heard that a famous County Supervisor, after many miserly years in power, ranting against supposedly lazy Mexicans, had just gotten the roughest jolt of his life -- under-estimating the mood, as well as badly underestimating the e-lective power of the local Mexican community, found himself goosed right out of his good office. Pow. Just like that. Too bad. He had to go back to his used car lot and highly profit-able real estate business in Los Altos or Los Gansos or Los Cochis. What a shame. What a loss. So it was happening to the piggy as well as the mighty. Well well well.

A weird circumstance. Despite his restlessness, Ramiro Sanchez was very much impressed by that electoral ticket. Living in his abandoned tool shed on the edge of the Western Grande, even more abandoned than the other shacks, Ramiro Sanchez enjoyed collecting his own places to work in, weeding, driving, spraying, anything, bug juicer. His ancestors had fought off the cindery blasts of mighty volcanoes, had dipped flaky fish out of deep cool lakes with their graceful butterfly nets, had fought off the greedy hacenderos, and before that, resisted the greedier Spanish gachupin conquistadores. The grito of Padre Hidalgo, still echoing in his soul, lay still, and unanswered. When oh when padre, do we stop stooping and start collecting our liberty and our ardor and our justice and our equality and our brotherhood of man? They were big ideals, no mere thoughts, gritty bits imbedded in his hard, lean flesh, in his muscle-hardened flesh, muscles hardened by climbing countless trees and ladders, working thoughts in rows, walking millions of rows, lungs purified by countless wafts of pure un-filtered air, fingers made deft and flinty and wrists locked hard.

"Hey, I said," repeated Zeke, scraping along a chair and jutting his big square jaw out into space. "How come you Mix cain't talk Merican lak me."

The silence thickened.

"Tell you what," he added, shifting a wad, rubbing foam from his mouth. His head bobbed as though trying to dodge a miniscule boxer. "Say, tell you what. I'll roll dice any man here nest round, hokay."

"Zeke," said Pepe softly, from behind the shadows. "You go get yourself home now."

"Zit," said Zeke.

"You had enough now," said Pepe.

Zeke rolled his gnarled, bumpy head and waited for his blobby eyes to focus themselves on Pepe. Pepe looked back at him steadily. "You know sometin, Pepe. You a no damned good chicano. But I lak you. You. You roll. Hokay."

"Christ, Zeke."

"No. Roll."

"Bullshit."

"Whatsa matter."

"You know."

"My dough ain't good as yours."

"You better believe it."

"You know what --"

"Yeah."

Zeke blinked, opened his mouth, laughed, "Haw haw."

"Hey," said Ramiro Sanchez quietly, from Zeke's left, "Why the hell don't you clear the hell out of here, flannel mouth."

Everyone's eyes swiveled instantly to Ramiro. Had he gone crazy? Ramiro leaned back, looking straight at Zeke.

"Hey," said Zeke, relaxing, unbelieving, blinking. "You sound funny. You sure do sound funny. Anybody ever toll you dot, son? Who you anyway?" Zeke blinked three times in a row, and shook his mangy head like a great snowy bear.

"Vete, pendejo," whispered Pepe fiercely to Ramiro. "You looking for a domingo fight? I know how to handle this one."

"Now, no, now you roll," repeated Zeke carefully to Ramiro, rounding every syllable sonorously, leaning forward, holding the cup of dice outstretched.

Ramiro did not move.

Nobody moved.

Zeke tipped forward.

Ramiro moved slightly aside.

The heavy man floated to the floor as gracefully as a sopping wet mop and splashed.

"Now you done it," said Manuel.

"Done what," said Ramiro.

"What'd you go do that for," said Pepe.

"Shut up, pop," said Silvestre.

"Let's get outa here," said Jesus.

Jonson was out cold.

"You guys get him out of here," yelled the irritated bartender, wiping three glasses dry at one time. "You hear me. I don't want no more goddamn raids like last week."

"Where do we take him?"

"I don't care. Just take him out."

It took three of them to raise Jonson's hulk. Pushing, hauling, grunting, tugging, they swung him out at last, like a prime sack of Idaho's pride, U. S. stamped as OK spuds.

Top grade. Made it. Another weird circumstance. What could they do with an inert body? They pushed him into Jesus' shiny new Chariot 666, fully loaded, fully intending to return him to his beloved in shack No. 6, finding themselves, however, rolling out along El Camino Real, all lit up with reverential restaurants and mapoline furniture stores and lit up gas depots and twinkling shopping centers and red tights outlets, and out to Alviso Road where the Guadalupe River dumped itself into the salt flats, cruising along a long thin ribbon of smooth black asphalt.

At one intersection a police car was waiting.

Jesus gunned the motor slightly. It immediately spurted forward. The bobbing red light blinked on and the black widow started its charge. The railroad signal ahead also flashed on. Jesus squeezed across the rakish tracks just in the nick of evening as the SP Express from Los Angeles flashed across his tail's exhaust, cutting off the hot pursuit. Then, in order to turn and pass his tormentor coming head on, Jesus drove the hearse into a dirt road in the darkness, bumping along, getting narrower, the headlights piercing the black gloom exposing growing mounds of stinking garbage. He stopped. Road's end. They all got out. They looked around. They unlimbered their beer filled hoses. They splashed a good long heartfelt piss into the black mire, soaking everything in reach. They were floating in the midst of a sea of garbage, all lit up by the light of the romantic moon, lovingly delineating every scrap, every crump of used paper, every bent straw, every spent can of lucky, every piece of string, every spawn of stinking, decaying, moldy, barnacled bananapeel. Mounds and mounds of pure useless garbage gently degenerating in the warm moonlight.

Suddenly Zeke Jonson jumped out the other side, shrieking "YEEOW!" like a gang of banshees were after him, hot on his tail, flopping and lurching into that messy garbage. He flopped. He rolled over. He flipped on his back. He got up, arms outstretched. He slipped. He slid deeper into the mess. He sloshed among his ancestral antibodies, in the garbage and the slush and the sludge and the slime and the mess of his primeval spirit coming home to roost at last, the last and final discard of the meatiest and most, most modern of civilizations.

They couldn't find him.

"Ah, let him be," said Pepe.

"Si," said Manuel.

"He'll sleep it off," said Jesus.

They backed out of there and purred politely past the patiently waiting black widow, expectantly parked in its accustomed station back at the fruitful crossroads of life.

Waiting   waiting   waiting.

5

Phyllis Ferguson, fat and blousy, stood smiling at her open door, waiting, waiting, waiting, licking the tears streaming down her full round cheeks. She'd heard the crash and heard the roar of a motorcycle passing through the compound. Anything the matter? In the bustling dawn, anything could happen. Silvestre, passing by, on his way back from the community latrine, stopped short in the dawn darkness, backed up, and went up to ask her, "Anything the matter, m'am?"

"No," she lied. "As a matter of fact -- why, yes, the faucet won't work."

Won't work? Silvestre followed her inside. His softly whistled pheew followed him inside. Never had he seen such elegance, such opulence, such corpulence, such a beautiful interior. Son of a bitch. Never had he seen such a beautiful carpet. Such a soft, thick, fluffy carpet. On the floor. Hombre. He could really lie down and really go to sleep on that carpet. Man. What a son of a bitchin carpet.

"What did you say?"

"I say, hombre, what a carpet."

The furniture was beautiful too. A tall highboy stood in one corner, rimmed with a gold-rimmed oval mirror shining above. A small frilly lamp with a pink globe glowed dully on a paradise night stand beside her Hollywood couch. The couch was

covered with an intricately woven moorishly arabesqued bed-
spread. The inlaid table, Delft china, mosaic chairs and all
the rest of the handsome furniture glowing and gleaming in the
semi-darkness made him feel like Pancho Villa really won the
revolution. Even the window was closed off with a thick luxu-
rious drape, almost as thick as the rug.

"Over there."

Over there was an exquisite Roman white-veined gray marble sink. He turned one faucet on. Nothing. He turned the
other. Also nothing.

Ah, he ah'd, dropping to his knees and tapping his forehead,
then tapping the control faucets down below.

Ah? she echoed.

Ah, he said again, opening and shutting them. Nothing.

You pay your water bill? he asked.

What water bill? she asked.

You don't....

No.

But the water is not connected.

That is right.

But --

But of course not, she admitted. Are you new here? she
said at last, lounging back on her soft sofa, running her arm
along its length, reclining. He stood there.

He stood there in the darkness, like a dummy, a raging
idiot, looking down upon the incredible beauty of her crossed
animal legs gleaming dully in the darkness, her robe fallen a-
way. More than hinting at the stark ripeness of her magic pad.
What the hell was she ever up to anyway?

Wait -- she said.

Whatever for, por el amor de dios, he husked.

Money first, she said, tapping her palm.

He'd already ripped his pants off, and he had to stop right
smack in the middle of his greatest desire and grope through
his goddamn pockets on his knees in the dark for his last lousy
two dollars. He would earn more money later that day picking
prunes, but right now he had to get his just desserts before
breakfast.

Ummmm, she sighed. Ummmm, he grunted, pawing her
yielding blubber down to the softly, magnificently carpeted
floor, pulling off the rest of her robe, pressing her bare bottom
squeezing her titties, nibbling her generous nipples, perching
on her thighs, opening up, swelling up, hardening against
softening, squashing and pushing, ummmm, she sighed, rolling and bumping, fondling his pair of pendant prunes.

Man, he said, all relaxed. What a dandy --

What, she said.

What a dandy, dandy rug, he said.

6

Strange.

Very strange. Mr. Quill was sure he'd locked, padlocked, and doubled the latches on Zeke Jonson's car to the stanchion in front of No. 6, the Wells Fargo. But Zeke Jonson's beat-up though remarkably smooth-running old Chevy was not there.

Not --

No, not in its place. Jonson was three weeks, three blasted weeks behind in his rent. That wouldn't do. Not do. Not at all. No. No sir. No no. Not not. Now, Mr. Turner --

Mr. Quill walked up the dusty, sandy, dirty compound yard, very nonchalantly smiling and bowing at all the suspicious pickers' wives out hanging the laundry, or just hanging out, sidestepping the screaming kids, and quite deferentially examined the ground around where Jonson's Chevy should have been firmly fettered. His practised eye caught signs of scratching and scuffling in the sandy grit. He should have been an Indian agent. Yes. Ah yes. He should have known. A temporary forgetfulness on his part. That zephyr Zeke, that unholy son of a bitch, being a master mechanic of course, simply got out his little portable acetylene torch and gently bit through each chain.

Mrs. Jonson, red-eyed, scragglyhaired and screwey, came out looking like a well-stuffed, well-hidden eel.

24

"You looce shomting?"

Mr. Quill, quivering, shook his generous jowls.

"You look for dot miserable rotten no cood sunavabitchen Zeke? Ah?"

Mr. Quill stood still, still swaying, saying nothing.

"Well because he come in stinko this morning again all cover all over with stinko garbage from head to butt and he said to toll you to go to hell he was going to show you how he gots a chob and he be back later with the rant if it's awe right which you. You wanna trow me out?"

Mr. Quill sighed, shook his head slowly, and walked off as Mrs. Jonson slammed the door so hard his teeth rattled.

No sign of anything. No links. No bits of chain. No car. No nothing. Quill realized he'd made one more maladjusted misjudgment of human frailty. There was no end to the price he had to pay. Was there no justice in this rank world?

MAN KILLED IN BAR BRAWL
CAUSED BY ROLLING DICE

-- ran the terrible headline. Simply terrible. Now why couldn't that happen to Jonson? Simply terrible. When would grown men learn to resolve their just differences in a more peaceful manner? He read on, filled with morbid curiosity:

> (A. P.) -- Gilbert got up and left the bar, saying that he would be back in about five minutes. He did return, and after stepping up to the bar he deliberately gave Sullivan a shove, pulled out a 45 and fired once.

RAZING OF SHACKS ORDER HALTED

-- ran another headline. Well. Finally. Hmmm. Mr. Turner had his way after all. The power began to flow once more in the proper direction. That put Mr. Quill in a happy frame of mind. He liked music. Da da de de da de de de hmmmmm hummmmmm da da dit. "Good morning ladies and gentlemen, or is it evening, haha ha --" The music was interrupted by a special news broadcast:

> Now look here Mr. ran Mrs. America,
> I have nothing but your sordid interest
> at heart for this is none other than Rat
> Barfy from Hono with another lulu for
> you in the middle of an island da dum
> in the middle of the good friendly old

Pacific. Ma, it's clear here tonight.
My theme tonight, however, lazy gen-
numen is -- believe it or not -- equality.
That's right. I shall now proceed to
prove to each of you that equality does
not exist. EQUALITY DOES NOT EE-
XIST. There you are. I have proved...

Mr. Quill sat down. He had to.
The profound logic was almost too much for him.

Yes, Lincoln was wrong. Yee, honest
old Abe was all wet, that reprobate,
dead wrong in proclaiming that all men
are created equal. The U. S. Constitu-
tion is wrong too. And the Supreme
Court Justices, while I'm at it. Anybody who believes in equality is wrong.
Wrong, wrong, wrong. Just think it
over, my pinko freakybop nincompoops.
Thank you. I'll thank you more if you
remember to send in your ten cents,
that one thin dime, to this here broadcast, that keeps me going, yawl hear
all you cotton pickin cats yawl?

Mr. Quill hurriedly wrote down the station number as he'd
forgotten to send in his thin dime the week before and he wanted
to be sure that that that marvelous Mr. Ratatat Barfy kept
going zing with his magnificent broadcasts, even if it took his
last dime. Barfy was so much righter than those other pinko
freakybop commentators. He prayed silently that Rat Barfy
would be able to keep it up forever. Goodness knew he needed
him, and what was good for Barfy was good for the century,
and the mad, mad country, for his poor, poor country growing
strangely more and more socialistic every day in every way.
Even growling Howlin Mad Nolan, that wonderful Governor,
when he wasn't plotting his next sales tax raise, in order to
help cover the rent on his $1,000 month mansion, had nothing
but praise for Rat Barfy.
    It shouldn't have mattered to Mr. Quill the kind of private
life Mr. Turner led which certainly, as he well knew, if anyone did, was far from blameless. It shouldn't have mattered
to him the devious turnouts that Mr. Turner's busted psyche
was capable of undertaking, the somersaults, the crooked
leaps.
    But it did matter.
    It was Mr. Quill's job to keep books, booze, hog, fat, and

26

pig bristle together. Besides minding The Stores. He was not Mr. Turpitude Turner's moral forager, true. If anything, it was the other way around. That still didn't help any, for Mr. Quill constantly had to face one terrible dilemma after another.

For one thing, he couldn't quit yearning for a raise, yet he couldn't force himself to broach the subject.

Which was a frustrating dilemma. Mr. Quill simply did not dare test their relationship. How long had it been since he'd dared squeak up and question any turpitude of Mr. Turner's, no matter how crude? For the years that he'd been manager and chief warden of the Western Grande barely managing to scrape by on the stringy prunepicking celery salary the scruffy old scrooger paid him, the only thing Quill had managed to grow was madder. There were some glowing moments when he felt he was really quite mad. It was dawning on him that he was staying on, not simply because it would be extremely difficult for him to ever find, if not nigh impossible, another job of at least equal responsibility and prestige, even in a cult factory, herding dung; it was also dawning on him that these miserable migrant workers gave him a kind of a floor.

At least he had some souls he could look down upon.

Which in turn kept his sanity up.

There it was. A fact. There were others who were actually in more miserable straits than he. Mr. Quill suspected he badly needed this kind of propping up. Chuck and Olive Pope, now, in Cabin No. 7, the projected Post Office, now weren't they really and truly the most miserable human couple ever, he'd ever seen, unmarried, she pregnant, and and he a retard?

Quill raged, raged in the dirty silence of his dreary cell, ruminating, bitterly swallowing his bile over and over. His badly beaded little eyes rested on the large old-fashioned tin-typed poster of Black Bart which, in fact, represented a resplendant Mr. Turner in one of his youthful theatrical disguises before becoming a monster of Satan in undisguised arrogance, a genuine curl on his surly lip, a real western gambler, a pig-headed, bigmouthed, narrowhipped, thickskinned, blackhaired varmint who was so loose and so lowdown mean as to masquerade as a minister. And with mean little red eyes.

Mr. Quill, standing there in his greasy little room, swimming in selfpity, looking on in envy, in mock contrast, potbellied, pearshaped, broomstick armed, he, Mr. Quill, realized that the only feature in which he came anywhere near close in comparison to Black Bart, as impersonated by Fred W. C. Turner, were in his mean little sunovabitchin red eyes.

Since his eyes, therefore, were his best feature, Mr. Quill narrowed them still more as he muttered his worst imprecation. "Dzang dzang," he dzanged, looking about him. Dzang it all, the day I quit, he fantasied, that miserable day this whole shebang, this entire stupendous Western Grande will sink sloppily into its own mud, into this sickly bay of oblivion, and scatter everything in it to the four......... quite a windy fellow.

Remorse, perhaps. But not shame. No, not shame. Inter-twined with pride, perhaps with a little shame. The sun climbed higher, burning off its morning dew, as all of Santa Clara County sang another hosanna of hallelujah. With all of its hun-dreds upon thousands of acres of ripening plums and cots and cherries, the county was certainly in grave danger of overdoing it -- of feeding the world in all its sunny exuberance.

As manager of the Western Grande, a degrading position for so many, many years, Mr. Quill was imbued with a cer-tain feeling of emptiness, a profound defeatism. Once upon a time he had been a moral, model, normal, reasonably sappy young man with the usual loafer's chance for some kind of dis-creditable success. Keeping himself alive, say. His only guilty fling at matrimony ended in his bride's snapping her cork and leaping abruptly out of the church foyer shrieking, "Oh my God what am I doing?" As his meaningless years flopped lazily by, literally killing time, he gradually uncov-ered all of his unlimited shallowness, which was quite exten-sive indeed. But hardly anything he could brag about, or put down in an application blank. His talents suffered least, he found, when saying yessir and nossir to anybody, anybody at all, first as night clerk in flop houses, where he didn't have to mess with real human beings, then eventually graduating to become charge d'affaires of Mr. Turner's hobby lobby, this great greedy business venture, this sleeper for agricultural migratory vagrants, this marvelous tax loss.

If seven members of the same migrating family of vagabond farm workers could be smothered together into one low-priced vestibule, everyone was happy. The family. Mr. Quill. Mr. Turner. The only alternative left such a feisty family was that of sleeping squashed together in their car or by the roadside -- a toe-to-toe togetherness that was never hinted at in any of Lord Hume's books nor by the Larks, the Ladies Auxiliary Royal Kitchen Society, of which Dame Jean Turner was social chairwoman -- as in the good old days of yore and gore.

Mr. Quill's perpetual, long drawn-out one-sided war with his boss was not entirely devoid of subterranean pleasure for Mr. Quill. Mr. Turner himself had also started out exactly like Quill, on the bottommost rung, except that Turner was smarter and luckier. Beyond that, Mr. Quill had never had to meet a payroll.

Frederick I. C. B. M. Turner, in fact, with his xenophobic

penchant for combining thrift with opportunism, shameless guile with dishonesty, ruthlessness with crooked timing, and no feeling of guilt whatsoever, had managed to acquire clear title not only to the Western Grande, but to numerous other choice properties up and down the whole county, on both sides of El Camino Real -- now that Padre Junipera Serra's famed Royal Highway had definitely passed into history -- through tax defaults, sly but legal business deals, faulty titles, subtle machinations, governmental kickbacks, agricultural subsidy supports, and sincere but steady pressures shrewdly applied. Las Vegas, Mr. Turner piously believed, was for suckers. Traffic in human mistery paid off so much more excitingly, so much quicker, and what was more, so sincere. After all -- didn't everyone?

Friendly Adroit Turner, warming himself in the Drawbridge sun, used Santa Clara County as his own private Santa Claus. He was nobody's fool. Even Mr. Quill knew that. He also suspected that Mr. Turner was very carefully trying to develop an instant public image so as not to be too meanly thought of, and possibly even become loved in return. Was that really too much to ask? he once said to Mr. Quill. If it was, then the injustice of it all excited him all the more. Gaining public love and keeping his excess wealth too. What more could anyone in this exalted position ask? Others had done it. Now it was his, Turner's turn to enter history. He was determined to go down in history not as the son of a bitch he had been all his life, a grandiose sinner, a rotten, heartless exploiter, but as some kind of innocuous, thoughtless, asinine benefactor. The more indecent the public praise the better. It wasn't that he gave a shit for humanity as a whole or individually, which he very carefully avoided. Being ultrasmart gave him the added advantage of knowing he didn't have much of a chance of founding a brilliant college in his name, at least not in this area -- he just didn't trust college graduates in any case, no matter what the college, so many of them turned out freakybops who never had the slightest idea what it meant to have to meet a payroll-- therefore he liked indulging himself in fantasies such as imagining himself the avatar of a mighty bit of westermania.

Now that he was a serious candidate for the title of Mr. He Who Screwed Everyone, Mr. Turner was turning more and more to rewards psychic and artistic, something truly precious, something he had never even really wanted: the undeserved adulation, warmth, and respect of his fellow men. This was the greatest challenge of his replete, satiated, fully stuffed barrenness of his spiritually sickly existence. Where other weaklings begged for rope or the Pope or any handy help in their ultimate horror of impending departure from this valley of tears, Turner was counting on a false recount to turn the trick. Not without plenty of good reason and precedent.

Forces were constantly directing Fraud Turner toward imposing goals. Being rich and envied was really the easiest part of it. Once he had a puppy as a small boy and that was the last time he had ever experienced any human compassion. All he had had to do was to hang onto his Fresno vineyards for twenty odd, very odd years, steadily exploiting the life out of hundreds upon hundreds of highly vulnerable, mobile, and easily intimidated Mexican braceros invited up from our friendly neighbor south of the border, hiring them, his fellow human beings, to pluck the fruit he grew, at prevailing starvation wages, and not ever think of them again, or their health, or their hunger, or their families, or their education, nothing, while watching his bank accounts fatten and fatten aaand fatten. He had even reached the point of wanting to open one of those fancy numbered accounts in Switzerland just for the prestige of it. He already had all the tricks against the I.R.S. he ever wanted, being a member of the clan of millionaires who boasted never paying a single penny in income tax. It sure was a good feeling all right. Screwing the defenceless pickers on the one hand and screwing the government and society on the other. Pretty neat. It was all so pat, so neat, so logical. What a dandy world. It was much, much, much better than --

In his younger days, while waiting patiently for the crap shooters to show their true colors, down south in Los Angeles, Freddy Turner had actually been hired as a cowboy extra for very early western pictures. This pseudo-western background served as a sort of substitute hobby-cum-business for him, thereby keeping him out of heavier munitions. This lucky turn actually activated his thoughts toward learning how to rob defenceless people and still stay within the law.

All the buildings in the Western Grande had, therefore, false fronts. All in proper tradition. And they were all specialized.

In back and to one side of No. 12, the Bar-Noon Saloon, stood the huge, ancient, thicktrunked hangem oak which afforded in hot weather an enormous arc of refreshing shade. This tree happened to be the only vegetable hereabouts to have some authentic claim to fame. As its overhead nailed-on sign proclaimed, it proved to be the real "Hangman's Tree" of local fame.

This tree had been much used and abused in pioneer gold rush and vigilante days. From its heaviest limb, not readily seen either from the entrance nor the highway, hung an abominable straw effigy, swaying at the slightest passing zephyr. This dummy bore another stupid plaque of its own -- "Black Bart" -- in dire warning to all dastardly runty nogood hustling rustling varmints thereabouts, another notch in the coarse sequence of Mr. Turner's macabre humor. It was in his western roles that he played the villains' parts gladly, and many times. He often bragged about having to shave in order to appear even more convincingly villainous.

Mr. Quill was privately convinced that his boss's aberrations were the natural byproduct of deep-rooted natural greed. Mr. Quill was never really comfortable with this "gristly jest" of Mr. Turner's. The idea of Black Bart, the swinging dummy, simply made him want to throw up.

7

Lupe listens.

Rocking back and forth in her worn-smooth Salvation Army rocking chair, in the gloom of yet another long sunny afternoon. Trying not to wonder when Manuel would get back from the day's picking. Feeding the bottle to baby Cati. Bueno. Listening to Manuelito running his plastic car vroom vroom back and forth on the splintered floor. A lucky fever, passing so quickly. Que bueno, for they didn't have or even know a doctor. Mariquita in the corner, splashing water in an open pan, adrift in her own small sea of dreams.

A pride of motorcyclists racing back and forth out on a distant street. Bueno too. The cyclists gun their powerful phaetons proving to an indulgent world how easy it is to make so much noise and enormous their maquinas were. Bueno for them. Vroom vroom. A great shortage of gods, good mechanics, and water in an open pan. Mr. Jonson in the next hut never talks to anyone, always working on his entirely rebuilt old car, tinkering forever, polishing and testing it, buying new parts for it like a small boy after a new toy, gunning and testing it over and over, as though perpetually perfecting a hopeless prison break, with Mrs. Jonson throwing things out at him every once in a while to remind him she was still very much around.

31

And the radio. Lupe keeps the radio tuned to her favorite
San Jose station, a whining singer, a girl, wailing:

        como palomas volaron
        todas mis ilusiones....

....there go all my illusions, flying away like doves -- that is
La Malpagadora, the wailing singer, crying over one who re-
pay s a good deed with a bad one.
    Blue Angeles, Navy pilots zooming over Moffett Field over-
head, rip a puffy white cross upon the clear blue limitless sky,
shredding the peaceful air to bits, letting their entrails scatter
and fall like thin puffs of melting cottony icecream to the hot
land down below.

        los celos me vuelven loco,
        y poco a poco....

....jealousy is driving me crazy, and little by little --
    A thick green carpeted caterpillar clambers up a branch.
Manuelito has brought it inside to study its silken mane shimmering softly. A huge, clumsy caterpillar road-building monster, raging and snorting out on the boulevard like a giant
bull lumbers into rest position after half a day's work, its
shiny chrome glinting in the hot sun. The squat workhorse
tractor under the plum trees growls louder, taking another
endless turn around the numberless rows.

        la verguenza mas
        grande del mundo....

....ah, the greatest shame in the world. Si, si, Lupe, pushing a fork into the moist earth of the plastic pot sitting on her
sill, recalling dimly that avocados were said to have originated
in her homeland, in southern Mexico, and avocadoes were luxuries beyond their reach. The slim little plant never cease d
fascinating her. The large brown eggshaped stone, supported
by toothpicks, had split and sent out its tender tendrils, roots
down, slim stem up. Now a foot high, it had half a dozen long
narrow leaves radiating in fan fashion, like petals on a flower.
A small, healthy, vigorous plant. She had set it out and nour-
ished it herself. Like herself. Another child. A child of the
earth. An earthling. This treelet would never reach maturity.
She knew that. She'd lost too many others. It would never
bear fruit. The odds were too great against it. It would never
shade her nor her children. But still -- it was alive. She refused to let it sadden her. There was hope. And life. Espe-
ranza y vida. It was hers. And no one else's. How she found

the heart to keep watering it uselessly she didn't know. What ever happens to the almighty rich? The poor pay nothing but misery. I'm willing dear God, querido dios, to do anything to get my children to school. To feed them succulent dishes. To clothe them in bright orange clothing. To do anything to get us out of this endless trap of misery. But what? What can I do? Que puedo hacer?

In her dreams she has many nightmares. Their shack catches fire. The smoke chokes them to death. The flames sear their flesh horribly. An earthquake swallows her children. Manuel is with another woman. She wakes up in a hot damp sweat. Shaking. Trembling. A shrill dry cry freezes in her throat. The border patrol arrives in neatly dressed swastika uniforms. It does no good to argue that she has a legitimate immigrant's card. They tear her away from her husband. They take her children. They swing their iron crosses like truncheons. Lupe runs, runs, runs. Scared. Crying. Looking everywhere for her children, her baby, Manuel. The sheriffs smash the doors down with rifle butts. The windows are nailed shut. Her potted plants are all crunched beneath their heels. They turn their rifles on her. She doesn't care. Fright turns to fury. Mr. Quill refuses to give her any more food. He makes her take her garbage back. The kids grow pale, thin, and disappear. The train crashes into their shack. The sun beats down on their nude prostrate bodies. The avocado plant wilts, shrivels, and finally becomes a thin, twisted black thread.

Maybe, if only Manuel could only work for--Mr. Schroeder!

She had her daytime nightmares too. Manuel was loyal to Mr. Turner, who always hired him when there was work. They never spoke of it. It was just understood. Lupe couldn't go talk to Mr. Schroeder, and Manuel wouldn't. She would sometimes grow wild with Manuel. "Do you know, tonto, why Señor Turner wants you around? Tonto! Because he wants you on tap and cheap. That's why!"

But woman, said Manuel patiently, flattening his hands --

Ah, the world composed of two worlds in one, the very poor and the very rich. How unbearable. A large world. A very tiny precious world. Crushed. Mr. Schroeder had a small orchard, and he also had a big nursery planned and under way. He was always covered with dirt, like a worker, always running around, always working as hard as any picker, always on his own. She liked going with Manuel to Mr. Schroeder's nursery for the small plants Mr. Turner ordered. She liked to look down the crammed, packed rows of tiny plants. All kinds of bushes and saplings and baby fruit trees set out in small fruit cans, all jammed together. So much like small children, those little plants. They would be set out to start new huertas,

33

rich new generations of neat new rows for the rich, for the already rich, more thousands of new trees for the fruit pickers
to pick. Couldn't Manuel do that kind of work? Couldn't he?
Of course, he replied. But they were in debt to Mr. Turner.
And besides where would he get a plot of land--"And all Señor
Turner is interested in is his business." But of course, how
true, my corazon, but wouldn't you also say that is also true of
your good Mr. Schroeder? "He is like a machine!" True again,
mi corazon, heart of my heart. But how would Manuel pay off
their debts? How would they pay rent on the outside? Where
would they live? She was afraid of Señor Turner. She hated
him and she was afraid of him at the same time. She was a-
fraid of him .... all the time. She was afraid he could turn
them in to the immigration authorities any time he wanted to.
Or get them arrested. Or get the police after them. Or the
border patrol. Or lock them up. Or chase them back to Mexico. They had seen it happen to others. Not once. But many
times. If you wanted to stay here on this side of the border in
these glorious United States of America you kept your mouth
shut. And you picked fruit till you dropped, and you never
complained about the meager pay the growers liked best to pay
-- until or unless they were forced either by the government
or by a threat of a strike to pay more.

Lupe wanted to go back to Mexico. Oh how she yearned to
go back. But she wanted to go back properly. Like any tour-
ist. Like any visitor. Not running. Not thrown back like a
dying discarded unwanted fish into the sea because it isn't big
or fat enough or sleek enough or rich enough. How would they
ever find work in Mexico, where there was even more poverty?
Where grown men with families worked for ten and twenty cents
an hour? Let alone start a business of their own? For that
poor reason, they should be grateful and willing to work for a
dollar an hour for the rich bastardos here. And what would
she ever do, dios mio, if Manuel's livelihood were stopped?
It seemed a lie, but this was her daytime nightmare, even
worse than the night frights. What if something should happen
to him? "Do you not ever stop worrying, mi querida? Your
angel black hair will turn white from so much worrying," he
teased.

"Do not call me that, you heathen," she cried, pounding his
back, making him laugh. He was turning her into a heathen
too, what with his blasphemous indifference to God.

The blond guero kids out in the compound courtyard were
laughing and shrieking and yelling and hooting among themselves.
Her own Manuelito, no angel himself, either, also fought back.
Eh, Manuelito -- watch out, you guero cheese eaters. You
lazy Mexican, they taunt. Hey, you hear Mrs. Jonson give her
cat a kid's birthday patty? Hey, how about a mail order busi-

34

ness -- you could mail chicken enchiladas to Texas, eh, Manu-
elito ha ha. Chulos amigos eh. A big put-on. One of the
guero kids yells Hey Manuelito, you got Mexican brains?
   Yeh, chua. Hey, you mutter got two tits.
   No, tree.
   Sure I got Metsican brains.
   What you got.
   Bird brain.
   Bird turd.
   You don't like me.
   What you gonna do.
   Stuff this here tamal down you troat.
   You an what else.
   Hey you too.
   No a goofball.
   Gimme my car.
   You gave it to mc.
   Ma!
   I'll give you these marbles.
   No.
   Did Manuelito.... have Mexican brains? If so,... was some-
thing wrong with that? Was that all that was wrong with them?
There was plenty wrong somewhere. Else why did they work
so hard and still suffer? There was something wrong with the
gueros too, the poor anglos, the blond blue-eyed dollar dolls
with scrambled eggs, stuck here in the Western Grande just
like themselves. So it wasn't just Mexicans. She could see
that all right. Olive Pope in No. 7, the fake Post Office, gos-
sipped to her in absolute confidence that the Jonsons were from
Alamaba where they were considered something like poor white
trash. Trash was basura which was garbage. It was with
great difficulty that Lupe wondered how the white gueros could
treat their own kind like living garbage too.
   Slowly and patiently and shyly, Olive Pope filled Lupe in on
the Jonsons. One bright Alamaba morning, one or two or three
years ago, it was horrible, and how could they, but a garbage
collector discovered it. How could they have been so criminal?
A cry came from inside the garbage can. The collector took
the lid off. He looked inside and burrowed among the trash.
Wrapped up inside a thick rolled-up newspaper bundle he found
an infant baby. It was tiny and alive. It had just been born. It
was whimpering and squirming. He took it to the police who
immediately took it to a hospital. There was nothing, absolutely
nothing at all wrong with the baby. It was just hungry. It was
alive and healthy and well. About all that could be said for the
Jonsons was that they didn't murder it deliberately. The police came to arrest them. What happened was Mrs. Jonson
had gotten herself pregnant by another man. And Zeke of course

wanted no part of it. You either, he told her, get rid of the
kid. Or else I go. They had no other children. They jumped
bail, entered the migrant stream, and had been on the season
as migratory pickers ever since. All year round. It was ideal.
Unless they returned to Alamaba, Mrs. Pope said, the police
would never, could never hope to catch up to them.

Lupe was horrified.

She'd never heard of such a terrible thing before. She
couldn't imagine its being true. It was an unimaginable, un-
forgiveable act, entirely beyond her mental capacity to understand. How could a woman give up her natural baby? Whatever
the provocation? Even dumb beasts fight to the death to pro-
tect their young. What kind of unspeakable beings were these
people? I'd die first, she whispered, crossing herself......
Where was the love? Was there no horror, no sin these gueros
would not commit? No crime?

And poor Mrs. Pope herself. Another problem case. A
sweet, an unbelievably whitegoldenyellowhaired young goddess,
fatter than an avocado, ready to drop her own baby on the world
any minute now, and possessing not one single ounce of brain.
Olive howled a lot. Chuck, her so-called husband, slept a lot.
Hardly anybody ever saw Chuck Pope up. He went out at night
like a light, like an owl, like a night owl, leaving Olive howling
and bawling and weeping and sobbing and crying. Sometimes
Lupe would ask her a simple favor, like where to throw the
coffee grounds, just to take her poor mind off her troubles, so
as not to stuff up the garbage troughs, and they found they could
laugh and giggle and have a good time now and then together,
sharing their miseries. Mr. Pope pushed dope. So what.
Manuel said everybody else said he did. So what. The Popes
were behind in their rent too, in debt to Mr. Quill, to Mr.
Turner, to the finance companies, and to everybody else. Mrs.
Pope often borrowed whatever food she could from Lupe,
mostly cooked beans.

Occasionally there were fights among the compound residents, fierce drunken brawls at night, out in the dark courtyard, in the dark of the moon, banging and heaving and grunting
and hitting and crushing and smashing and socking. Lupe had
to beg Manuel not to go out. And then....... silence. By the
bruises and black eyes and cut lips the following morning, Lupe
could tell who had been at it. Often they turned out to be the
best of friends.

At times, in place of nightmares, she had happy dreams.
In her dreams, Lupe prayed they would some day live like civilized people or at least like Pepe and Serafina and their growing children. Pepe had started out as a poor bean picker himself years before, down in Ventura County among the oil der-
ricks, and now they owned their own house and their own lot,

and they had their own car, and they were sending all their children through school. The eldest, Rosa, nineteen, was already out of high school and working. She worked in the cannery from time to time in Sunnyvale, making good money. Margarita, seventeen, and Daniel, sixteen, were still in high school. Joey, Linda, and Carlitos, the younger ones, were all in grade school. They all worked together as a family unit summers, picking prunes, like dozens of other Santa Clara families, helping with the family budget, without losing any school, easy work, each contributing his little bit. That was right. Rosa was big and mature and irresponsible. She must soon catch herself a husband. Margarita was already a slender young woman. Daniel seemed lost. He was not interested in studying anything the high school offered him, and that was truly a shame. He was good in sports and he bragged he would win an athletic scholarship to some big university. Was it too much for Lupe to dream that her own little Manuelito would also some day go through school and -- perhaps attend college as well?

Standing in the rosy powdery sunlight in her frayed quilted light green robe, her black hair gleaming in the dazzle of a magnificent morning sun, Lupe gripped the bright green stem of her mop and sloshed it in the orange plastic bucket, making her own rainbow. Scattered about her feet on the ground were discarded bits of dissected toys, a torn blue wading pool, a small redbanded yellow boat, a redecorated red-orange truck without wheels, and several magenta, mauve, tan, black, and white building blocks. The children enjoyed digging up the soft friendly brown earth. It was just another day and, like all days, full of wonder and stunted promises and twisted dreams. There was so much that begged to be done, and dreams to be dreamt, and promises to be fulfilled, and anxieties to be assuaged, and demands to be met, and obstacles to be overcome, and so much life burning, bursting, aching, praying, yearning to be lived, to be lived, to be truly, really lived.

And so little fun.

8

"Que tal, compadre!"
"Que tal, comadre!"
"Que tal, viejo!"
"Quiubale, hermano!"
"Que tal está tu cola, chango!"
"Igual a la de tu iguana, tu esposa!"
"La tuya!"
"Tu tu tu!"
"Ja ja ja!"

Good friends, buenos amigos, having fun, cars crunching into Pepe's dirt driveway, Lupe's and Serafina's children running about in happy squeals, a warm sultry afternoon sun glorifying summer's Sunday, as buenos compañeros flock together. Pepe's house is on the opposite corner of Mr. Turner's glum plum orchard, a long, long acre away from the Western Grande compound, and a minute step toward civilized living.

Corn tortillas and hot green chile. Saucy cheese taquitos. Enchiladas and hot green salsa picante. Empanadas. Tostadas. Chiles rellenos. Tamales. Little red chile peppers. Chile pequin. Everything with chile on it. Serafina beside herself, smiling and pleased at all the pleasure her company, her compadres and compatriotas were giving her.

Oh, man, groaned Danny, a different thinker, in a low voice

beside himself barely in his sister Margarita's hearing, heaving in dismay, his thick black hair combed gracefully back, in thick, fat, glistening waves. "Man, look at 'em go. Look. There they -- oh boy. Man. All that hot air going bloop, all afternoon too. Hi blah hi blee hi blo hi bloop blee. Ain't they nothing to drink yet? Hey it's hot man, and all they do is sit and yap. Cheese."

"You shush," whispered Margarita, pleased.

"Why should I?" he said. They both well knew why. Papa Pepe was why. He could very angry was why.

"They are friends and family," she said. Out of the corner of her eye she caught Ramiro Sanchez sitting quietly in the farthese corner of the room by himself, leaning against the wall.

"Oh. Oh, man! I mean, great!" Danny rolled his handsome brown eyes in mock anguish at his sister's mild reprimand. Suddenly he sat straight up at Manuel's approach and lifted a cold can of cool beer from Manuel's passing tray.

"Cheese, what am I supposed to do, sis? Huh? Keep ah quiet? Keel over? Huh? Keel over in a dead faint huh?"

Manuel, tall, heavy, slowthinking, moved with deliberateness. He spoke only when addressed, and then answered only briefly. His reticence had a knack of driving Lupe mad. Then, after many sighs, she resigned herself to his silence, as though realizing that her garrulousness coupled to his inertia helped them get along together beautifully. There were times when even she tired of hearing only her own voice. Now that she was in her true element here, with a crowd of her own countrymen, a crown to joy, she felt a little lightheaded, a little better, a little homesick too, and a little fun at last.

Serafina, formless, a blob, heavy, her own children grown or growing large, except for little Carlitos; Margarita, and Rosa almost ready to fly the coop; cradled Lupe's tiny Cati in her ample motherly lap, alternately feeding her the bottle and chuckling with the men and laughing at their thighslapping jokes. Now that they were resting from the fields, and all the dirt and grime and backbreaking work were behind them for the week, they could relax and laugh and sing and laugh.

On the blue springworn sofa sat Pepe, heavy, fat, and contented. Beside him sat Alberto, and Jesus, and Santiago. Alberto Fernandez, the informal leader of this traveling quartet, was the only one of the four who could manage to keep them cemented together without bickering for their important summer travels. The fourth member, Silvestre Salazar, sat on the floor by himself, drinking his beer alone, surly and quiet. The covering material on the sofa was torn open in spots, revealing yellowed foam rubber within. A short thick table, with four short stumpy brown screw-in legs twelve inches high, occupied the floor at their feet, was filled with cans, glasses, and all kinds of appetizing enticements.

Dan, snapping his gum, fidgeted on the edge of a round brown leather hassock as though ready to spring into a spree. Margarita, sitting quietly beside him on a white kitchen chair near the kitchen door, had her hands folded on her lap. Alberto cast furtive glances at Margarita's sister Rosa sitting stiffly on a stuffed rocker near the front window. Rosa's thick frilly ruffles belied the heat that filled the buzzing, friendly, laughing room. She had spent the whole morning bathing and putting her makeup on and dressing.

"Have you already forgotten that friendly foreman at La Casita in McAllen?" said Alberto of Jesus. "Or is it that you don't care to remember that you are a Texan?"

"Si," grunted Silvestre.

"Well, I'll tell you," said Jesus. "Yes, I do miss him, all right. Si. Poor guy. Poor fellow was in danger of losing his wiglet when the celery didn't get in. Mama, but was that water fria. I just didn't like standing in freezing water and barefooted too para acabar la chingada so early in the morning so I do the only thing I know to do and I say to hell which you."

"Just what means that, paisano?"

"It sure got hot there."

"What you think it means, pendejo."

"You can say that again."

"Si."

"You better believe it."

"All foremen are poor slobby bastards."

"Si."

"He sure did hate to fire us, though."

"Si, he sure did all right."

"Si, si."

"He sure got opset over nothing."

"The union hall said hell they were lucky to clear fifty thousand."

"Hey, cucaracha, how come you know the business."

"Si. Fonny. And I never met a payroll either."

"No, no. It is truly nice here in your Santa Clara, Pepe."

"It sure is."

"Your freeways for example. That is only one way of many marvelous examples of how many, well, for example, how much you are civilized people and know how you say to appreciate things here. We sure don't get chased around by those Texas those gorgeous Texas Grangers so much here either."

"You better believe it."

"Si."

"Pues, Alberto, surely you could have thought a little more and found some other even more marvelous example."

"Are you meaning that in an engineering sense, Jesus?"

"Un momento, amigo. You are causing me to absolutely stop and think about it for a moment or two."

"Well, amigo, if it hurts you that much, I beg of you, please do not strain yourself on my account."

"That is a very very complicated subject."

"You mean because you are not of the engineering clan."

"And after they fired us, I decided I deserved I felt I said I would some day have to grow my own maiz and go swim in it especially when I am filthy rich."

"Well, you are already halfway there, compadre."

"Well, as for me, I'm going to raise hell and lots of it."

"Cheese," whispered Danny. "You hear all that? They nearly started a fight."

"They did not," said Margarita. "Shhhh."

"I'll tell you what else I miss most in Texas. I miss that bug poison they sprayed all over us while we were picketing fifty paces apart. They sure had to use a lot of spray."

"Hell, man, they do that right here in California. Chavez and his bunch of grape pickers got sprayed at Delano."

> O the yellow rose of Texas
> is the sweetest rose that grows --

hummed Silvestre.

"You admit therefore to not being an engineer."

"I also admit to not being rich."

"In what sense."

"I did not think there was any doubt."

"How about a floating swimming pool."

"Why, to float when you can't swim, sure."

> O the yellow rose of Texas
> is the sweetest rose that grows --

"When it comes to celery in icy water, I am a coward."

"Me too."

"We are all like."

"Like peas in a pod."

"Please, please do not speak to me of peas."

Manuel, sitting on a short wooden stool brought in from the back yard, rested his beer between his feet on the floor, engrossed, thinking, his forehead wrinkled. Rosa got up and tripped prettily to the kitchen. Ramiro Sanchez, sitting quietly, glanced casually at Margarita. When she got up too to go into the kitchen, his eyes followed her, watching the kitchen door, turning around each time someone passed through.

"Then permit me to ask this of you, cuñado. How can they be building so many freeways? What I truly mean is, are they all going somewhere?"

"You can go entirely around this entire magnifico bay --"

"Hold it there, tomato picker. What he means is -- what are they all so necessary for?"

"At last I am looking at someone possessing a glimmer of the fundamental problem."

"Pues, hombre. That is clearly a philanthropic problem. You must forgive me as I need another minute or so to think."

"You are certain that is all you will need, you short-eared son of a jackass of a depraved burro?"

"You must have known my grandfather."

"I think this borracho of an Alberto is attempting to intrude another imitation metaphysic or something."

"Your grandfather also held back the best part of the brain."

"But not as much as your grandparents."

"Gracias for that, amigo."

"Por nada, amigo."

Rosa returned. She carried a trayful of more antojitos and delicacies, pushing the door open prettily with the back of her shoulder. Her brilliantly oranged lips were parted as though in temporary astonishment, her eyes wide and dark-pooled, lashed and heavily mascaraed with light blue eyelids. She carried a studied look of slight surprise. Where Papa Pepe was severe with younger Margarita, to a less extent with Danny, he was completely indulgent with Rosa. She had only to roll her eyes and snap her palate in the most open manner, Lupe noticed, and Pepe would smile with fatherly pride and pleasure. Since Ramiro's arrival, however, there had been a slight undercurrent of tension among them all. Something bothered Pepe about Ramiro, and these two did not share the hot dog good times the others were enjoying.

Rosa lingered by Ramiro, offering the tray. "Take another," she said. Smiling.

Ramiro nodded. He kept his eyes on the kitchen door.

Margarita still had not come out.

Yes, thought Lupe, and look at you. Lupe didn't like Rosa's blatant pushing. What an ugly manner of insinuating herself into the men's attentions. Ugh. With all that heavy makeup on, and those new clothes. Rosa was being spoiled by too many American ways, earning and keeping her own money, with no responsibility. Just look at you. Lupe controlled an ugly urge to stick her tongue out. She was furious without really knowing why. This visit wasn't going right. Lupe downed a whole can of beer at a single draught, spilling some on her only good dress, something she'd never done before. Manuel, startled, shook his head, looked at her, then straight back at Rosa's wiggling rump. He couldn't help it. No man could. Lupe was growing livid, and therefore dangerous.

"It was the rain," offered Manuel, attempting his initial debut as a belated life of the party.

"Oh, YES,"breathed Rosa shrilly, using Manuel as antenna so as to attract other poor men. Lupe's anger grew colder. "It certainly was a wonderful and very wet rain."

"No, no," said Manuel. Clearing his throat.

"For the growers it was,"Serafina quickly cut in, trying her motherly best to head off the gathering thunderhead.

"I thought it would never stop,"insisted Rosa, crinkling her pretty crinkleproof rain dress.

"I admit it was real bad for the camotes,"said Manuel, furrowing his eyebrows, getting absolutely garrulous for him, which was also very, very dangerous. "Very bad. Yes. Very, very bad." He shook his head showing how bad it really was. What was also very, very bad was the lethal look Lupe was looping at him, nearly flattening him sideways when he finally connected with it. He immediately claimed his more modest and more natural silence once more, into safety, and retreated into his natural dark mood. Rosa, gaily indifferent, chortled and moved on.

Santiago Martines, grinning from ear to ear, getting plastered, slipped from his can, saying nothing, contributing nothing but the warmth of his presence, grinning all the while, laughing silently at everything that was being said, his easy smile and broad hefty laughter entering at appropriate times, a marvelous audience, always at home no matter what was said or by whom or for what reason. He didn't care what anybody said so long as somebody said something.

"If it's bug spray --"

"I don't mind a little --"

"How about hay fever."

"It isn't just talk."

"Let's suppose -- you ask the gueros to stop it."

"I say, goddamn it, let's pull the strike."

"Sure. You can say that. It's easy with no family."

"Sure. But you win too."

"Sure. Sure. I know."

"They are saying the comunistas --"

"Bah."

"Why must we worry? Haven't we got enough to eat?"

"Comunistas are like the flies. The more misery,the more flies. Therefore, the more comunistas. Bah, what do gringos know about misery? Or compassion? Or sympathy --?"

"Amigos, amigos, we are getting --"

"What you say? Free? Free money?"

"I toll you. They actually give it away. Free."

"Do you mean to remain seating there in plain day in plain

43

sight in your fonny close and stoffing chile in your big open mouth and claim they are paying people for doing absolutely no work whatsoever? At all? Is these what you mean man?"

"I assure you."

"Nothing at all?"

"It is a coll social spurity or something. Or unemployment involvency. Something like that. Pepe he knows all there is to know about it. Ask him. Also publicity welfare."

"But how is it done, hombre. Damn, I moss know. Where you go sign up, man. I want sign up bad, man. Just toll me. I never realize how this was sotch a goddamn wonnerful contry all right just just until just this minute, pal."

"Si, Jesus. Now you listen carefully. You just go into that unemployment office with your bunch a bananas peel, like you mean business see, and you know forst thing right off they ask you, is you o is you ain't a comunista. What you say?"

"Who? Me? Jesus Avila from Camacho? A comunista?"

"Thass what they will say."

"But I am no red, man. Do I look rojo? I am too illiterate to be even a committee, let alone a filthy, dorty, stinking red."

"Nevertheless. Thass what they will say anyway, tonto."

"It just doesn't seem logical. Here? In the U.S.?"

"Now just how would you know that?"

"But all I want is to get my feelthy hands on money, money, more and more money, easy money, lots a money, feelthy rich with money. Now you tell me please, does not that mean, if logic interests you, that I am a deep-dyed capitalista?"

"Jesus, you do not care beans for logic."

"Jesus, you are confusing money with dirt."

"Jesus, you are not a thinker."

"Jesus, are you dumb."

"Jesus, not even a Samson could straighten you out."

"Jesus, they will throw you out anyway."

Jesus thought. "You don't say."

"Si."

"Just for asking for a little money."

"Si."

"This is sure one goddamn fonny contry all right."

"This is why I am trying to say, compadre."

"Well, my frens, I think I know now what is my trable. My mind starts to think of all that beautiful lovely green money here, there, all over, and then I remember all, I remember the ten million or so prunes I still have to pick before I die."

"Si."

While they downed a toast to that, Ramiro Sanchez got up and slipped quietly through the kitchen door in back.

9

"All right, Schroeder. Here. Read this. Here it is in black and white. What the hell more proof do you need, man? Go on. Convince yourself. Read it. Don't take my word for it."

Drawbridge Courier
Thursday Nineteen

Pickers involved
FRESNO (TP) -- Pickers were deeply involved in the drive to recruit and organize farm workers in the Delano vineyards. Investigation has revealed, disclosed the Senior Mop-up Senator from Fresno, that known pickers were active in previous strike actions, and unless steps were taken immediately and firmly, free enterprise in the farmfields will soon fall to the communists, who are known to be opposed to hunger.

"Whatever else is done," said the Senator forcefully, "whatever other steps are taken, all the signs are there, there's a picket born every minute, and if nothing else time is of the essence in a very real sense of the word. Let us give thanks," he added, "to the brave beleaguered growers, investors, and gamblers who have the hearts and purses of the American consumer in tow. Let us also give thanks to our great

45

Governor, who is really Howlin Mad, and to all the Rat Barfys for their undiminished zeal."

The Senator is up for re-election this month.

"Now," sputtered Turner, turning apoplectic. "What more evidence do you want? First Delano, then Modesto, then all of San Joaquin. Then us. Well, I won't have it. You hear?"

"You won't have it I hear."

"Now get this, Schroeder. To get rich quicker, you've got to be smarter than the average picker. And that ain't so hard. If we keep them out of school and in the fields. Well, we've gotten this far. Now we've got to dispense with these goddem vicious sonsabitchin union raccoons."

"You got to fight."

"Right. You. Got. To. Fight."

"Or down you go."

"Right. Or. Down. Now you listen to me, hear me good, Schroeder. This ain't no laughing matter. First, don't give in one single inch or else they got you by the balls, er, they'll rip out everything you own by the roots." Turner pointed his thick black blazing cigar at the slender man's thinning hair.

It sure had been a real nice day. As a planter himself, Schroeder appreciated nice days. Turner was more than just a good customer of his. Turner was pure prune power, orchards, hundreds of acres of prune, driers, packers, pickers, the works. Schroeder, however, couldn't help being curious about the older man's ploy. Why was he testing him? Was senility setting in? Turner's mansion, a comfortable enough residence, was built of sturdy granite set amidst a large rocky section of wooden hills, with endless acres of plums and apricots set out endlessly on the flat slopes below, a flat checkerboard table top, with the mansion as the centerpiece, the sky as chandelier, and the ground as their table. "Half wild," Turner was fond of saying. "Like me." The resident property was all hidden, fence off, a huge private compound. The entry driveway was half hidden by large, rapacious bushes. A visitor had to be shown the secret entrance the first time. The wild dogs were kept in locked cages on either side, snarling at anyone passing, ready to be sprung loose by a button from the house. The Turners didn't really need all eighteen rooms, but they were comfortable enough. They never knew who might drop in. Perhaps children had been anticipated, children who never materialized. Schroeder's own son and daugher, both away at college, had decreed the place too creepy, good only for sp0ok parties.

"You must exercise extreme care. Besides being smart, Schroeder. Once you have your working plans laid out, and your capital, all you've got to do is follow through. Naturally the first million prunes are always the hardest, if not impossible for most people. But one can always try cots. You have to irrigate. Do you realize what it means to irrigate, Schroeder? I mean, to really irrigate? The wetness of water?"

He droned on and on and Schroeder nodded drowsily, sitting relaxed sunk deep in the soft, thick, comfortable horsehide sofa. He was wondering what his wife Georgia and that ESP nut Jean Turner were having to talk about. He took his time thinking, taking light thoughtful puffs on his fat aromatic cigar. This screwball Turner had the darndest ideas. But he sure knew how to build a greenhouse. Business made the wheels willing to whir. He looked past the huge plate window, down at the darkening surface of the Bay's long gray sheen. The sun had already sunk into the Santa Cruz Range to the west.

Jim Schroeder's face was deeply tanned from the sun, leathery and wrinkled from the winds, a quick, sensitive barometer of inner concerns. Truner droned on.

"Even if most people want to help the poor, that majority has absolutely no right, either ethical or otherwise, to use democracy to force their twisted amorality on the rest of us. I've worked like a slave, I know what it is to work like a slave, to earn my better-than-average allowance. I was born with my God-given right to use my money as I want. And now I am being robbed of both. Incompetents are made the funkies of nincompoops, and mind you I like my rest much as anybody But every weekend? They want every weekend off? How inhumane, how insane, and how immaterial is humanitarianism."

"And hypocritical."

"Of course."

"Of course."

Turner was quick in his movements. His skin was pale, sallow, and smooth as a baby's bottom. His paunch protruded slightly beneath the flap of his large flowery imported sport shirt. In the growing darkness, since they hadn't turned the lights on, the flowers were gradually disappearing. He and Mrs. Turner were great fans of Mexican artifacts. Every year on their trips to Acapulco and Cuernavaca and Mexico City they picked up carloads of priceless trinkets, zarapes, ceramics, pottery, jewelry, and especially genuine ancient Mayan sculpture. Turner enjoyed scattering these artifacts all around his place. Since becoming unscrupulously rich from exploiting hundreds and thousands of Mexican migrant pickers, he felt it was poetically fitting and ironically just that he use those ill-gotten gains to exploit ancient Mexican culture too for his hobby, as a vapid pastime. He planned his self-obsolescence as a kind of a private see to go down in.

Turner liked thinking of himself as an amateur philosopher and minor historian, protecting and passing on the cultures of the past, not merely a money manager, although money of course always came first. Non disputatum, as he liked to add. In his more serious moments he could articulate pure fabrications, claiming for one thing that he had cracked the ancient Mayan code and knew exactly what they thought and said, but he wasn't about to share his discoveries with those dum-dum archeologists who thought they knew so much but who never had to meet a payroll. These Mayan statuettes therefore helped buttress his own hypocritical opinion of his stunted inner self, with no one the wiser. He chased off all the experts because they politely disagreed, the nincompoops.

Turner smiled and took a deep satisfied puff of port. "You goddem right I know. I ought to. Those domed intellectual dum-dums trying to organize the dumb plum pickers make me sick. They come over here and theorize and bastardize and write pamphlets when when when but when it comes down to hard, hard work, like you and me, see, to real hard work, ah, where was I, and uh oh yes, and logic, they want none of it. You ever notice that? Now take the pickers. You ever see a picker who ever had to meet a payroll? No. And you won't. Not while I'm around. The pickers are perfectly happy with the way things are. I never met a picker who didn't say he was happy working for me. They all say they'd be happy to be my slave. And believe me I've asked hundreds of them. Thousands. They are the happiest people on the face of the earth. That's why I like going to Acapulco. The service in those hotels is absolutely terrific. I really envy them because I'm miserable practically all the time. And let me tell you another thing. I speak their launguage even though I don't talk a word a Mexican. Oh, I know sombrero and mañana and saludos amigos and crap like that, just enough to get by, you know. Now they would be in miserable shape if I weren't around to create employment for them. Isn't that right? What else could they do? They don't have any capital because of course we don't let 'em have any. Just keepum alive. That's what makes 'em happy. They don't know anything because there's no sense letting their kids go to school either. So what else could they do? You mark my words Schroeder. You've got to keep control over every single square inch of soil. You don't let 'em plant one goddem single stalk of corn or boom you're in trouble. Before you know it those goddem reds will be telling you when you can wipe your ass, if you'll pardon the vulgarity. They'll check your ledgers, your books, your accounts receivable, your toilet paper, everything. They even tell you when and where you can piss too, if you'll pardon the indelicacy again."

Well, thought Schroeder, this fellow has it made. Worked hard all his life. All past. 'All leveled off. Turner could easily live off his interest alone if he wanted to. Avocadoville in Escondido. Peaches in Tagus. Date palms in Assyria.

Grapes in Fresno. Oranges in Cairo. Cots in Sunnyvale. Wineries in Madera. Grape juice in Napa. Years at it. Building. Planting. Blasting. Extending. Adding. Replanting. Pruning. Cutting. Cultivating. Irrigating. Growing. Wining. Dining. The works. And finally cashing out. Always on top. Always -- "Now here's the way to get really rich."

And: "You know what it takes to be a prune picker?"

And: "Five fingers."

And: "Sweat your butt off. Then what. Then they come along, those nervy government crooks siding with those greedy pickers wanting to peel you back down to the nutty core. More more more. That's what they want. Makes me more sick."

That new gang up in Sacramento must be bugging him awful bad. But who? Schroeder thought Turner was happy with the last election, with the way the new Governor Howlin Mad Nolan was cutting medicare and increasing students' tuition and decreasing education and raising sales taxes and dropping property taxes and relieving the rich and soaking the poor. What was Turner mad about anyway? Something was sure bugging him. The report of the State House Un-American Festivities Committee was fresh out in all the papers. The Senator from Fresno, intimate friend and fellow plunderer of Turner's, who also owned a nice thick slice of the Delano vineyards and lots of cotton, had just helped himself to a nice fat helping of fat federal subsidy price supports, another royal screwing for the public, and was at that moment successfully fighting off those "goddem radicals who want to limit subsidy payments to a maximum of $20,000 to say any one single so-called farmer."

In the middle of Delano town was the Maginot Line against this encroaching socialism first of the grape pickers, then ultimately of all agricultural workers everywhere.

This was California.

This, the richest, the greatest, the most productive chunk of rich earth in the world, this munificent cornucopian state pouring forth an unbelievable glut of gorgeous peaches, a blizzard of plums, a plethora of apricots, pears, and tiger lillies, a bloat of tomatoes and ravishing radishes and cool cucumbers and bugproof lettuce, carloads of magnificent verminfree vegetables a mile long, was only just getting started. Soon, when the new waterways were laid down, with concrete irrigation moats crisscrossing the entire state, siphoning off the headsoaking rains from the copious northern rivers bringing the spring washes down in long, clean, sleek, white cementine canals to the enormous stretches of burnt dung-brown nerveless acres west of the San Joaquin, all of them already bought up at worthless prices by expectant farsighted corporation heads, to the coastal ranges -- all these areas would also be brought into agricultural production, doubling

and tripling the harvest, creating a true breakthrough, an incredibly overflowing breadbasket for the whole world. Quite
a remarkable, sophisticated invention, as the U.S. headed toward its glorious 21st century, combining big land combines
with perpetual migrant slavism.

"I don't trust that new fellow, that rat Ramiro or something. "

"No? Why?" Why should Turner express interest in one
single lowly picker?

"Because he's, well, he's, goddem it, he's too happy. "

That figured. Turner making points.

"I bet you he threw the brick through Quill's window. "

"Poor Quill, " said Schroeder.

"I'm not blind. I know it was aimed at me. "

Another point.

"Then, it could have been Zeke Jonson. "

Point point.

"Or one of Mrs. Ferguson's boyfriends. "

"You mean customers, friend. "

"Maybe even that retarded bloke, Pope. "

"You think he's got the head for it?"

"Ha, ha, good joke, Schroeder. That's what I like about you.
Always see the humor in everything. And top of it all I've got
to fight off that swoopy city hall bunch. Inspectors. And their
goddem ultimatums. I'll snap them in two --" snapping his
fingers.

"Do you mean it?"

"Are you questioning my integrity?"

"Who? Me?"

"Aren't you listening to me, Schroeder?"

U.S. growers could grow ten times the amount of food the
world could ever possibly consume, and then, as at Ninevah,
plow nine-tenths under again, paying off the big combines with
taxes siphoned off industrial complexes, growing richer while
the world grew poorer and starvation increased apace. Turner
called it The Law of Ultimate Consumption, meaning people
were entitled to embark upon some form of sublime cannibal-
ism. The big growers had every right to be frightened of the
organized crime taking the dastardly form of unionized pickers
picketing. For these poor bastards, these ignorant, uneducated,
unwashed, disorganized, barely human migrant fruit pickers
were actually trying to demand higher wages, cutting Turner
baby's freedom to visit Acapulkey or Honeylululu any goddem
time he felt like it. Damn their hides, was there no limit to
their picketing or their greed? It was healthy outdoor work,
too. What more did they want? A great big gooseberry in
every pie dish of pure cream?

"Can't you see that, Schroeder?"

Schroeder thought: was Turner taking an interest in exporting his labor? By importing tomatoes from Sonora and Sinaloa in western Mexico? Importing the labor was getting more difficult. It sure had made him lots of pots of honied money. Nationals. Wetbacks. Alambristas. Descamisados. Braceros. Migrants. Commuters. Green carders. Seasoners. River crossers. Night riders. They all met and they all fulfilled the same conditions: cheap traveling rotating convenient exploitable farm labor. When they were needed. Not a moment bebefore. Not a moment after. Use 'em fast. Then kick them off the land. Bring 'em on in here. Then disappear 'em fast. Back to Texas. Where they came from. Back into the woodwork till they were needed again next summer. Cheat them good too. Cheat them on the boxes. Cheat them on the breaks. Cheat them on the conveniences. Cut the water. Use them up. Pay them their their miserable forty centavos an hour. Kick them out. Then let them enjoy their miserable misery elsewhere. Not here. Back to San Antone or Mejico or wherever. Until we meet again. Hasta la vista, you all. Love you pickers. Didn't Turner love them enough? And, loving, care? Once the crop was in --

"And mind you, mark my words, I mean really rich --"

Turner was fond of quoting his favorite Senator, the passionate defender of the poor defenseless landowners, that famous softhearted softshoe Senator who vowed not once but many times "I hereby vow I'll not send Amurrican boys to pick Amurrican stromberries because they're just not built right for stooping. Er, the boys, not the berries."

"So to hell with 'em I say --"

A great beginning. A marvelous song of gratitude. And as it was in the beginning, so it should be in the end, if Turner had his way. And what was there to stop it?

"So into the burning hell with 'em I say --"

And: "Keep 'em off balance. Keep pushing 'em. They'll knock you off your perch. Say, do you like to go fishing, Schroeder? Catfish. Ever try fried cod? Good cod. Almighty fish. Grapes good good with cod too. Cool. Grapes grown on the vine, go on strike, first thing you know the oranges pop and then and then the lemonaides, the sassafras, the tangerines, tamborines, and then only God knows what else. Mandarines."

"It sure is one hell of a nasty problem all right."

"You better believe it, Schroeder."

"Sharing."

"Right. Er, what do you mean, sharing?"

"Socialism. It's our most important product."

"Yeah."

"Your big combines are always making secret pricing schedules so as to drive small people like me out of business."

"You're wrong, Schroeder. Dead wrong. As my great granddad always used to say, buying real estate is not only the best way, the quickest way and the safest way -- but the only way to become wealthy. "

"Neither dead nor wrong, " muttered Schroeder. "The bank turned down my request for another small loan I need to add another room. They say I can't make it as a one-man business. But I'll build the damn thing myself. "

"Good for you. That was for your own good, Schroeder. You don't want to overextend yourself. Right? That was just for your own protection by better business heads wiser in the ways of investment than you. Or your crops. "

"Nuts. "

"Yeah, well, they're good, too. "

Georgia Schroeder and Jean Turner came in, chatting toge- ther, from the outer veranda and entered the unlit living room. Through the big plate glass the black flat void of the bay was ringed with hundreds of shimmering lights. A string of pearls sparkled across the blackness, where the San Mateo bridge spanned the lower bay.

"Well, hon, " said Georgia. "We'd best be going, I guess. "

"Why haven't you turned the lights on, " said Jean, turning the lights on herself. "This is so spooky. "

"Yeah, " said Jim.

"What's the rush, huh?" said Turner. "You mean you're leaving already?"

"You're a darling, Frederick, " said Georgia, smiling her warmest, brushing an unspeck from her blue suit. "You know how Jim has to get up early. I won't have him driving on an- other drink. He can have all he wants when he's home. "

"Thanks a lot, dear, " said Jim, getting up.

"I think that's so sensible, " said Jean.

"All right, " gruffed Turner, trying not to hide his vexation. "You women. You see -- you see he gets you home all right, then. "

And, later: What was the rush, hon?

Well, you can always have another.

What a mother.

You were all set to start a fight.

Me?

I know you.

I was keeping quiet. It was damned good scotch.

I know about that too.

All right, home it is then.

Shifting hard.

Purring.

Silence.

Then, And I won't have you fighting when you can't win.

Not even if it's my own fight.

She hugged him and squeezed his arm. Sure, sweet --
My own wife.

Tigers, leopards, and the jungle's law....

You know, hon, I was ready to claw her eyes out myself.

How come?

Do you know what she had the holy nerve to tell me? She said she -- she actually complimented me on the marvelous way I made my suit carry over another year, and how she wished she could. Could my foot!

10

Dawn.

Outside, the coolest night.

Outside, the soft, plush, lingering sheen of nightlight.

Within his breezy airconditioned shack Manuel lay half asleep in the middle of the biggest apricot orchard in the world, nothing but apricot trees all around, in one of a long double row of splintered boards nailed together and called a shack. A migrant's shack. He struggled to come awake. Everything seemed to be plugged up. A distant roar closed in steadily. He awoke in a cold sweat. He sat up abruptly in the cold darkness.

The roar grew louder and louder. He leaned forward, hunched in his worn, torn covers, and peered through the grimy window. A huge black monster was butting through trees, moving and pitching about, its headlights piercing the armor of night, then swinging away again as the roaring lessened. Manuel smiled. The roar of a tractor. He rubbed the sleep from his eyes. He stretched his aching arms and shoulders. He thought of Lupe and the kids back in Drawbridge.

On the very brink of the full onslaught of summer's punishing heat, with the plums and pears and apricots fattening madly on every vine, branch, bush, and limb in every section of every county in the country, pickers were needed right now immediately on every farm and orchard everywhere and all at once. The frantic demand for pickers increased rapidly as the hot days mounted. That sure looked good out there. What a cool job that was. Driving a tractor at night. Maybe he could get Ramiro to teach him to drive one.

Manuel well knew what his physical energy was.

His physical energy was his total wordly wealth.

No matter how anxious he was to work, he did have his limit. He had to rest his body. The finger joint he'd injured still hurt. He missed Lupe's chatter. He'd signed up with that shrewd contractor, Roberto Morales, that shrewd, fat, energetic contratista, manipulator of migrating farm worker s, that smiling middleman who promised to deliver so many hands to the moon at such and such a time at such and such an orchard at such and such a price, for such a small commission. A tiny percentage. Such a little slice. Silvery slavery -- modernized.

Roberto Morales, an organization man, was a built-in toll gate. A parasite. A collector of drops of human sweat. An efficiency expert. Had he had not been Mexican, he would have made a fantastic capitalist, like Turner. He was Turner upside down. Sucking blood from his own people. With the help and convenient connivance of Turner's insatiable greed.

The agricultural combine's imperative need to have its capital personally plucked when ripe so as to materialize its honest return on its critical investment in order to keep its executives relaxed in blue splendor in far-off desert pools, was coupled to the migrant workers' inexorable and uncompromising need to earn pennies to fend off stark starvation.

Good money.

Good dough.

Good hard work.

Pick fast.

Penny a bucket.

Check off.

Get the count right.

Cotsplumsprunespeachesbeanspeas.

Pods.

The seed of life.

And: -- don't complain....

Manuel lay back in the blackness. As the darkness receded and the light of day started creeping imperiously across its own land, he thought that these powerful orchard land owners were awfully generous to give him such a beautiful hostel to stop in overnight. The skylight hotel. There the land stood. A heaving, sleeping mother earth. A marvelous land. Ripening her fruit once again. Once more. Ripening it fatly and prégnantly for the thousandth time. It must be plucked said the wise man. For it cannot hang around on limbs a minute extra. At no man's convenience. As soon as the baby's ready. Lush and full of plump juices. Hugging its new seed around its own ripeness. The plum and the cot and the peach and the pear must plummet again to earth. Carrying the seed of its own delicate rebirth and redestruction back home to earth again. A clever mother earth who in her all-but-unbelievable generosity was capable of giving man fivefold, tenfold the quantity of fruit he could himself eat, five times fifty, and yet the pickers were never paid enough to satisfy their hunger beyond their actual working hours. And yet it was called a moral world. An ethical world. A good world. A happy world. A world full of golden opportunities. Manuel simply couldn't figure it out.

What was wrong with the figures?

Why was mother earth so generous? And men so greedy?

You got twenty-five cents a basket for tomatoes. A dollar a crate for some fruit. You had to work fast. That was the whole thing. A frantic lunatic to make your barely living wage. If you had no rent to pay, it was OK. You were ahead, amigo. Pay rent, however, stay in one place, and you couldn't migrate after other easy pickings. The joy of working was looking over your dreams locked to hunger.

Manuel studied the whorls in the woodwork whirling slowly, revealed in the faint crepuscular light penetrating his shack. His cot was a slab of half-inch plywood board twenty-two inches wide and eight feet long, the width of the shack, supported by two two-by-four beams butted up against the wall at both ends beneath the side window. The shack itself was eight by twelve by seven feet high. Its roof had a slight pitch. The rain stains in the ceiling planks revealed the ease with which the rain penetrated. Except for two small panes of glass exposed near the top, most of the window at the opposite end was boarded up. A single, old, paint-encrusted door was the only entry. No curtains. No interior paneling. Just a shack. A shack of misery. He found he was able to admire and appreciate the simplicity and the strength of the construction. He counted the upright studs, level, two feet apart, the double joists across the top supporting the roof. Cracks and knotholes aplenty, in the wall siding, let in bright chinks of light during the day and welcome wisps of clear fresh air at night. The rough planking of the siding was stained dark. The floor was only partly covered with odd sections of plywood. Some of the rough planking below was exposed, revealing cracks leading down to the cool black earth beneath. A small thick table was firmly studded to a portion of the wall opposite the door. A few small pieces of clear lumber stood bunched together, unsung, unused, unhurried, in the far corner. An overhead shelf, supported from the ceiling by a small extending perpendicular arm, containing some boxes of left-over chemicals and fertilizers, completed the furnishings in his temporary abode.

It was habitable.

He could raise his family in it.

If they were rabbits.

The first rays of a brute new day clinked in through the small rectangle of panes. The ray hovered, then peaked, then rested on the covers pushed up by his knees. He recalled his mountain trips with his uncle to the great forbidding barrancas near Durango in Central Mexico, and stopping to rest in the middle of the wild woods, and coming unexpectedly upon a crumbling, splintered hulk of a shack that was all falling apart. It barely gave them shelter from the sudden pelting storm they were trying to escape, he as a young frightened boy, but shelter it was--and how beautiful that experience was, then, for they were free, daring, adventurers, out there in that wilderness, alone and daring, with nothing between them and God's own overpowering nature, alone. They belonged to nothing. To no one. But themselves. They were dignity purified. No one forced them to go or stay there. They were delighted and grateful to the shack. For the protection it afforded them. Though it was hardly more than a ratty pile of splinters. Far worse than this one he was now occupying. . . . but also somehow far more beautiful in his memory.

And now. Here he was. Shut up in this miserable shack. So sturdily built. Thinking how it sickened him inside because it was more a jail cell than a shelter. He didn't care how comfortable and convenient the growers made the shacks for him. They were huts of slavery. What he wanted was an outlet for his pride. A sudden fierce wave of anger made him want to cross the shack with his fists. There had to be some way to cross the ungulfable bridge. Why was necessity always the bride of hunger? To be free. . . . ah, and also to be able to eat all one wanted. My heart, mi corazon, why did work always have to blend with such misery? The welcome warmth of the sun's early rays, penetrating more, warmed his frame. But it was a false, false hope. He knew it. The work that lay ahead of him that day would drain and stupify and fatigue him once again to the point of senseless torpor, ready to fall over long before the work day was done. And that fatigue wasn't merely so bad to bear as the deadly repetitious monotony of never changing, never resting, doing the same plucking over and over and over again. But he had to do it. He had no choice. It was all he could do. It had to be done if he wanted the money. And he had to have the money, if he wanted to feed his family. The brain in his arms was his only capital. Not very much, true, but it was the only sacrifice he could offer the money gods, the only heart he could offer on the pyramid of gold.

His life. La gran vida.

Wide awake now, fully refreshed, his whole body lithe and toned, Manuel was ashamed to find himself eager to start in work, knowing that he would do well, but ashamed because he could think of nothing he would rather do more. The final step.

The final the final the final the final the final the final step.

To want to work oneself to death. A la muerte. It wasn't the work itself that bothered him. It was the total immersion, the endless, ceaseless, total use of all his energies and spirit and mind and being that tore him apart within. He didn't know what else he was good for or could do with his life. But there had to be something else. He had to be something more than a miserable plucking animal. Pluck pluck pluck. Feed feed feed. Glug glug glug. Dressing quickly, rolling up his blanket roll and stuffing it into a corner to use again that night, Manuel stepped coolly out into the morning sweetness and breathed the honeyscented humidity rinsing air rising from the honied soil, and joined the thickening throng of his fellow pluckers milling about the large open barn serving as a cookout. Feeding all the pickers was another of the fat man's unholy prerogatives, for he cheated and overpriced on meals too. Roberto Morales, the fat man, the shrewd contratista, was a bully man, busily darting his blob about, exhorting his priceless pickers to hurry, answering questions, giving advice, in the cool half-light, impatiently, pushing, giving orders. Manuel, in order to avoid having to greet him, scowled at his toes when Roberto came trouncing by, saying, "Apurense, compañeros, hurry, hurry, hurry, amigos." Sure. Amigos. Si. Si. Frens. They all gulped their food down hurriedly, standing. Just like home. Paper plates, plastic cups. Wooden spoons. And bits of garbage flying into large canisters. Then in the still cool nightlike morning air, like a flood of disturbed birds, they all picked up their pails and filed into the orchard.

The apricots were plump.

Smooth.

A golden syrupy orange.

Manuel popped two into his mouth, enjoying their cool natural sweetness after the bitter coffee. He knew he could not eat too many. His stomach muscles would cramp. Other pickers started pull ing rapidly away from him. Let them. Calmly he calculated the struggle. Start the press sure, slow, and keep it going steady. Piecework. Fill the bucket, fill another, and still another. The competition was among a set of savages, as savage for money as himself, savages with machetes, hacking their way through the thickets of modern civilization back to the good old Aztec days, waiting to see who'd be first in line to wrench his heart out. Savage beasts, eager to fill as many buckets as possible in as short a time as possible, cleaning out an entire orchard, picking everything in

57

sight clean, tons of fruit, delivering every bit of ripe fruit to the accountants in their cool air conditioned orifices.

The competition was not between pickers and growers.

It was between pickers -- Jorge and Guillermo.

Between the poor and the hungry, the desperate, and the hunted, the slave and the slave, slob against slob, the depraved and himself. You were your own terrible boss. That was the cleverest part of the whole thing. The picker his own bone picker, his own willing built-in slave driver. God, that was good! That was where they reached into your scrotum and screwed you royally and drained your brain and directed your sinews and nerves and muscles with invisible fingers. To fatten their coffers. And drive you to your coffin. That sure was smart. Meant to be smart. Bookkeepers aren't dumb. You worked hard because you wanted to do that hard work above everything else. Pick fast pick hard pick furious pick pick pick. They didnt' need straw bosses studying your neck to see if you kept bobbing up and down to keep your picking pace up. Like the barn-stupid chicken, you drove yourself to do it. You were your own money monkey foreman, monkey on top of your own back.

You over-charged yourself.

With your own frenzy.

Neat.

You pushed your gut and your tired aching arms and your twitching legs pumping adrenalin until your tongue tasted like coarse sandpaper.

You didn't even stop to take a drink, let alone a piss, for fear you'd get fined, fired, or bawled out.

And then, after all that effort, you got your miserable pay.

Would the bobbing boss's sons stoop to that?

His fingers were loose and dexterous now. The plump orange balls plopped pitter patter like heavy drops of golden rain into his swaying, sweaty canvas bucket. His earnings depended entirely on how quickly he worked and how well he kept the pressure up. The morning sun was high. The sweet shade was fragrant and refreshing and comfortable under the leafy branches. The soil too was still cool and humid. It was going to be another hot one.

There.

Another row ended.

He swung around the end of the row and for a moment he was all alone, all by himself. He looked out far across the neighboring alfalfa field, dark green and rich and ripe. Then he looked at the long low Diablo Range close by, rising up into the misty pale blue air kept cool by the unseen bay nearby. This was all his. For a flowing, deceptive minute, all this rich, enormous terrain was all his. All this warm balmy baby air. All this healthful sunny breeze. All those hills, this rich

fertile valley, these orchards, these tiled huertas, these magnificent farms all, all his.... for his eyes to feast upon. It
was a moment he wished he could capture forever and etch per-
manently on his memory, making it a part of living life for his
heart to feast joyously on, forever. Why couldn't he stop? Why?
Why couldn't he just put the bucket down and open his arms and
walk into the hills and merge himself with the hills and just
wander invisibly in the blue?

What Manuel couldn't really know was that he was complet-
ing yet another arc in the unending circle that had been started
by one of his Mexican forebears exactly two hundred years before -- for even the memory of history was also robbed from
him -- when Gaspar de Portola, hugging the coastline, nearing
present-day San Francisco, climbed what is now Sweeney
Ridge, and looked down upon San Francisco's magnificent land-
locked Bay, overlooking what is now the International Airport.

Both don Gaspar and don Manuel were landlords and land-
less at precisely the same instant of viewing all this heady
beauty. And both were equally dispossessed. Both were also
possessed of a keen sense of pride and natural absorption with
the ritual and mystery of all life. The living that looked mighty
good in a flash to Manuel lasted a good deal longer for don Gaspar whose stumbling accident swept him into the honored and
indelible pages of glorious history.

Manuel was now a mere straw among the enormous sludge
of humanity flowing past, a creature of limb and his own driving appetites, a creature of heed and need. Swinging around
another end run he placed his ladder on the next heavy limb of
the next pregnant tree. He reached up. He plucked bunches of
small golden fruit with both hands. He worked like a frenzied
windmill in slow motion. He cleared away an arc as far as the
circumference of his plucking fingers permitted. A living model
for da Vinci's outstretched man. Adam heeding God's moving
finger. He moved higher. He repeated another circle. Then
down and around again to another side of the tree, until he
cleared it, cleared it of all visible, viable, delectable, succulent fruit. It was sweet work. The biggest difference between
him and the honey-gathering ant was that the ant had a home.

Several pickers were halfway down the next row, well in
advance of him. He was satisfied he was pacing himself well.
Most of the band was still behind him. The moving sun, vault-
ing the sky dome's crackling earth parting with its bronzing
rays, pounded its fierce heat into every dead and living crev-
ice. Perspiration poured down his sideburns, down his forehead, down his cheek, down his neck, into his ears, off his
chin. He tasted its saltiness with the tip of his dry tongue.
He wished he'd brought some salt tablets. Roberto Morales
wasn't about to worry about the pickers, and Manuel wasn't

worried either. Despite the heat, he felt some protection from the ocean and bay. It had been much, much worse in Texas, and much hotter in Delano in the San Joaquin valley and worst of all in Satan's own land, the Imperial Valley.

No matter which way he turned, he was trapped in an endless maze of acpricot trees, as though forever, neat rows of them, neatly planted, row after row, just like the blackest bars on the jails of hell. There had to be an end. There had to be. There -- trapped. There had to be a way out. Locked. There had to be a respite. Animal. The buckets and the crates kept piling up higher. Brute. He felt alone. Though surrounded by other pickers. Beast. Though he was perspiring heavily, his shirt was powder dry. Savage. The hot dry air. The hot dry air sucking every drop of living moisture from his brute body. Wreck. He stopped and walked to the farthest end of the first row for some water, raised the dented dipper from the brute tank, drank the holy water in great brute gulps so he wouldn't have to savor its tastelessness, letting it spill down his torn shirt to cool his exhausted body, to replenish his brute cells and animal pores and stinking follicles and pig gristle, a truly refined wreck of an animal, pleased to meetcha. Predator.

Lunch.

Almost too exhausted to eat, he munched his cheese with tortillas, smoked on ashes, then lay back on the cool ground for half an hour. That short rest in the hot shade replenished some of his humor and resolve. He felt his spirit swell out again like a thirsty sponge in water. Then up again. The trees. The branches again. The briarly branches. The scratching leaves. The twigs tearing at his shirt sleeves. The ladder. The rough bark. The endlessly unending piling up of bucket upon box upon crate upon stack upon rack upon mound upon mountain. He picked a mountain of cots automatically. An automator. A beast. A ray of enemy sun penetrated the tree that was hiding him and split his forehead open. His mind whirred. He blacked out. Luckily he'd been leaning against a heavy branch. His feet hooked to the ladder's rung. His half-filled bucket slipped from his grasp and fell in slow motion, splattering the fruit he'd so laboriously picked. To the ground. Robert happened by and shook his head. "Whatsamatter, can't you see straight, pendejo." Manuel was too tired even to curse. He should have had some salt pills.

Midafternoon.

The summer' fierce zenith passed overhead. It passed. Then dropped. It started to light the ocean behind him, back of the hills. Sandy dreams. Cool nights. Cold drinks. Soft guitar music with Lupe sitting beside him. All wafting through his feverish moments. Tiredness drained his spirit of will. Exhaustion drained his mind. His fingers burned. His arms flailed the innocent trees. He was slowing down. He could hardly fill his last bucket. Suddenly the whistle blew. The day's work was at last ended.

Ended!

The contratista Roberto Morales stood there.

His feet straddled. Mexican style. A real robber. A Mexican general. A gentlemanly, friendly, polite, grinning, vicious, thieving brute. The worst kind. To his own people. Despite his being a fellow Mexican, despite his torn, old cloth - ing, everyone knew what kind of clever criminal he was. Des - pite his crude, ignorant manner, showing that he was one of them, that he'd started with them, that he grew up with them, that he'd suffered all the sordid deprivations with them, he was actually the shrewdest, smartest, richest cannibal in forty counties around. They sure couldn't blame the gueros for this miscarriage. He was a crew chief. How could anyone know what he did to his own people? And what did the gueros care? So the anglo growers and guero executives, smiling in their cool filtered offices, puffing their elegant thin cigars, washed their clean blond bloodless dirtless hands of the whole matter. All they did was hire Roberto Morales. Firm, fair, and square. For an agreed-upon price. Good. How he got his people down to the pickings was no concern of theirs. They were honest, those gueros. They could sleep at night. They fulfilled their end of the bargain, and cheated no one. Their only crime; their only soul grime indeed was that they just didn't give a shit how that migratory scum lived. It was no concern of theirs. Their religion said it was no concern of theirs. Their wives said it was no concern of theirs. Their aldermen said it was no concern of theirs. Their --

Whenever Roberto Morales spoke, Manuel had to force him- self not to answer. He had to keep his temper from flaring.

"Now," announced Morales at last, in his friendliest tone. "Now. I must take two cents from every bucket. I am sorry. There was a miscalculation. Everybody understands. Every- body?" He slid his eyes around, smiling, palms up.

The tired, exhausted pickers gasped as one.

Yes. Everyone understood. Freezing in place. After all that hard work.

"Any questions, men?"

Still grinning, knowing, everyone realizing that he had the upper hand, that that would mean a loss of two or three dollars out of each picker's pay that day, a huge windfall for Morales..

"You promised to take nothing!" Manuel heard himself say- ing. Everyone turned in astonishment to stare at Manuel.

"I said two cents, hombre. You got a problem or what?"

"You promised."

The two men, centered in a huge ring of red-ringed eyes,

61

glared at each other. Reaching for each other's jugular. The other exhausted animals studied the tableau through widening eyes. It was so unequal. Morales remained calm, confident, studying Manuel. As though memorizing his features. He had the whole advantage. Then, with his last remaining energy, Manuel lifted his foot and clumsily tipped over his own last bucket of cots. They rolled away in all directions around everyone's feet.

Roberto Morales' eyes blazed. His fists clenched. "You pick them up, Gutierrez."

So. He knew his name. After all. For answer, Manuel kicked over another bucket, and again the fruit rolled away in all directions.

Then an astonishing thing happened.

All the other pickers moved toward their own buckets still standing beside them on the ground awaiting the truck gatherer, and took an ominous position over them, straddling their feet over them. Without looking around, without taking his eyes off Manuel, Roberto Morales said sharply, "All right. All right, men. I shall take nothing this time."

Manuel felt a thrill of power course through his nerves.

He had never won anything before. He would have to pay for this, for his defiance, somehow, again, later. But he had shown defiance. He had salvaged his money savagely and he had earned respect from his fellow slaves. The gringo hijos de la chingada would never know of this little incident, and would probably be surprised, and perhaps even a little morti-fied, for a few minutes. But they wouldn't give a damn. It was bread, pan y tortillas out of his children's mouths. But they still wouldn't give a single damn. Manuel had wrenched Mora-les' greedy fingers away and removed a fat slug of a purse from his sticky grasp. And in his slow way, in his stupid, accidental, dangerous way, Manuel had made an extravagant discovery, as don Gaspar had also made two centuries before, in almost exactly the same spot. And that was -- that a man counted for something. For men, Manuel dimly s u s p e c ted, are built for something more important and less trifling than the mere gathering of prunes and apricots, hour upon hour, decade upon decade, insensibly, mechanically, antlike. Men are built to experience a certain sense of honor and pride.

Or else they are dead before they die.

11

Cati, back in her orange-crate crib inside the dark room cried in deliberate rhythm, no strain, just annoyance.

Lupe listened to her attentively a few moments. Then, satisfied, she stepped outside. She scanned the courtyard, studying each scrubby tree, bush, and unpainted shack. All deserted. All the children were out of sight. Where could her Mariquita and Manuelito be? She went around in back and searched among the trees filling the flattened land in long monotonous endless rows, row upon row of neatly cleared prune trees, all, all, all belonging to the royal turtle, Mr. Turner.

The roar of the tireless tractor in a far corner of the orchard gave her a momentary fright. The tractor was churning the earth, planing it, flattening it. Manuelito was frightened of the big monster machine while Mariquita curiously was not.

Lupe continued standing there, torn between the distant motor's rumble and the baby's lessened whimper. It was like having a nightmare. But she was awake. Why should she be frightened? A jet's evil whine pierced the far horizon, entered her piece of sky, and roared low through the late afternoon's glide on its streaktrack to nearby Moffett Field. From El Camino Boulevard came the steady hum of traffic and an occasional truck, partially muffled by the intervening trees.

63

From another corner of the Valley, further west, came other ominous sounds, the bangbangbang of hammering carpenters hanging up new new spanking brand new sweetsmelling houses in clusters of ten ten and twenty and thirty brand new boxes to meet the growing prosperous demand, where the trees were growing only yesterday, bearing fruit, maturing, and then ripped up out of the earth. All kinds of noises funneled down to her, from the sausage freeway, from the roaring towns, through the bustling trees, rumbling and groaning, roaring, blicking, blooping, banging, knocking and clicking hells. But none of those noises contained her children's yells.

Where could they possibly be?

She looked into the crib. Assuring herself that her Cati was indeed asleep, sound asleep, her little eyes shuttight, breath - in her soft delightful baby rhythm, Lupe set out for the arroyo in her robe and house slippers. The earth, the soft, rich, pliant mother earth was rich and true, supporting healthy trees, so rich and proud and so evenly spaced, trees as well cared for, better cared for than some children she knew. She walked toward the dip that led to the arroyo, reached it, stood there prnsively a few moments, listening, then stepped carefully sideways down the gentle slope of the dry creek. The bed of the dry gully was a sinister rubble of many different-sized rocks, pebbles, and boulders. Not a sign of either Mariquita or Manuelito. Where could they be? Back at the house? Should she return? Panic started coiling her nerves taut. She fought it off. Where should she go? She tried to swallow but her mouth was dry. She could go in any of six different directions, out there in that vast rich endless maze of an orchard, under that wide open balmy sky. The sky began to darken. The wind moaned low. The branches reached for her. The trunks blocked her way. The stones bruised her feet. The invisible dust choked her. The children knew how to do their necessity outdoors when no one was around, like a pair of small animals in their natural habitat. Why had she talked so long with Olive Pope? The air was sweet, sickening her. Suddenly she star- ted recalling her own sweet childhood, how she had survived, out in the open country among fields of tall corn and in el monte, in the underbrush of the hilly slopes high in the mountains of Jalisco. Ay Jalisco....

"Mariquita!" she called, barely able to scream above a whisper. "Manuelito!"

They did not answer.

She quickened her step. She thought of the baby all alone.

She'd never left Cati alone before. She tried to force her- self to go back to the shack. A sharp pain suddenly stabbed her chest, probably from walking too fast. She had to run. She stumbled among the boulders, climbed up the side of the arroyo, then cut diagonally out across the orchard. Cool streams of air filtered down from the Santa Cruz range, through the trees, but her brow got hotter. Oh, they were all right. Por dios santo. Oh, they had to be all right. Ay dios mio. She reassured herself over and over, mumbling, talking to herself, forcing herself to run faster. The pain in her lungs made her slow down again. Ay dios, where could they be? Where could they have gone to? Where should she go? They had to be somewhere. Somewhere near. Why did she have to hurt so?

Beyond thought, grieved to distraction, imagining everything terrible, she turned and ran and changed her direction and changed it again wildly and angled back once more. She saw the rumbling tractor in the distant plums, angling toward her, lurching, a terrible monster of a machine that chopped and chewed the ground so easily. A wild spasm of pure fear shot through her all of a sudden. She broke into a thumping, waddling run, her feet frozen to the ground. The -- machine -- ! The driver, one of Mr. Turner's regular hands, saw her and grinned and waved. He kept pushing the snorter. On the next turn, when he saw she was not simply waving a greeting at him, but trying to make him stop, he halted. The rumbler stopped.

"My children, mis niños!" she cried.

"Hah?" It was hot.

"My Manuelito!"

"Hot, eh!"

"You have not seen my little boy, my little girl?"

He finally understood. "Nope." He mopped his head with a small kitchen towel.

She turned her head. "Mariquita!" Her shriek shattered the enormous silence. The driver watched her, grinning, shrugging his shoulders, oblivious to her great peril, ignorant of her concern, indifferent to the great pains surging through her chest. She looked down at the freshly churned earth, half expecting to see a tiny leg sticking out. With a painful sob, she turned again, and rushed back toward the compound.

Then she saw it -- a tiny shoe. A small, brown, unlaced boy's shoe atop the freshly flattened earth. She snatched it up. It was Manuelito's shoe. Manuelito -- ? The rest of the earth around it was packed solidly flat. Her head started to whirl. She dropped to her knees as though in prayer. Then, animal-like, she started scratching at the hardpacked earth with her fingers. Her fingernails broke. It was no use. Pale with fright, her face drained of blood, almost out of her mind, she leaped up and ran the rest of the way to her hut. She found Manuel standing inside the shack. She could not speak. Her breath came in painful gasps. She was on the verge of fainting.

"Mi corazon," said Manuel, clasping her firmly. "What is the matter with you? Come, tell me. Calm yourself."

"Ay, ay, ay --" was all she could gasp.

"You are all out of breath, mi corazon. You must sit down. "

"No, no!" She waved the child's shoe at him. "Don't you, you, you, the children, ven, los niños, ven, they are, are --"

Manuel followed her. Instead of going in the direction she wanted, however, he led her around to the back of the hut.

And there they were.

The two of them --

The two of them, Manuelito and Mariquita, playing peacefully, digging in the dirt under the big oak tree. She had not seen them. They had returned during her absence. Of course Manuelito was without his one shoe, and, with a mixture of anger compounded by frustration, she snatched them both up to spank them sharply but instead embraced and kissed and hugged them hard, squirming and complaining, tears streaking down her perspiring face. She was laughing, crying, and sobbing, all at the same time. She nearly fainted again from the relief.

12

Sleep had left her.

Throwing back her covers, Margarita tiptoed barefooted to the window and ducked under the drawn window shade. She liked looking out at dawn. Her favorite game, whenever she awoke early enough, was looking out through the window when dawn was coming on. She was half dreamy, half awake, in a world alone, all her own, all by herself, the only real privacy she could ever find. She loved life, she loved the world and everything in it. She was thrilled with the bigness of her capacity for love, and most of all she loved watching the way she sun came up faithfully every morning, lighting everything up so beautifully. The sky began to barely burn light gray on the horizon, exposing the profits of the nearby Diablo Mountains as a long, low range of hills, darker than the houses and orchard trees on both sides of the Drawbridge High School buildings. Some of the lights were still lit on the school grounds, burning with a light purple glow on tall thin posts.

She heard the motors of the powerful, heavy trucks along the nearby Bayshore Freeway, taking produce up the Peninsula to San Francisco, or up the other side, the Nimitz Freeway to Oakland. She liked the peacefulness of the countryside under its cool misty cover and, as the the got ready to lift itself above the mountain humps, its rays lit the undersides of some long, love slivers of clouds, setting them aglow with a wedge of silvery orange fire against the gradually lightening, brightening gray sky. She liked it just the way it was. It was so peaceful and calm. She wished she could stop it, the whole process, that it would stay exactly that way forever. She hated the thought, she hated the prospect of having to face another day filled with hatreds, fights, and unknown ordeals. She knew life could be so beautiful, but its beauty eluded her. What did she have to do to suck the joy out?

High school, everybody said, was supposed to be so much fun. It wouldn't be bad if only the kids would leave her alone. The Anglo boys teased her unmercifully. "Hey, Margarita -- give me one of your sexy looks." That was their way of complimenting her. Well, she hated it. The blonde girls were jealous, mean or nasty, and always superior and often suspicious of her. But why? Why? She didn't like having the world split between Mexican and Anglo, but that was how it was, and she tried to make the best of it. She wasn't always successful. The teachers were all right. But so innocent. What it was, they really didn't care. They didn't like getting involved. They didn't want to probe too deeply. Besides by instinct they couldn't help siding with their own kind, with their own Anglo kids, against the Chicanos. Or else they'd do something worse -- they'd be patronizing toward her, dripping with false sympanthy, and that was much, much worse. She could stand on her own feet. She didn't need any special favors. All she wanted, wanted, all she asked for and seldom got was plain, simple, decent, ordinary kindness. Most of the kids fortunately were indifferent toward her and left her alone. Some of them, however, the tormentors, liked occasionally going out of their way to be real mean.

Drawbridge High wasn't a big school. It was brand new, though, with long low pretty pinkstoned buildings. Only two years were in, and Margarita was keeping pace with its growth and progress. She wished oh many times she wished she could quit school altogether. Not for any reason she could put her finger on. She was just plain unhappy. What good was school doing her? She didnt' find school stimulating. She liked to study things she liked, but what was the use? And all the kids were always yapping away about which college they were going to go to. No thank you. What, and go through all this stupid nonsense all over again? What good were books if people insisted on being so mean? And what good was studying if no one gave you any credit for knowing anything? She knew she could learn anything she set her mind to. She knew she could get all the good grades she wanted to, just by concentrating. But why do it? When all they did was laugh and tease and poke fun at you and your looks? Lucky she wasn't ugly like some of the jealous gueras, but she sometimes felt it was better to be a repulsive, ugly blonde guera than pretty, Mexican, and dark skinned. That was the way it was. And that was the way it was always going to be. What good did it do to be ambitious? And a girl? And a Mexican girl? She knew those things bugged Danny too, but Danny at least had his sports and the track team and the swimming team, and he could laugh and play big man and fight back and so they respected him. But she didn't want to fight back. She was always being goaded and annoyed and insulted in mean little ways. Always having to smile back. Always having to go out of her way. Always avoiding conflicts. She didn't like it. That was why she wanted to quit. She wished she could.

The sophomore class was going to be added in September, and the senior class the following year, and she could keep pace. Because it was such a new school, besides, maybe she was better off here. She really didn't care. There was no one she could confide in. What was real keen was that the school was right behind her house. She didn't have to ride for miles and miles like some of the kids. She could look out her bedroom window and over the back fence into the school yard.

She heard a softly scuffling sound, little feet scudding across the floor. The steady tinkle of pee running into the toilet came faintly to her. It was Carlitos, her littlest brother. He came up to her. "What you doing, Margarita? Huh?" he husked, tugging her pajamas.

"Hush, Carlitos," she said. On impulse she bent down and kissed the top of his ruffled head. "You go back to your bed, hear, and get some more sleep."

"But I'm all awake, Marga."

"You try. For me. I bet you can."

"OK. I try."

It was still very dark out. A minute later she heard his peaceful breathing again, in deep rhythm. She wanted to die. She admitted to herself that she secretly liked the way boys looked at her. She knew she thrilled at their longing. But she didn't like the way they teased her unmercifully. They always did it in front of other girls. For their benefit, it seemed. She couldn't stand being teased, toyed or played with. She knew it was their way of flirting with her but still she didn't like it. She was really too grown up for them. They seemed so like children, immature and spoiled. She was already dreaming of having a proud blue prince for a husband, a lover who would give her everything she wanted from life, who would fight for her and relieve her emptinesses.

There were some Anglo boys she liked but she would never dream of letting them know. The Mexican boys, the Chicanos, treated her diffidently, either with distant disregard, as though waiting, or, some she didn't like, with mean looks of longing in their narrow black eyes. Some of them scared her, but not in a mean way. She would always take care of herself with that kind. But the Anglos, the gueros, who liked to jostle and joke. .... She wished she could stop smiling at them when they did it and show her anger but she smiled each time they hurt her and she did it only not to give her hurt away and also and espe - cially for the gueras. The gueras considered her their rival maybe because the boys teased her and paid her so much attention. She could tell. She could tell from the way they studied her from the dormers of their lightly made-up eyes, and from the way they smirked behind their upraised arms. As though making believe they were only coughing. But also really making sure she saw.

A girl once came up to her one morning as classes were starting. She stared at Margarita full of meanness. Margarita's pride senses a new trouble. She was dull with fights.

"Hey you," snarled the girl, waving her stiffly lacquered golden blonde locks at her.

"Yes?" said Margarita, hugging her books.

"You. You keep away from my boyfriend."

Margarita kept away from everybody's boyfriends. She stared back. She said nothing, waiting for the explosion.

"My Bill. You keep away from my Bill. He's mine. You hear?"

Bill. Margarita knew at least four boys named Bill. Which one?

"Now you keep away from mm, spic. You comprainda?"

Margarita, bigger and stronger than this whey-faced hate-filled slut, turned away, before her tormentor could have the satisfaction of triggering her temper, or of seeing the tears that were already stinging her eyes. Before the unclean guera could mouth more of her fool sappish Spanish at her, before the indecent wretch had a chance to utter that most loathsome of their favorite phrases, you dirty Mexican, Margarita turned and fled. She didn't want to have to smack her. That would have proved only that she was stronger, but not smarter. So Margarita would have to do her best to keep away from the slut's "Bill," whichever one that might be, and all her normal and natural impulses to play and banter and yet flirt with boys would again have to be bottled up still tighter. They would tease her all the more, calling her stuck-up and conceited and vain, and the gueras would then smirk all the more. There were moments when she wished she could just die.

Slowly, shyly, timidly, the sun's edge peeked above the distant range, a tiny pinpoint of fire at first. She looked at it in fascination. A brand new sun. Another brand new kind of life. A brand new hope. It glowed fiercely. It shimmered. It hung suspended. It nestled for a split instant between a cradle of small peaks like an incandescent orange topaz. It grew bright, hotter, and more dazzling each fragment of a second. She imagined it to be a giant sizzling jewel, perhaps an engagement ring that her princely lover came all the way across the heavens to give her to wipe out all the misery she was suffering. Then the yolk burst. The orange ball tugged itself free of the mountain peaks and blazed so fiercely it burned everything in sight -- the trees, the morning mountain, the school, her eyelids. Too bright. Too hot for her to look at directly any more.

She turned her eyes away, seared, sizzled.

It was going to be another hot day again.

Where did she come from? Why was she here? Lupe often talked about Mexico and Guadalajara, but Mexico was nowhere for her. It was as foreign to her as Belgium. Did that mean she had no home? In Mexico she had seen that, except for the very rich, just about everybody was very poor. Two extremes. At least here in her country, in the U.S., everyone that wanted to could work and not be ashamed of being poor, or partly poor, or poor in the sense of not starving but perhaps not having everything you saw in sight in all the shop windows or TV ads or big discount houses. Or even of being just a poor slob of a worker, for everybody worked at something. Still, there were times she couldn't help feeling she didn't belong, even though she had been born right here in Santa Clara, an American born, a citizen by birth. What good was it? What was the good of being born a perfectly good, honest, private, legal citizen of the United States of America if everyone was going to snarl Mexican to your face like it was some hateful word? Where did she belong then? Back in her mother's home town? In her father's? In Salpinango? In Guadalajara? Would they send her back there? But what if she wasn't from there, from any of those places either? What then? She didn't belong there, in old Mexico, either. She was California born. California . . . . . which once was Mexico. California -- which once belonged to her people, for hundreds and thousands of years. And now she didn't belong. In Mexico, on her two brief visits, the native Mexicans there always considered her as an American. She also sensed they also thought her family was very rich because she had pretty clothes. True, she had brought her prettiest dresses; but she'd made most of them herself, and had earned the money for the yardage either babysitting or picking prunes. How could she explain that they weren't rich? That although her father earned more money in a month than most of their relatives earned in a year still didn't make him rich because the cost of living was so high in the U.S.? But how do you explain to poor people, who are poorer than you, that you aren't rich? The answer is. . . .

The answer is, you don't explain. You can't.

The sun vaulted higher. Margarita continued standing there, letting its hot head press down hard on her cool forehead. Its heat felt odd, against the cool pane of that early morning hour. Summer -- and summer picking. The household was beginning to stir now. Her mother was moving about in the kitchen, moving pots softly, putting water on to boil, and her sisters in the bathroom were running water. They were all getting ready for another outing, another day's prune picking in family sum-mertime.

Prune picking was essentially and practically a family job. It was more fun and more practical that way. The prune grow-ers preferred families to single pickers. The Delgado family lived right in the middle of the biggest prune county in the world, and there was nothing, absolutely nothing to gathering prunes. Papa Pepe went off to his regular job in the cannery when he wasn't running crews for Roberto Morales. Daniel, big man, would have nothing to do with prune pricking. Mama protected him. Serafina liked spoiling him. Daniel liked strutting about showing off his flamante clothery and driving his dad's car around town when Pepe didn't need it or used his pickup instead. Danny chauffered them to that day's picking, then went off on his rounds, looking for big things to do with his big time with other big do-nothings. When asked what do you do that for by his older sister Rosa, he'd reply laugh-ing, Sure -- what for?

The orchard owners were good employers. The prune gath-erers got as much work as they wanted, and in return they always showed up and executed their agreed contract as prom-ised. It was a good agreement, and mutually beneficial. The prune pickers didn't have to travel around the country, like so many hapless migrant workers, so many now that they were coming in thick like flies to help with all of the heavy crops now ripening, the apricots, the pears, and later the walnuts. The pickers got their wages, and the growers kept their land. Everybody was happy. Even the bankers. Serafina was espe-cially happy to see Mr. Turner so pleased; it was a sure sign that his bank vaults were probably spilling over, and nothing made her happier, for that meant more work for her and hers. She didn't care how much richer the rich got. She didn't like all that radical talk among her compañeros about how the rich ought to be stripped of every dollar and every hectare of land. That was terrible. The rich had earned what they got. They worked hard. They suffered. They sometimes lost, she had heard. They risked their capital. And without them, where would she, and all other poor families be? No, it was good to have good, fat, rich, and -- yes -- even greedy capitalists in their midst, for that way they all had work and they all could work to their hearts' content, from sunup to sundown if

71

they wanted to, to be able to keep alive. They should be grateful, not critical, her compadres. How ungrateful they were!! But she pardoned even them, for they did not know what they did in comdemning the poor, abused capitalists.

Serafina found she could always work her brood as a family unit just as much or as little as they pleased. All they had to do was put in time pretty steadily to make it worth the while. It was necessary to get up early to get out to the orchards. At summer all the kids thought of was playing, for nothing, so outdoor work was good for them. Pepe shrugged his shoulders, letting mama control this aspect of the family's recreation. Pepe took care of the heavy bills, the house payments, the car, the utilities, the food. The money mama wanted and that the kids helped earn helped her buy extra clothing and small luxuries for themselves. It wasn't any longer needed just to keep themselves alive, as had been true in the past, and as was still true of many migrating families she knew.

Daniel drove them over to the new section. Mr. Schroeder was there with Manuel, looking down the rows of trees, in his brandnew green pickup. Laid out in many rows, plenty of shade in the long slanting rays of the sun, the kids leaped out of the car like so many dolphins, happy, yelling, hooting, and rolling over each other.

Then the long, monotonous day's work began.

Under each tree was a layer of small round plump plums, film-covered with bloom, all ripe and ready for drying into prunes. The tractor had done its work a few days before. The earth had been leveled smooth. There was nothing to it. Stoop over, or down on your knees, gather up handfuls of the small ripe fruit, and fill your bucket. Then carry bucket to crate. Then crate to box. The kids were all quick and full of energy, and it was half play for them as well as half pay. Mama didn't care how much or how little they did so long as they didn't wander off out of sight or step on any of the fruit. She didn't have to tell them not to eat any either. They knew. After their first day's severe stomach cramps, and after being forced to run to the outhouse every five minutes, they soon learned to respect the silent power of those plump plums.

The boxes, gathered by Manuel in a flat electric car, were then taken to the driers, the hot ovens going full blast night and day, turning the fresh round light purple balls into sweet, black crinkleskinned energypacked prunes. Margarita worked hard. She wanted to forget the misery that kept creeping into her mind, lingering, poisoning her thoughts, tying her mind up in thick black knots. She wished she could kid around and laugh and play like her small brothers. At the end of the work day, at six p.m., when they were all exhausted, Danny showed up and they all crept into the car, almost on fours.

"Hey, sis," said Daniel. "How come you're not going to the big summer hop?"

"Shut up," said Margarita, staring blankly out the window. "You just shut up and leave me alone."

"You better leave your sister alone, hijito," said mama.

Danny knew better than to push her. He drove them home in silence. In bitter, tired, frustrated silence.

13

The hot July air was dry, crackly, dusty, and larcenous.

Manuel maneuvered the coughing, dusty, dry sedan along the bumpy, also dusty, also rutty lane, flanking long rows of other cars already parked in the huge open field out in that blistering San Jose sun. He swung past the last cat in the last row and hugged to a stop.

"Vaya, hombre," said Ramiro. "We made it."

"You had doubts?" Manuel jumped out. He stretched his arms, legs straddled. Ramiro pried the door open for Lupe. Cati was cradled asleep in her lap. Manuelito and Mariquita leaped out in high glee and jumped and jumped about like wild dolphins. Lupe warned them about the other cars moving about the huge open lot.

Once inside the Flea Market gate, the two children twisted loose and ran flipping about joyously. Just like a giant carnival. Throngs of people, crowds milling about. There were stalls and tables of every kind, shape, and size. Mountains of wares of all kinds of notions invited perusal.

"Ah, look at all that magnificent chorizo," said Manuel. "Let us buy some chorizo right away before -- !"

"Por el amor de dios," said Lupe. "Not just now. It is much too hot out. Let us buy it on the way out."

"Sure," said Ramiro. "Let us buy the place out."

They stopped and gawked at every tidbit offered along the way. The variety of goods on open display was incredible. Everything under the sun. Some new. Most old. Somewhere, some place, someone had something for sale, cheap and good and beautiful. Bueno, barato, y bonito, the three B's. In from the Valley, back by the lower lip of the bay, behind Drawbridge, near Alviso, on the edge of San Jose, off the county road leading to Milpitas, buried among huge huertas and endless orchards full of flowering plums, way out where the creep-boxhouse builders had not yet begun to blast, was the market of the fleas, the county's biggest hot air open market.

At the Table of the Dolls little Mariquita's big eyes bulged even bigger. On the long narrow table, out in the bright sun, were rows and rows of dollas. Big-eyed dolls, bulging dolls, burping dolls, ragtag dolls, thin, skinny dollas, mopheads, towheads, frowzyheads. Green tarantula dolls with long spindly arms. Fat little baby blue dolls with red eyes. Brown dolls with blue marbles gleaming for eyes. Yellow dolls, pink dolls, checkered and ginghamed dolls, black dolls, and sad dolls, glad dolls, white dolls, all sitting dolls patiently awaiting their fate. Neurotic and phlegmatic dolls. Piano playing dolls. Bulging dolls. Judy dolls. Hopeful dolls. Cheap and expensive dolls sitting democratically side by side. Marinated dolls. Babushka dolls. A wide sampling of pitiful dolls. Mariquita dolls. Mariquita stared. She stopped to look at one especially sad doll, a muñequita linda, a sad little frayed doll. Manuel wouldn't let her fondle it. He pulled her away.

"Why not let her hold it?" said Ramiro. "Everyone does."

"Two for the price of one," croaked the hairy fairy doll squatting under her beautiful beach umbrella. "Any two."

"No, no," said Lupe, shooing the children away from the smiling witch. "The idea. We have got to buy food. We can not buy toys."

Ramiro pulled a bill out of his pocket. He scooped up the sad rag doll, plus another brilliant China doll, and tucked them into Mariquita's surprised arms. He also immediately bought a harmonica for Manuelito.

The shoe stall, full of all sizes, makes, colors, shapes, and styles, was chaos compounded by confusion. Lupe looked at a pair of long needlenosed black pumps marked "Made in Italy," turned them over and over, felt them, squeezed them, weighed them, sighed with them, and walked on. Long, long rows of tables and stalls stuffed with merchandise, marmalades, and marmadukes, some new, some used, but most of it helplessly shoddy. Fluttering swings, tattered awnings, enclosed shutters, little cubicles with waiting smiling merchants within. Shady overhead lattices overhead. From one enormous overhang, shaded by a high flat overhead roof, reminding Lupe of the huge open air market places of her girlhood, came the persistent drone of a determined auctioneer's voice over a loudspeaker:

"Now hear hear this hear this ladies and gentlemen I have here have here this this have this beauti beauti imp beautif imported now get this girls get this cutlery kitchen kitchen knife important antler antlered hand handled look look at it at it glee gleam look at it glisten listen it listen to it glisten and it goes for a song I mean a note wham I mean what am I bid what am I bid make an eff make an off an offer a noffer make it fast make quick make it furious take advantage now it's a steal for it will soon it will soon be soon be gone be gone and you'll be sorry fifty fifty cents who'll make it sixty sixty sixty sixtysixtysss eh eh six seventyseventyseven going once going seventy going twice SOLD seventee three cents to that there handsome ah gentleman in back there. And now folks wait don't don't wait if there are any more of you sports who fell in love who fell for this I mean with this piece with this lousy antlered piece of cutlery I say there are four not five nor six but four more exact duplicate copies of this same putrid piece of antlered junk which you can also have right now right now I saw this very minuet at this magnificent giveaway gift prize of only seventee three cents a piece oh so come on up now don't rush before they are all gone and you'll be sorry."

But all four were sold before Lupe even thought of pinching Manuel's arm to try to get one.

They stood there at the back of the transfixed crowd, listening to the charmer's hypnotic chant, watching one gleaming object after another pass in review before their very own eyes. A mixer. You want a mixer, corazon? Of course she wanted a mixer. But how could she be sure it worked? Suppose they got stuck? And what would they do for food money? Was it any good? Was it really new? Did it really work? Could they really afford it? Then someone snatched it up and it was good and gone forever too. Like everything else. And so, one after another, all afternoon, the candlesticks, a teacup set, a kerosene lamp, a set of genuine silverware, a huge pewter soup toureen, two hi-fis, a golden Aladdin's lamp guaranteed to work when rubbed, a silvertasseled lampshade six genuine European handpainted oil paintings, and much, much more. A house, Lupe wondered what is a house? A six-diced bug box. It turns into a home gradually with the things you buy for it and find to fill it with, with furniture and rattan, with warm clothing and bright throw rugs and sparkling dishes and heavy pots and gleaming copper pans, tables and chairs and drapes. And you always want more and more..... and that nude painting? What did Manuel know about art? It was a most indecent painting. Well..... she'd show him.

75

The endless rows of bricabrac, the discards of every nation, everywhere, in alleyways, in hideaways, on top of discarded end tables, piles of lumber, brand new garbage cans, tools of every kind, hammers and boxes of straightened nail and spiraled screws and seesaws and twisted screwdrivers and rusty pliers, plumbers helpers and carpenters aids, architectural calipers, surgeons' scalpels, sandblasting pumps, and much, much more. A regular bazaar. Bargains and bargains and bargains. But they resisted, shaking their heads at every table. The kids ran about playing game from one magic display to another, darting back and forth and in and out of the rows.

The hot sun started waning, ending one more day, and the hawkers saved their voices. Some did extremely well, some poorly. Everybody bought or sold something. Now or die. Do or dee. Sell off and plan the world all over again. Try some other combination next time. Nobody wanted any line that did not work, and the mounds kept getting smaller, shrinking, and the buyers kept on coming. There were so many things. Lupe bitterly realized that they were too poor to buy even the truly genuine bargains, not even the discards. They could buy only necessities. Bargains were really only for those with extra cash lying around that wasn't needed for bills, to be used to scoop up two socks for the price of one, or a special disaster slightly dented, or a deliberate sale leader, or something they wouldn't buy in their right minds but on impulse. If it didn't hurt. Like a $50 Hawaiian blouse. Or a blue plastered Venus de Milo. Sure, everybody in town could buy anything they wanted any time they wanted, could twist their little finger and fix their dollhouses up with sliding drawers and ama - thystine settings and eggyolk curtains for dessert. Sure. Fat filly mignon for brunch. Sure. Roasted turkey delight for breaking fast. Sure. Broiled tom toms for kicks. Si si si.

The produce section sported mountains of large orangutan tangerines, stacks of sacked potatoes, inverted funnels of snap beans, green beans, stalks of ripe heavy corn with kernels the size of golden nuggets, the newest California gold. The vendors kept yapping about bread and the staff of life, that flaky loose white fluff, loose and pale and lifeless as the gueros themselves. But the corn, hombre -- now that was really life, golden yellow life, rich life, real life. Vida.

"Shall we buy some corn, then, my heart?"

"No. "

Now they were really tired.

The dust and the heat irritated their arms, hurt their eyelids, and entered their pores. The jostling, juggling crowd helped keep their nerves jumpy. Even primo Ramiro was not smiling or laughing any more. The excitement was dissipating. The rest rooms were filthy. The children were crying. The crowds were annoying. The dust was suffocating. A bottle of soda pop barely kept the kids quiet a moment.

Like ants the milling throngs had arrived, had sprawled all over the offerings, had picked over the morsels they liked, and then streamed out once more back to the dusty parking lot, carrying their choices, having left some money behind, having bought some momentary happiness, some glistening thing, some new gadget, some old necessity, or something blue.

Only at one stall did Lupe dearly want to give in: at the ceramic stand, where the garishly colored flocked bulls from Tijuana stood in tight, even rows. Not the bulls; she didn't like them; they were terrible; but behind them were some tall slim Greek maidens, heads demurely bowed in pure innocence, wrapping all the premise of an angelic world in their long glowing robes, with only the barest peep of sandaled toes peeping out. She wondered why God had been so careless as to give her such a lumpy figure. She dreamed of a paradise where she might hold herself slim and erect and virginal all over again, with thin breasts barely protruding through her silky gauze gown. But these thinlipped goddesses, these blood blond tresses caused her to wonder what kind of poison was darkening her mind. Dark was the color of blood, and dark the long silken stands of her own trensas. Dark brown, like rich coffee, were her eyes. Not light. Not pink. Not pale blue. And yet .... she wanted to own one of these white goddesses. Why? Suddenly she felt a surge of wanting to smash them all, as a child would in full anger. She would smash them to bits. She would send the chips flying in all directions. She would grind them back to dust, back to marbly golden dust, turning the dust into paste with her tears. What new form could she make that would make her glad? And then the pale dress came back to her again and again. What could she, a mere woman, do? Pray? More? Pray more? Pray what? Ay dios de mi vida. Ay por dios santo. She wore out her rosaries. She kneeled. She clasped her hands in prayer. She prayed hard. All the time. Cooking. Sleeping. Walking. To all the saints. Todos los santos. To Saint Manuel. To Santa Isabel. To Santa Margarita. And to her own namesake above all, her own Virgen Guadalupe. Would she hear? This far? Outside her own land? Her own dark virgin? Ay ay ay. Virgen Guadalupe! What turmoils had been stored up for her and for her dark people and for her own dark precious children! She -- when would the bright bells ring out for joy? When would they delight? When would there be light like the sun lighting the whole world with pure delight and easy laughter?

"Come, mujer," grumbled Manuel, tugging her arm. "Do

you want to stay here all day and stare at those stupid statues? Do you want to have one? Is that it?"

"No," she lied, whispering, half in a trance, shaking her head. Manuel would give it to her if she asked. He was even more a child than she in that respect. Her eye fell on one of the huge urns on the ground, a thin-walled, light fragile jug. She wondered: what if she could raise her avocado plant in that? That way they, that way, they could, they might..... On impulse, she pointed to the huge urn. Manuel bought it. Ramiro lifted it clumsily, wrapping both arms around its body. Though it was not heavy, it was fat and cumbersome. It cost both men some effort to push and heave and many clumsy grunts and groans before they were finally able to wedge it in the back of the sedan. There was barely enough room for Manuelito beside it. Mariquita was squeezed up front with the big people and the baby.

"Tell me something, Ramiro," said Lupe, as the car started bouncing its way out through the dry ruts.

"I shall try."

"Do you like Margarita?"

Ramiro turned his head and laughed. "Well, what a --"

"Yes. I see," said Lupe. "As I thought. Now. Tell me this: why does Pepe hate you? What have you done to him?"

"I? To him? To Pepe?"

"Why do you not apologize to him?"

"To Pepe?" echoed Manuel. "You are crazy, mujer. Why should Pepe hate Ramiro? That is good for a big laugh."

Lupe started crying softly. Soft, large, heavy tears started dropping down her cheek, splashing onto baby Cati's blanket.

"Now what is the matter, corazon?" said Manuel.

"Nothing," she sobbed. She refused to say any more.

"You," said Ramiro, "are a big pendejo."

"I?" said Manuel. "But why I, en el nombre de dios?"

"Because -- you did not get her the Venus."

Lupe's tears and moans gushed even wilder. Both men shrugged. They had to shut up in the presence of such uncontrollable feminine outpouring. Heaven was only home.

78

14

Upon leaving the Flea Market, they drove a while along several borders of enormous cultivated fields. "Tomatoes," said Ramiro. "Looks like the one we'll be picking tomorrow." In the distance a long train of boxcars snaked along the Southern Pacific track, threading its way north to San Francisco.

Lupe saw, or thought she smelled -- smoke. But there were no fires anywhere. The salt flats ahead were impossible to burn. The garbage dumps weren't smoking either. To the left stretched endless green acres of alfalfa. No fires there either.

"It is burning," cried Lupe. "The car -- the car is burning up."

"Stop the car," said Ramiro. "She is right. It is coming from the car."

Manuel pulled over and stopped on a soft shoulder in front of a high hedge. He turned the ignition off. They listened. In the quiet heat of the afternoon they heard a loud hissing noise. They got out and watched a huge cloud of white steam escaping loudly from beneath the car. A Blue Angel, rippling low and furious across the purple sky, trailed a long plume of pure pure white smoke and they barely heard it, so that --

"It is the mad motor I think that is on fire," offered Manuel, scratching his head.

"No, no, hombre," said Ramiro. "Can't you tell? It has got to be the brakes."

"Idiots!" said Lupe, exasperated. "Can you not see it is coming from underneath? It is the differential."

"Bah!" cried Manuel. "What differential, mujer? You do not know a car part from a sheep part."

"You had better catch a control over your obscene language especially in front of company and especially before the children and most especially of all if you also do not wish to sprout another part in your sparse hair, poco pelo."

Ramiro lifted the hood. In amazement they traced the great cloud of white steam to the radiator. With great care, using a baby diaper, Ramiro loosened the cap. Instantly, a small, powerful geyser of white hot steam shot straight up. He bounced back out of the way, and they all stood back with great respect as the furious energy gradually exhausted itself.

"Now what did you do that for?"

"But it was nothing I did, mujer."

"You were going too fast."

"I? I? Going too fast?"

"Yes. Wasn't he, Ramiro."

"You are certain it is I you are speaking of?"

"It is probably plugged up, primo."

"And what, pray, could possibly plug it up?"

"Quien sabe?"

Yes indeed -- quien sabe. It was clear and dry out in that fine summery air. Incoming planes, dropping down, leveled off for Moffett Field. The alfalfa kept right on quietly, persistently, inexorably growing greener by the moment in the warm dry air as though nothing unusual was happening. The more alfalfa grows the greener it glows, but how the green grows no one actually knows, except the gringos who put it all in the money bank to fester another crop, another year, another bank, another acre, another section, another county, another state, another fat year, year after year. In that heat came the wail of Manuelito and the whimper of Mariquita, announcing they too were on fire, they were very thirsty, mama, they wanted water, agua agua, and they wanted it right away. It wasn't a good idea to drive a waterless wagon around a lot. Ramiro, peering around the hedge, discovered a house sitting there and a lawn in front of it.

"Hello," he said.

"AGUA!" wailed Manuelito.

"What is it?"

"Shall I go see?"

"Agua, agua!" wailed Mariquita.

"No, I'd better."

"Let us go together, primo."

"Andele, pues."

Manuel and Ramiro walked politely up to the door. They knocked manfully. They waited patiently. They studied the plane-studded sky expectantly. They looked at each other blankly. Hands in pockets, they bounced on their heels rhythmically. Ramiro saw a buzzer and pressed it long and hard, forever.

"Nobody's home," cried Lupe. "Par de idiotas."

"A pair of what? What did your woman just call us?"

"We are just making sure, corazon," said Manuel.

"Yes, we want to be sure," cried Ramiro, mopping his brow.

"Sure? Sure of what, idiotas?"

"Now I am sure, primo."

"What do you suppose that thing is over there, primo?"

"What is what?"

"Precisely. Excuse me, perhaps my eyes may be off just a little, but is not that a faucet I think I see?"

"Yes. I think you see, for I see it too."

"Will it reach the car?"

"I have my grave doubts."

"Agua, agua, agua!!"

"Wheel the car in here?"

"Even graver doubts."

"Oh no, it would not do to drive the car in here."

"Not without widening the hedge."

"No. Nor without permission, either."

"You are as usual correct again, primo."

"So that is out."

"Out. Si."

"What are you two idiotas conferencing about?"

"Agua, agua, agua!!"

"In that case, primo, what would you suggest we do?"

"Shall we look for a pail?"

"Excellent! A marvelous idea."

They looked. There wasn't, of course, a single pail for miles around. Not a pail, a bucket, a pan, a pot..... mi carrito for one single simple little bucket. Mariquita toddled up, chewing on a white paper cup. Ramiro asked her politely for it. She said no. Manuel reached down and rashly pried it out of her clenched little fingers, crushing and tearing it. Mariquita ran screaming back to her mama, who then screamed at Manuel.

"You just shut up, mujer," said Manuel. He was trying hard to keep from running out of problems.

She said, "What was that you say, you desgraciado hijo de tu maldita chingada? How darest thou speak to me, me, in those, in that, in short, in such, in such --"

"Stupid?" offered Ramiro politely.

81

"In such a monstrous manner!"

"No, she's just upset," said Manuel.

"Yes, it must be the heat."

Yes, she was hot. Ramiro came up to the car holding the invaluable cup of clear cool priceless water. Was the cup full? No. As the water had been steadily depleting itself through the tear, he was lucky to have half a cupful by the time he reached the whimpering radiator. He went back for another. After six trips, three of which served to replenish the children's thirst -- until Lupe thought of sending them directly to the spigot for their sparkling drinks -- to the source, ah, that lifegiving fount also helped to give the kids something playful to do as they sprayed themselves and watered the owner's land at the same time. But Manuel was also getting very tired, seeing that the job would not even begin to get done at that turtle pace.

"Isn't it too big, hombre?"

"Si, si. It is pretty. And big, too."

"But not too big."

"No, maybe not. Maybe not too big."

"No, you don't --!" cried poor Lupe."

"I do have to admit, however --"

"You pair of monsters!"

"-- that it really is pretty big all right."

"Now that is not a bad admission, hombre."

"You two keep your clumsy chickenfingers off it."

"Not bad. No, not bad at all."

"You will break it, you two, you you you --"

"But on the other hand it is not too small, either."

"No. That is also equally true."

"You can say that again."

"It certainly is not as tiny as those useless paper cups."

"Or otherwise we shall be marooned here all afternoon."

Lupe opened her mouth and closed it several times, as though gasping for air, or testing her gills. It was getting very, very hot. Another Blue Angel snorkeled hot against the booming ripe hot sky, causing Manuelito to set up an even longer and hotter banshee howl. Now he was getting hungry as well. Lupe, like Atlas, shrugged. She resigned herself to the inevitable. To the fates. After a great deal of tugging and pulling they freed the huge holiday urn at last from its cozy seat and between them lugged it safely to the faucet. By tipping it on its side, and by pressing the pipe with the thumb, they managed to squirt a fairly generous amount of water in. But it still wouldn't do. They had to stand it up. Ramiro used Mariquita's paper cup with far more efficiency for he had only to bend up and down, up and down, like a snorkel bird. Still, he wouldn't have put a fire out. Manuel saw Manuelito tossing around a used tomato can with a Warhol soup ad pasted on and promptly confiscated it, touching off another enormous howl. By working steadily they raised the level in the urn little by little. Lupe tweaked Manuelito's little ear good.

"How much water can fit into that priceless radiator?"

"Beats me, primo."

"Shall we give it a haul?"

"Bueno. Vamonos."

Together, they placed a palm under the huge urn. Grasping the upper rim with the other hand, they grappled. They hove. They heaved. They hoisted the hummer barely an inch off the ground.

"Dow -- dow -- down, hermano!"

"Hokay!"

They let it drop gently back on the grass. It made a gentle blunt clunk. It also made an accompanying ominous-sounding dull clunk.

"I didn't like that sound, primo."

"Let us say nothing to our little sister, primo."

"Bueno. Good as done."

"Is it possible it might be too full?"

"Si, I think that is a very great possibility, primo."

Leaning the monster over, both of them holding on carefully, they managed to slosh half its tender contents out on the watery lawn again. This time, lightened, they heaved and staggered the thing to the car like a pair of crippled pigeons, with a certain flair of success. They lifted it up, then tipped it over. Passengers in passing cars slowed down a bit to take a long unbelieving look, almost causing a series of new accidents. They managed to spill a small fraction of the precious liquid into the radiator itself, and the bulk of it over all the working and stationary parts of the motor, thereby cooling it off as well as seriously risking cracking the block. Even though the radiator filled quickly, the urn was still half full.

"Pues, primo --"

"You wish to know what I think."

"Basta!" cried Lupe, meaning Enough!

"I think --"

"Don't you dare, you two unhandsome imbeciles!"

"Well. Now we are incomplete, cousin. Before --"

"And underdeveloped as well."

"Si, mi corazon."

"But, little cousin, we must do it."

"Si, mi corazon."

"If you two dare to pit to pot to put that that monstttttt --"

"Si, mi corazon."

"-- inside the car full of water I shall get out and walk."

"But it is not full, mi corazon."

"Si, it is only partly fluvial, my little cousin. "

"Exactly. Ramiro is speaking the exact truth, corazon. "

"The water needs a radiator, and, and --"

"Can you imagine what might happen if the water boils--?"

"Si. If the water boils out again?"

"Si. As it will surely do. "

"Si. And if we aren't near another oasis such as this -- "

"Si. Such as this marvelous one that dios placed right --"

"You two, you pair of heathens, you leave dios out of this."

"Si. And what if the motor should crack in two?"

"Si. And the whole thing explodes and sends us flying?"

"Si. Flying to heaven with Blue Angels and no license. "

"Blue Devils!" she spat. Poor Lupe. In the face of such overwhelming, overpowering logic, what could she do? She did what she had to do. She shut up. She set her face to stone, allowing the silence to degenerate to consent. She took her place in the middle of the front seat again, letting those two maniacs wrestle with their monstrous vessel of their conscience, sloshing another twenty galoons loose all over inside the back of the car.

"Well, it has gotten a quick interior ablution. "

"Si. How dorty the car used to be. "

"Used to be ?"

"Well, we'll do the outside as soon as ah if we get home. "

"Never mind. I want the children up front here with me. "

"But why?"

"Because they will drown in that stupid ocean back there."

Timorously, Manuel kicked the ignition on. The needle pulled away from its red hot spot on the indicator and settled rapidly down to normal. Back on a main street once more, they drove into the first large red, white, and blue chevron service station they saw. While gassing up, they incidentally asked the gas attendant what he might think the matter could possibly be.

"You really want to know. "

"Sure. "

"It's your brakes, man. "

"We already thought of that. "

"No kidding. How about, say, come to think of it, I did he hear a peculiar kooky knock in your directional transmission."

"Be careful, man, how you speak of my wife. "

"Manuel, he was not --"

"Say, now I got it! You guys got your welt belts on?"

"You mean seat belts?"

"Fan belt. Fan belt's all shot. I should know. "

"You haven't lifted the hood yet. "

"That's right. Well, then, let's run the hood up my good man and take us a good look. Let's see. Where's the damn hook? In front or in back? Say, ah --"

"Ah. Is it?"

"No. But I'm happy to tell you it is something worse."

"It's not the generator?"

"The generator? What's that? That thing over there?"

"No, no," said Ramiro. "That's the hot box."

"No kidding. I sure didn't think they used them any more."

"Say, Manuel. It is not leaking out any more now."

"I noticed that too."

"No. It all boiled again is why?"

"Wow, you guys must be putting me on. You can't run a star, a car, or even a gasser without water."

"Heck no."

"Wow, are you guys ever lucky."

"How's that."

"Look. Just looka this here windshield wiper, man."

"It looks all right to me."

"No. It's shot, man. I mean, man."

"It's the middle of summer. You especk rain?"

"Sure. It could. Any minute now. Say, you see a cloud?'

"Where?"

"Wow. It's gone already. See what I mean?"

"I think we'll take a wild gamble it won't."

"Wow. What a pair of swingers. Well OK then, if --"

"You sure do a pretty good hose job."

"Yeh, well, heh, heh, say, ain't that a heck a lot of water squirting through your water hose pump oscillating grater?"

"Huh? What? Where? Who?"

"Nah. That's the refractor."

That young brash efficient attendant tore off the old water hose, dirty and thick, black and rotten, scraped around all the bases to get all the accumulated crud off, dove into the office, brought back a new hose, and reamed it on. For a mere three bucks, three lousy bucks and seventyfive cents it was good as new, new clamps, new everything -- "Ha ha they always mak these clamps you got to buy them new too ever time you need a new hose job thirty cents apiece, amigos!" -- more gas, fresh new soda pops for the little critters, water all over the station floor, coming out of the john after Manuelito finished flushing too, connect her up, kick her over, just like brand new over again. They pulled out as another enormous river of water streamed happily from the broken crockery in back.

Just as they prepared to enter traffic again, Lupe said, "Shhhhh! What's that?"

"Mujer, pero mujer, you always are hearing something."

"Shhhh! I hear something going thump."

"She's right again, primo," said Ramiro, sighing. "Something is going thump all right."

Sure enough. Something was going thump thump thump. Better get out and look. Ramiro got out and looked. "Manuel."

"Si."

"You better get out here and look too."

Manuel got out and looked. They both stood there, looking. "Hey. A flat, eh. What do you know."

"Si."

The smart station attendant, smiling and smelling all business, came running up,grinning from foot to forelock.

"Hey, great. You guys look like you just got a flat."

"Yeah."

"That's terrific."

"You got any nails in your driveway?"

"Hey, great joke. You got jack?"

"Nope."

"No jack, Manuel?"

"No, Ramiro."

"Just a -- how about a spare, mister?"

"No. No spare either."

"No spare?"

"No."

"Are you in the process of meaning to tell me, cousin, that we have been drifting all over this wide open county without having either a spare or a jack in the car?"

"Si."

"You got jack!" cried the attendant, breaking into smiles.

"I already said no to that, fella."

"I mean dough, fella. Wid dough you can fix anything goes wrong with a car. Only two bucks for this flat. A bargain. Change, jack, patch, latch, air, new, everything you like. You guys sure are lucky, that's for sure, wow."

Manuel looked at Lupe who looked at Manuel; he shrugged his shoulders. "Well I guess it's OK, fellow. You win."

The skinny friend, the energetic station attendant beat it back to his cave, came out like a flying squirrel with his little pouches puffed out, grabbed the air hose on the way, snaked it into the flat deflated tire, inflated it without removing it, ran his ear all around the tire until he found the air leak, punched it through with an awl that he'd threaded with thick cord and goop, plugged it into the hissing leak, snipped off the thick cord, stood up, brushed his slacks, saluted, then held his palm out as the air hose slithered back into his hole all by itself.

"That will be exactly two bucks, fellas, without removing the car, or taking the tire off, or putting it on, and all in less than thirty seconds, a record I guess. I just timed it myself. Pretty good hay!"

15

"Plenty good fat corn, mi vida, my life!" Manuel planted a big kiss on Lupe's attractive neck, then guzzled down the other half of his glass of red vino. "I shall make you a necklace of beautiful green esmeraldas, greener than your eyes, you watch, you witch, my chula, my precious wife, you wait and see!"

Lupe brushed him off, smiling, happy to see him happy. "How many times must I tell you my eyes are not green."

"Beautiful, beautiful --"

It was nice to hear his compliments. The dust, the never-ending dust from the outside, the dirt and earth and grease and grime covering the torn linoleum floor with its gritty film exasperated Lupe more than anything else about the shack.

"Get away," she said, pushing him with her elbow as she swung the wet mop around.

"Eh, mujer," he said, stepping back cautiously. "You are in a bad mood I see."

"No, I am not," she said, looking up, becoming genuinely annoyed that he could be so dense. "It is you."

"But you are the one who just struck me."

"I did not."

"You jabbed me with your elbow, mi corazon," he said as politely as possible, trying to show how wrong she was.

87

"You are the one who is wrong. You were standing in the way, and I must do my work, and you ran into me."

"I suppose you think that I do not work."

Though it was late in the day, the heat was still punishing them through the open unscreened door. The heat of anger,born of exasperation, escalating on frustration, pushing through the coolest part of her composure, tempted her temper.

"I suppose," he repeated deliberately, "that you do not think I work."

So. He was looking for a fight. Well, she was ready. He would find out. Her nerves tightened as he walked over to the crib and fondled the sleeping baby's head.

"You will wake Cati up," she said, trying to control her rising anger.

"So?" The infant, startled, moved and wiggled her legs, scowling and wrinkling her tiny features. Then she let out a short, sharp, strident yelp, her eyes still shut tight.

"There, I told you. Couldn't you leave her alone?"

"But I did not wake her. I only --"

"Yes, I, always I. You never realize that it is I who must fight her when she's awake, and feed her, and change her."

Frowning, Manuel lifted the screaming infant in his strong, rough, calloused hands. He pressed the child's face to his shoulder. The baby's shrieks gradually subsided. "Que paso, gordita," he murmured, holding her coconut head to his face, smelling her. "That baby smell is good. That baby sweat, I like it." He walked over to the kitchen table, picking up a diaper and the can of talcum powder along the way, and swiftly removed the baby's soaked and pungent diaper. He dusted her bottom with the talc, then pinned the clean diaper on. "There," he said quietly. "Now you have a nice dry diaper on."

Lupe slammed the mop to the floor. "SO! You think you are the one big help do you? What do you do about the dishes, big man? And the floor? And the dozens and dozens of times I change her diapers when you aren't around? And tonight's dinner? Why don't you take me out to dinner? You're ashamed to, isn't that it? You're ashamed to, isn't that it? You're ashamed of my clothes. Does it not ever bother you that I haven't one single decent thing to wear?"

"Enough, mujer."

"Why? Why is that enough? Are you pleased with yourself?" Crushed between misery and frustration, Lupe felt a sudden release from her anger. What was the matter with him? Couldn't she, couldn't he see how she she she was suffering? Complaints. What complaints. What was she complaining about. How long was she going to have to put up with these stupid pressures? "All this running around, running from house to shack, from town to village, from farm to farm,

never having the rent, or change for the laundry machines?"
She barely stopped for breath. I've had enough, you hear.
Enough. You think you can drag us from place to place and
give us a few frijoles --"

"Enough, mujer," said Manuel in a low voice.

"Si -- frijoles. This is what you call the good life, eh.
And even boast of it. In Mejico -- and nobody can tell — "

"Woman, mujer, I said enough, basta."

"What? What enough. Go on. What are you going to say.
Are you going to try for a better job. Is that it, or what?"

He looked at her. He put the baby slowly back in her crib.
Cati started screaming again. He put his hat on and turned to
the door.

"Sure. Of course. Go on. You big man. Go on out and enjoy yourself. Drink. Andale, borracho. Run. Run away.
That's the way. Go on, you coward. And when you get back
you can be sure of one thing: You can be sure that I won't be
here nor will any of the children."

He left. He closed the door quietly behind him.

Her fury mounted. She knew what he would do. He would
go to the Golden Cork and in broad daylight get a good drunk
on. That was his historic way. He would stay drunk for a day
and a night. And he would be no good for work for another day.
And he would put in danger all the confidence he'd spent these
weeks and months building up. He would say he was sick.
Just another drunken Mexican was what his bosses would say,
and so would that evil contratista, Roberto Morales.

She snapped. She just didn't care any more. Anger shattered her usual selfcontrol and paralyzed her good sense.
She slammed clothing into the old cardboard suitcase that had
been standing in the corner. Manuelito's pants, underclothes,
and Mariquita's dresses, and the baby's diapers. "Where we
going, mama?" The two youngsters, in from the shade-speck-
led out-of-doors, danced around her feet. "I don't know, I
don't know," she cried, pushing them away from her. "Somewhere." They backed off, respecting her great anger. Holding the baby in one arm, the box in the other, she held the
screen door open for the children to scamper through. As
she turned to release the door, she felt herself grasped
firmly around the waist, and lifted clear into the air. The
box was snatched from her hand.

"You put me down!!" she screamed, kicking.

"Not until you promise to behave," said Manuel. He carried her and the baby bodily back into the shack and set her
down. "Why must you do this to me, my heart?"

"Why? Why?" she screamed back. "Because I am going
out of my mind. That is why. What did you think?"

"But I do not see why, corazon," he said softly. And then

in a flash she saw that he really did not see. She buried her face in Cati's blanket, crying along with her.

Outwardly, physically, Manuel was rough and strong. Inside he was soft and kind and even innocent. He really did not see the many hurts and the many complications that constantly chipped away her reserve, her resolve, her plans, her peace of mind, her dreams. One moment angry, in the next instant she crumpled in a heap to the floor, bending over the baby moaning, sobbing, rocking back and forth. "Why why why? God, God, God." Sobbing over and over. "Por que por que por que? Dios, dios, dios."

"Mi corazon," said Manuel tenderly, sitting beside her on the floor. Lifting the crying baby gently away from her. "You must stop. Come. Don't cry any more."

Little by little she composed herself. He kept murmuring to her, embracing her, and soon her sobs subsided. "I'm all right," she said after a while.

"You are quite upset, my heart, why? What is it that is twisting you all up?"

He truly did not know. "Nothing. No, no. Nothing."

"Then listen to me, Lupe. I have a big idea. Let us go down to a restaurant tonight for our dinner.

"No, no, Manuel. You know we cannot afford it."

"But you need some diversion, some distraction."

"That is why you offer it?" she said, a little sharply. Suddenly she was afraid her anger would return; he felt it too.

"No, corazon, no. Well, yes, maybe, in a way. And why not? I have earned a good packet today."

Yes, he'd made good money that day. But what about tomorrow? More important -- what about November? And December? She held her tongue. She was tempted by the restaurant, she loved having a meal served to her at a table, but her practical nature won out. "No. I'm much better now, Manuel."

She stood up. He stood up beside her, solicitous, watching her, and with a great surge of warmth she realized she'd pushed too far. Embracing him, she said, "You bruto, you can go to the store the for tortillas if you want to. Do you want to? I'll make tacos."

Ay, tacos! His favorite dish. Because of the hard work it took, all that frying and spluttering hot hot fat, he knew she was in control of herself again. He would get her a little pot of geraniums.

Sold..... Her memories came flooding. To the neighboring colonia.... After getting home one day, after going through all the super specials in the supermarket that day they discovered the tortillas mildewed, the bread hard, the cans dented, and rat claws in the hamburger. It was all so cheap, and who

forced them to buy it at all?   After that,   there was however a
gay fiesta for everyone, for everyone likes to dance and sing
a little.

Maiz..... out of corn can come so many good things, tortillas, thin, round, suntoasted, and substantive. Tortillas
have weight and substance. They are thin and heavy, not like
those puffy white slices of spongy fluff called white bread.
Lupe remembered her aged grandmother in Salpinango making
tortillas solemnly, flap flap endlessly with her palms, pat pat
with flying fingers, and then, on special occasions, turning
tortillas into crisp fold-overs for tacos. Or rolled over a
cheese or bean filling for enchiladas, thin and long and soft
and rich and spicy with chile. And the masa from corn meal
for tamales, ay ay ay, also for special feasts. Thick, fat,
plump, and tender, flavored with hot spicy meat, tamales
were wrapped in corn husks to be steamed long and lovingly
in huge ollas. Those finger licking foods that had filled her
childhood days with happy joys brought a poignant tear of frustration to her eyes now and then.

Sickness..... There had been disease and hunger in her
childhood too, and often. Two of her little brothers had died
as small boys. And ignorance. Here in America she dreamed
of a chance at keeping her children in school so they would not
suffer from her ignorance. Every family back home had children who had died of some sickness or other. She'd die if
anything happened to her little cherubs. She'd kept them all..
.... all three. Here there were good doctors, despite their being so cold and expensive. Manuel was just now earning good
money in these hot days, and for a good part of the year. She
should not complain. Later, they'd figure out how to get through
the rest of the year. On those cold, rainy days they would get
by. Somehow. It was a precarious life. But there was always
some fruit to be picked somewhere. Or to be canned. Or
processed. Or weeds to be plucked. They paid cash for everything. They never dreamed or thought of trying to get credit.

Summer.... A big patriotic bug, zizzzzing, bit Lupe on her
upper arm as she was hanging diapers to dry in the sun. She
screamed. A big painful welt developed, and it remained a
long time. She thought it would never go away.

Superstition..... When Lupe mentioned how much she'd
like to own one of those stylish new wigs, Olive Pope told her
of a wig she'd once bought in another town, and how one evening, when she was all alone at home, she saw a shadow in
the hallway -- a woman's shadow -- and no one around -- and
it made her scalp creep. When she got up close to investigate,
the shadow disappeared. The next day she told her friend,
who told her that the woman's hair had probably been cut from
her corpse in France and her soul had roamed the world over

until it finally located it and now her original spirit wanted her own hair back. Olive threw it in the incinerator and was never bothered by the phantasm again. Lupe's own scalp tingled at the hearing of it. She was very glad she didn't have a wiglet of her own now.

Braceros.... Fellow workers of the Rio Grande, you have nothing to lose, not even your citizenship, because you have nothing. Fellow Mexicans, get yourselves a little green card, become an international commuter, cross over the border, work for fifty/sixty cents an hour, break the strikes, help the big growers out of their dilemma, because they don't know their moral ass from a whole dollar, come on across until they squeeze you dry, knowing you are hungry, hermanos, knowing you are willing to be exploited and willing never to complain, and they'll bring you over in their big trucks without any brakes, pick you up right at the border crossing, good service, and tell you you can pick good and hard all de ditty day long, to your heart's content, if your back doesn't break, squeeze you in like hot sardines, put blinders on and ear plugs in, then put guards on your compound gates, just like the good old natsi days, so you can't have no visitors, and after you air through, after all the fields are plucked clean, you are really through, and you can go back to your happy land, back to your sleepy hacienda, back to your family, back until we whistle again, eh amigos from across de borda. But in the meantime we sure can sue you use you you you. We got this nasty U.S. Mexican scum over here on this side that ain't worth forty cents an hour who are frying to get uppity on us trying to make us pay more and more all year so we sure do need you kind gentle folk from down south there. For if we didn't have you strike breakers we'd sure have a pretty hard time keeping these locals in their goddem places. This way we just tell your govenmint and our govenmint in WashDC that we just cain't get agric pickers nohow fast enough because they all lazy sunloving slobs ain't wanting to stoop over just a little bit each day a little hot for the big fat wages we pay for we cain't afford really to pay no more or else we go broke man, so we get these braceros you see man these lovely green cards commuting at our convenience, who don't mind eating shit as we just tell them simply and honestly and frankly what they can do and what they dasn't do and what they muss do and we locks em up in our big Texas compounds you see. Efficiency. We must have the plocks cropped. See. Just like running trains on time yawl that hiddler chap he wasn't such a bad feller when if you stop to think about it because trains is sure important to us man but shee-yit we cain't have this scum yelling and yapping at us for ten more cents each and every hour when they hain't worth the forty goddem cents we offer.

What the hell do they think? We is made o money? They think is is a goddem fwee country? They got another goddem sweet tooth motherpowerful thought coming to them let me tell you buster because we rangers now we don't take that kinda sheet fum noboddy heah? So we gets these mex you see and we puts em to work and we worked em and we worksem and we really works em and then we sends their asses flying back to their old madre tierra again see. Hey we even takes insurance out on their worthless hides. What you think o that? Yessirree we puts an insurance policy for life on em and if any goddem thing happens to em whilst they working for us you know get a hand crushed or get chopped up in a combine or trompled by a tractor or clipped by a truck or burned to a crisp in our ovens or torn to bits by a shredder, sure, then, what they got to complain about? Pure accidents, but man how them city peppers love to play them up. See see see. Shee yit fugging iggorant bastards mex why they think they are any iggorant nogoods, why they cain't even talk murrican rite lak usns real januwine murrican citizens, U. S. M.

Brotherhood of Man at Twilight..... But were they not all brothers? Lupe asked. Were they not their brothers and cousins and primos and uncles and compadres across the border? That new batch of traveling pickers, camped outside in the rows, clustered in groups around their campfire, twilight in the orchard, beside their pitched tents. As Lupe walked by, dressed for her market shopping, she felt embarrassed. All those young Mexican migrant pickers sighed softly as one, her compatriots, green card transients, but loudly. She walked straight past them, Manuelito and Mariquita trailing behind her, without turning her head.

"As for you, my precious, I would put a gun to my head!"
"AY - AY - AY - mamacita!"
"Two guns!"
"A whole battleship!"
"For you my princess I would leave my wife and ten kids!"
"You are already all mine in my dreams!"
"Let me change your name to mine, I promise!"
"Angel of light!"

A Salesman..... The representative of the old shakedown type actually showed up. He stood there, after knocking on the splintered door. Hungry. Smiling. Neatly dressed. Jacket and tie. Figuring, hell they must have something stashed away which is why they live like this. Manuel home at the time. She called him. Manuel politely fended off the friendly old joke approach. But when the determined and dedicated sales person started getting serious, demanding a fee to help removate or restore some old mansion across the bay, some historic millionaire, which probably didn't even exist, Manuel started one of his slow burns. Finally he jumped him, and chased him clear across and out of the compound yard.

But who was going to care about them? Finally -- what could friends do? Nothing, really. Everyone must shake out all the lousy fruit he can. Make the best of a lousy lot, no matter how bad it seemed. Maybe the priests were right. Maybe that fanatical religious woman was wrong..... While Lupe set about preparing the meal, roasting the pork steaks, dicing the cucumbers, shredding the lettuce, peeling the to-matoes, chopping the chile for the tacos, she couldn't help sobbing as some anxiety oozed from her nervous body, from deep down, as from a baby after a heavy fit of crying. She wasn't pregnant after all. And now it was her period that was causing her extra strain. She had already formed the new criatura, a brand new, a perfect baby, in her imagination, feeding and fondling and embracing it in her dreams, and her heart ached as she let another sob escape from deep, deep down.

Manuel meant well. Pero en el nombre de dios, didn't she? Didn't she also mean well? Was there nothing she could her-self do to improve their lot? Couldn't she pick prunes her-self too? To do that -- but then what of the babies? She felt so helpless. She could do nothing. She would do something. They were in no position to dream of security, let alone of finger things. All the gringo guero heroes hijos de la chingada went to Hawaii or to Europe every single solid blessed summer, spring, fall, or winter. Didn't it ever occur to anyone that she'd like to go too? How could she broach the subject to Manuel?

"Manuel."

"Mande, corazon."

"Let us go to Hawaii this winter."

"What was that you just said, my heart?"

"Never mind."

Maybe he thought it was to pick crops there. And then last spring. A good stove. A small apartment model. Four bur-ners. No space for resting pots and pans, no block, no clock, no fringes, nothing extra. But it worked. It burned. It had a good oven. Connected up with the gas fine. Manuel fixed a wire grill for the top to hold the pots above the flame for there were no iron grills. The wire bent in the heat, tipping the pots off balance. Next month or next after that, Manuel prom-ised, they'd be in better shape. She knew what that meant. Next year, if they were lucky -- or next, or next....

Last week..... The refrigerator. They answered an ad placed by a private party in a local ad sheet for a twenty-dollar icebox. While they were there, the fat lady who adver-tised it showed them another, a gleaming white refrigerator.

"How much is that one?" asked Manuel.

"Sixty-five dollar," said the fat lady, stupifying Lupe. Lupe blushed. Of course she liked it, immensely. But -- how? They shouldn't even be looking at it.

"I have thirty dollars here," said Manuel.

The fat lady thought a moment, then said no.

"Thirty-five."

"Make it forty."

"All right."

Without any further trial, Manuel strapped the neat looking box to the dolly, tipped it over, and wheeled it to the borrowed pickup. It was too heavy for him to lift and the fat lady actually climbed up on the pickup and helped him guide it on. Back home, where he had no help, and he refused to let Lupe near it, things were different. "What's the matter with you, woman?" he said. "You want to get yourself squashed?"

Up on the back of the truck, he slid the box to the very edge, to where it began to teeter. Rather than get underneath it, which wouldn't be so smart, he wisely decided instead to rise up and ride it down. And down he rode. The thing flipped down so hard it yanked his heavy frame straight up into the air and both box and he thumped down clunk to the ground. After the first scare, he checked it out and found nothing broken. The motor started whirring immediately, silently, beautifully. What a relief! Oh Manuel, said Lupe, clapping her hands like a little girl. He opened the small freezer compartment door and put his hand in.

"There," he said proudly. "Put your hand in."

She did and felt an icy chill starting in along the aluminum sides of the inner compartment. She could hardly believe it. Their own refrigerator! She could buy frozen foods now and milk for two or three days instead of having to go to Mr. Quill's Store every day.

"What is that funny smell?" she said.

"You smell something funny?" he said.

"The box is clean so it can't be anything stale."

Whiffing. . . . he looked around the back of the box. The pungent ammonia-like odor came from somewhere around the motor in back but he didn't know what it was. But so what? It was working, wasn't it? Humming beautifully. In the morning they discovered what it was. They put their hands inside their beautiful refrigerator. And instead of being freezing, it was warm inside, even though the motor was still running beautifully. He had to go to work and the beautiful box just sat there, useless, for several days. The refrigerant, he learned later from Pepe, had leaked out. It would cost thirty-five dollars to have it repaired. He sold the box back to the fat lady for ten dollars and Lupe kept on trudging to the market for staples and to Mr. Quill's Store for daily needs.

Jean Angelica Turner..... Mrs. Turner was pure mystic.
Pure in heart. A very disconcerting woman. Lupe didn't dis-
like religious fanatics, though she preferred her own friendly
Catholic God, and she charitably excused Mrs. Turner her ex-
cesses, knowing she really meant well. Not one mean twist in
her nature. Or so she thought. Always smiling softly, politely, concerned. One day, Mrs. Turner drove up. Dressed
in her quiet, solid, comfortable finery. Delicately perfumed.
She timidly left Lupe a box of discarded clothing. Now you use
what you like, squeaked Mrs. Turner in a low concerned tone,
and what you don't like why you c an just throw away or give
away, say to Goodwill. Good Will. You do understand me,
Lupe? Si? Of course she did. But Lupe was too proud to admit she was too proud. When Lupe opened the box out of anger
and curiosity, her temper flipped. Oldfashioned dresses, all
wornout materials, nothing useful, nothing she could use,
worse than the trash at the Flea Market. What did that woman
want? Some relief? Lupe forgave her. She stuffed it all
back in the box, pushed the box out, and shoved it between two
trash cans in back. What Lupe didn't know was that Mrs. T.
was watching her frostily from Mr. Quill's office, while Mr.
T. was making the rounds with Mr. Q. Lupe couldn't see Mrs.
T.'s pink eyes glow red. Nor did Lupe ever learn or even
suspect that it was Mrs. T. who was responsible for the border patrol's showing up to check on their immigration cards.
And later, a social worker from County Welfare. But the social worker turned out to be a very sympathetic lady who said
she'd never seen such a beautiful bronze baby as Cati in such
excellent health, gurgling and happy. She was concerned about
the children's teeth, however, and suggested Lupe take them
to a dentist. Lupe smiled back, saying si, si, and thanked her.

The Goodwill Drop.... People always dropping things off of
va lue, by the yellow hut on the supermarket parking lot. Often
Lupe saw things they could use or needed, chairs, a tiny baby
feeding table, things they couldn't buy. But she was too proud
to retrieve anything. She used string for Manuelito's shoe-
laces. She patched clothing endlessly with needle and thread.
She used scotch tape on her only pair of good shoes, where the
patent leather peeled away. She made up shelving from old
planks and discarded bricks. Her heart yearned for an excellent dark walnut bookcase she saw leaning up against the yellow hut. She wore her old maternity slip. Old Christmas
wrapping pasted on a cardboard box was turned into an attractive wastebasket. A throw rug covered a worn spot in the
linoleum. It was dangerous only when Manuelito and Mariquita started chasing each other about the house. Another
throw rug covered the torn place in the middle of the old sofa

cot. Too poor to buy things from Goodwill, too proud to steal from them, Lupe threw Mrs. Turner's box away as an act of defiance, a blind, stupid way to get even with the universe. She paid the price. But in exchange she also felt the thrill of flying high. And the thrill of self-destruction.

She looked around and looked around until her eyes lit upon Manuel's half-empty gallon jug of cheap red wine. On impulse she poured herself half a glass. It was tart, puckering her mouth and burning her throat. Its rawness reached down into her stomach. She liked the taste of good wine, but this -- She drank it down nevertheless, like medicine, shook her head, poured and drank another rank glass. In less than one minute her head was reeling. She sat down and stayed there as wave after wave of dizzy heights passed through her mind. She was starting to glow all over when Manuel came in and placed the tortillas lovingly before her on the table. She was utterly relaxed. She didn't have one single worry remaining in her warm hot little brain.

"Take that!" she cried, happily slamming the pack of tortillas smack into his astonished face. "Hijo de la chingada cabronada maldita que fué la pendeja que te crió you bastard!"

16

Ramiro Sanchez, to the fruit born.
Ramiro Sanchez, General of the Flower Order.
Ramiro Sanchez, Master of the Bastard Prunes.

Ah, the poverty of luxury. Or was it the luxury of poverty. At any rate, he did what he could. He pulled his pants off the hoe handle, put them on, and stretched luxuriously. Now how would that look out on the Grand Old Culo, El Camino Real. Sticking out of a shingle. Here I am, world. Fruit Picker Suprema. Come and get me. Fruit Bum. Great. In every fancy shopping center.

A plump, fancy, shiny black widow spider, up in the darkest corner of his tool shed, watched him from the rafters intently and cautiously. He laughed. Deliberately, carefully, pawing her way with one long probing thin black leg, she spun another strand to her web. Spin away, Dame Turner. Enjoy your moment of gold. Let's all of us spin away together. Sure. Spin away you honey gray.

What a fanatical system. Turning men into beasts. Keep going. Forked tongues, forced work. From ding dong dawn to dusk. For money. Good reason. Good exercise. To your health. Kept him young in muscle, trim in tone, and bone taut. Fruit flies and better pickings. Brief, true, bruiting blaze of glory. Sitting in the darkness on the broad plank of

98

life that served him as temporary support for his sheltered bedroll, he pulled his work boots on. Hard to find himself woman. Stallion likes studding. Man to woman. Must work at it. First make money. Fruit picker. Then bum. In his dreams, Margarita's vision kept appearing, her soft, sweet smile, her long lustrous hair, and he felt a longing deep in the pit of his stomach. Spin away, my honey day.

Deep in his biarritz pit, he had only the dream of warmth, far, far out beyond his reach. Caramba, scramble, scrabble, scratch and scrounge you cromean rodent. Pick, hoe, till, weed, scratch, dig, cut, pack, and flex until your muscles sour. Then he'd earn enough to buy his own burial urn, a tux, a flask, and perhaps a bottled yacht or two to stare at in sheer envy while writhing away his years in stupid lockup.

From predawn blackness Ramiro picked ripe his fruit.

He picked to dusk.

He picked from prehistory into glassbright civilization.

From precolumbian artifacts to freeways to the future.

From Aztec elegance to the latest word in slums.

From first brute glimmer of reason to lastgasp of hope.

From hunger to insatiable desire.

From heresy's impulse to charity to shriveling frustration's deliberate larceny.

He worked harder than the dumbest animal that had ever penetrated any sylvan forest.

From the first crossings of the first Americans across Bering Strait, hundreds of generations of fatheads and grandfathers back, to the last tired gasp of eternal sleep.

And -- still they robbed him!

Man dumb.

Man invented.

Inverted man.

Man invented Ramiro to exploit the shit out of him in order to fleece him and float his own cheap alter image and gild the cage and call it survival and social justice to fit the punishment of birth and control of crime that doesn't pay.

Ramiro was also part -- pure devil.

He would find a way, some way out.

OK.

First: work.

He would keep his own brutish nature intact as long as necessary. Opportunities grew on trees. Please, boss. Soon he would find some way to overturn the whole cart. Since devils were also in charge, it would take devils to talk devil. So. They started low eh. So. They had to fight their way up with opportunities like old granddad eh. So. Turner had everything going for him, land, tanks, taxes, riches, satisfaction, and Mrs. Turner. And Mrs. T. her social security. So that was good enough reason to keep on pressing, squeezing, cheating, lying, shortchanging, robbing, denying, crimping, and holding back on decent pay for decent work.

Ramiro grinned.

White teeth through black stubble, Ramiro grinned and stepped outside, sniffing the cool cleansing smell of another God-pure dawn, unsullied by man, enjoying the steamy sordid and acrid smell of his own stream of piss.

He was hungry. Had no woman. Had no food. Had no land. How about a clod of first-class fired dirt, friend. What he could do with a clod of dirt. Sit on it. Dirt, the cheapest material on earth. And he couldn't own it. He picked up a clod bigger than his fist and sat on his doorstep. A transient? A fruit bum. No roots. What could he grow. What good was his manhood. How could he build. What could he build. What good was what he built. That dumb spider spinning her web. Was he no smarter?

He pressed the clod of earth. His father had always admonished him, "With corn, mi hijo, with corn you live." Yes. Sure. Corn nourishes, keeps whole tribes and nations alive. But where do you plant it? Where, padre? In this here clod? In this piece of flotsam dirt? He held the whole world in his hands. He would inject it with his manhood and make it boom into the biggest single stalk of tall corn this side of the Rio Grande. And hire some rangers to guard it. Then float it out into space. And make his own planet. Why not. Doom doom was his boom.

In his rising anger, stumbling among the rows of flowering plums, hating the innocent branches, despising the loveliness of the fragile white blossoms, he let the dawn's cool dew rinse his hot forehead. He carried his lump of dirt in mounting fury. It was getting heavier. Where would he hide it. In the crotch of a dead plump tree. How would he irrigate it. Piss on it. What more could a man want. His own fruit. Life. Why not let others enjoy their illicit loves. Children, hi-fis, two-story shanties. Why not. He smote the hard dry clay clod with all his might and sent the gritty particles flying all through that rich man's richly manured orchard, making it richer still. The dumb laws of nature. The dumber laws of man. Hundreds of millions of tons of turf, and hundreds of thousands of sick, hungry, desperate, undernourished mouths, and still the rich had to have still more. Every grit. Every nit. Every spit. Every bit. The richer you got the dumber you got. To hell with humanity. I earned it didn't I. It's mine mine mine mine mine minemineminemineminemineMIIIIIIIIIIIIINE! All mine, you sloppy two-bit cheap picking peasants, I am the King of the Greeds and long may I wave. The Song of Love. And still they took every last tiny grain of heaven, salt, and

100

earth. Air and rain everywhere. And still one had to buy water. Here he was, a graduate fruit picker, a proud picker, a skilled picker, a great grape picker, a honey picker, a June bride picker, a flea, lice, and bug picker. At last. Couldn't run away from it if he tried. Where was the pride. Corn hungry. Corn thirsty. Corn desire. Corn corn corn. Men with no rancho of their own. The little ranchos all gone. The big ones all owned by big land companies who didn't give one good goddamn for hunger, only for their balanced sheets. The Senator who grabbed and bragged that tiny farms were gone forever forgot what America was all about. America was God's gift to the little man and the Senator never knew it. Because Greed had termited his soul through. Monsters. But it was too late. Monsters. The monsters who lied and castrated blind Americans for the dirty work always came out on top.

Such malevolence. Such stupid malevolence. Why was he held down to such ignorance. Why was he born into the universe. Born with brain, not ganglion. The dinosaurs of greed lapped up everything in sight for millions of years. Hot knowledge was seeping through the cracks. Call the cops. Politicians blanching. The genius of evil always greater than charity, greater than hope, greater than love. Ramiro walked back and forth on the cracked, dry, parched soil between the rows, wrecked like himself, watching the corn stalks turning brown, bleached by the searing sun for lack of water, getting dizzy, ready to shrivel and die, useless, crumbling back to raw materiel for the earth to re-use, manure, over and over again. The love cycle. Fecal stench to rose perfume in one season. On the season. The bugs who ate well also fought back. What next ah. Would he know better next time in his next rebirth. As a bird. At least he'd be free. The gueros sure knew how to take care of the bugs. Fighting them off with magic potions. And knocking off all wild things with DDT.

Know - how. It was there.

Vast ecological know-how. It was also there.

Green glowing plants. They were there.

Rich and salable packages. Also there.

And yet -- why did they insist on men groveling in dirt, begging, picking. Refusing to let men work decently. Growers cried they couldn't will the plants to bloom in Heaven, February, etc. Putting the blame on nature. Neat. But they sure managed to pass their own final exams in comfort, their own winters of discontent in sheer comfort.

Human parasites. Worse than their own pests. Had to fight them off. Get them off his back, out of his system, out of his brain; out of his marrow; out of his prune pit; out of his inner ear. Those highhanded human demanders who offered steady work at cheap pay in order to rake it in from the dummies, the whole human race, who didn't care how a miserable man might feed his eleven children on a dollar an hour or relief.

Ramiro, child of scorn, held onto his resilience.

Ramiro, all winter he held onto his resilience.

Ramiro, he could bounce back.

Perhaps the day of Padre Hidalgo's anguished cry was gone.

Perhaps not.

Perhaps Emiliano Zapata's cry was also gone.

Perhaps not.

Perhaps the small farmer would return to haunt the greedy bastards who in the name of efficiency robbed an ordinary man of the last vestigial shred of his pride in a solitary spit of earth.

Bitterness was greed's Finest Virtue.

Efficiency was Greed's greatest contribution.

Perhaps -- they were Greed's greatest contributions.

Perhaps the numerous aunts and uncles and cousins Ramiro had left behind in his ancestral abode, also miserable, for at least he had steady work whenever he cared to find it, which was why he could never really complain, for at least he was in the happy land of unending plenty, and should never complain, where everybody and anybody had a magnificent series of opportunities stretched way out before him, provided he wasn't too darkskinned or too ignorant or spoke no foreign tongue or wasn't a migrant worker -- hey, perhaps, he,Ramiro Sanchez, king of the vagrants, might even be able to help his own people too, and become a new kind of Paul Bunyan, a folk-hero himself.

What a laugh.

The Turners and the Big American hunks of banana banks and the even bigger Land Comanches and the hugest of all Agricombines with their raping rapidly expanding conglomerate expansion plans and bayfilling proposals and their handsome piled-up automatic profits per year after year lied, screaming falsely, lying about rotting strawberries in order to reap cheap public sympathy and while their legitimate holdings and returns and increments and incredulous gains kept fattening into the tens of countless thousands of millions of unaccountable dollars, proudly, countless thousands of poor miserable migrant wretches kept hopefully trucking themselves patiently around the sunny countryside hanging on by the only cash they owned -- their agile fingers, their availability, their resilience, their strong backs, their silent treatment, their persistence, and their endless, useless hunger.

Here in this marvelous land of glut, the nation's fruits and vegetables could still be planted on the mobile backs of hapless human beings. What greater manure than human misery!

Like the captive peasants in Red Orient; like small farmers in sovietized societies who were all owed to the state except for a few chickens; like the Egyptians pulling endless blocks of dumb granite for dumber pyramids; so Ramiro and Manuel and all the other migrants in a modern, highly industrialized, prosperous, fantastically wealthy modern U. S. society were drained of their healthy mature energy, and prevented from contributing their explosive potential to a more humanized society based truly on dignity instead of rathood.

Ramiro grinned.
At least he owned his cloud of dreams.
At least he had his patrimony of frijoles.
At least his domain was not yet beggardom.
At least he was only a prince in beggar's rags.
The morning's mist grew headier.
The skies remained dark. A slight summer sprinkle started drizzling down again, giving more free irrigation to the swollen orchards. Ramiro laughed. His white teeth shone against the black joy of his blazing beard.
Ah, Tenochtitlan, he hummed. Here he was, a god again.

17

Peace was here at last. Papa was gone. Every once in a while papa Pepe took off. Margarita never knew where he went nor, for that matter, did his wife Serafina. Not that she cared. She had long before learned to be resigned. That way, Serafina growled, at least that viejo pendejo kept his machismo intact, his manhood, what there was of it. She'd said it so many times that Margarita never paid her mother any attention.

She heard a clink. How stupid of her. A dish slipped. She turned her head away from the running faucet, from the dish she was washing. Another mysterious clink, and another. Startled, she walked around the sink and behind the partition. Then she saw the cause: it was Ramiro, kneeling at the back screen door, working.

"Looking for something?" she said, in surprise.

He said nothing. He did not even look up. She was glad to see him there. He was taking out the lock screws. He then locked his eyes with hers, and she felt suddenly swimming, taken beyond her depth, but she wouldn't let him know that. and then he dropped them again, handsomely. She was glad to see his dark skin flush furiously. Smiling, she returned to the dishes. The woman in her soared strong. Her intuition was giving her signals. A moment later she heard him get up and she leaned forward to peer through the window. She watched him go into the back yard. She'd almost forgotten she'd been angry with him the other day, on his last visit to the kitchen, when she'd chased him off saying, sincerely she thought, that she never ever wanted to see him again, did he hear? That was then. She hadn't meant it of course, and she liked seeing him confused, and also his bold way of returning. She liked him. She was worried over papa's being annoyed with him. She did not know the reason for that. Vagabundo, Pepe had muttered. Her own papa. Pepe himself had started out precisely in the same way, a migrant, and had been on the season traveling all around the west for many years before finding himself able to settle down here in Drawbridge. Pepe had not only helped guide many migrants from Texas and Tamaulipas and Sonora to endless fruit picking jobs, but had also often contracted or subcontracted groups of pickers himself. Whatever it was Pepe had against Ramiro was beyond her depth. Men's fights.

Danny, coming through the kitchen, leaving his little brother and sister yelping in the living room, slipped an empty beer can into the sink's garbage, winked at her, and went out back too. She dried her hands and followed. A pair of motorcyclists, young heathens from Drawbridge High, roared across the wide fields with an earsplitting vrooooom. They frightened her. It was such a magnificent day, at four in the afternoon with nothing to do, no homework, no picking, all the cleaning done. A nifty, dreamy, sunny, summer Sunday. Threading through the warm air was a cool current of sweet breezes. A large splash of dark welcome shade from the old oak overhead. The rows and rows of smartly pruned plum trees reached back and around for years. It was a sweet time to be alive in. She wished she could tell everyone that. She stood still, watching them under the tree. Danny, like the good brother he was, ignored her. Ramiro looked up, down, around, everywhere but at her. He smiled. She was glad. She was gladder than glad. Almost giddy. She knew he wanted to talk to her. She enjoyed making him wait. She knew he wanted to approach her. She enjoyed feeling like a full woman, a fullblown woman, a mature woman. And that this was her real, true man. In time.

"But -- what's that?" inquired Danny the time killer.

"Nuts on a bike," said Ramiro.

"No, not them. That long ratchet you got."

"It looks broken."

"I mean," sighed Danny, with a long exaggerated sigh, "what I mean, man, is what does it connect? What's it sup - posed to do?"

"I think it's the spring inside that's broken."

"And you can fix it?"

"I can try."

Margarita felt it was safe now to join in. It looked like Ramiro was deliberately holding off talking to her first. "I didn't know you were a repairman."

"Aw, don't pay her any attention," said Dan, giving off his usual free legal advice.

"I said I would try," said Ramiro evenly, as though Margarita weren't present, alive, or even breathing.

She was delighted. "Did papa ask you to do it?" That was a dandy jibe.

"Look here, sis," said Danny, making a more determined effort to express his genuine exasperation. "Haven't you got any other goddamn thing to do somewhere? Sweep the floor or sew something or just get lost? Huh?"

"Do you really want me to go?"

"Sure I do. I said sure, didn't I? God, what do you want me to do? Get down on my goddamn beard and beg you? All right, gee, I sure would only I happen to know already that you're dumb enough to make me get on my heart, promising everything under the sun, and then not do it. She breaks promises all the time, Ramiro. Believe me, that's all she knows how to do."

"No, it isn't. That is not true at all. And you know it is not true, Daniel." She used his formal name to infuriate him more. She studied Ramiro's ever darkening face, enjoying herself immensely.

"Oh, yeh yeh yeh. Sure sure. Well, we know that part all by heart, don't we, Ramiro."

"Why do you have to ask him, Daniel? He can answer for himself, can't he?" Her bright yellow smock, invoking the sun, cinching her waist, furled out and circled broad around. Her long loose brown hair fell down in small ringlets and long smooth ripples. Her long slim brown arms folded, she leaned against the back of the house and continued standing there, motionless.

"Ah," said Danny. "Don't you listen to her, man. I mean, man, she's, well, take my word for it, man, just ignore her. Gawd, she sure knows how to butt in. A regular butt-in. You can't just trust girls. She's always got to stick her biggest toe in and she screams holy murder if you touch her."

"Maybe," said Ramiro, "she's just trying to get your goat."

"Yeah." Dan curled his fine-fuzzed upper lip almost out of sight. He'd just seen Classidium Clopper do it pretty good the night before on TV. It was terrific the way he did it. "Right. Say, Ramiro. Tell me something, will you. Say, what do you fellows do down Texas way for fun. You know, the hold ropes."

106

"Fun?"

"Yeh. You know. Fun stuff. The tricks. It's hot I bet. It sure gets hot here. Sometimes I mean. I mean it gets mean in summer. Well not too much because we do get cool fog from Santa Cruz. But nothing like hot down in Rio Grande I bet. Why?"

"Tell Ramiro how you got to know," said Margarita. "Especially since you've never been there yourself."

"See see see see see see?" spluttered Danny.

"How come you aren't smoking," she added, pushing the other banderilla in. "Papa isn't around."

"See? I said I bet. Didn'tI say I bet, Ramiro? Gaaaawd. Phew. Wow. Pow wow. Wow. And how are all the old gals down there in Rio Grande? Pretty good? Any rabbit spoofing? How fast you got to be? Any fastbacks? Any good road running? Tell me you're not ah tell me you ain't just kidding me, pal."

"I'm not kidding you, pal," said Ramiro. "And you would not like it."

"Why not?" said Margarita.

Danny shook his head with his eyelids rolled way back, reading something in the sky.

"You wouldn't --"

"Why wouldn't he?" she persisted.

Ramiro looked straight into her eyes, then bent down to study the lock assembly with deep interest. He pushed a slender screwdrive into the handle slot and exerted slight pressure. It was stuck. He squirted some oil in and tried again. He peered into it a long time. Two more motorcyclists joined the original pair, and practically ripped up the quiet residential Sunday. He pried at the works with both screwdriver and pliers.

"Say, Dan," he said. "How come those guys keep roaring up and down the streets like that?"

"Ah, punks."

From around the driveway Silvestre came into the back yard. "Hey, Ramiro. You hear that? What's all the racket?"

"Punks," said Dan. "The cycles out there."

"They sure nice machines. Think I'll get me one."

"What for?" said Ramiro.

"Listen, compadre," said Silvestre. His tone was low and threatening. "You keep your jokes to yourself. I got really tired your stale jokes long ago." Silvestre was strong, built like a bull, thick and heavy like a bull, mean and heavy like a bull. Not slender and strong like Ramiro.

"Boy, some girls sure are dumb," said Dan, magnetized by his favorite alltime topic, drunk or sober. "They sure -- hey, here's Rosa too. Hi, Rose."

107

"How many times --"

"-- I toll you not to call me a Rose," he mimicked.

"Danny, you are so conceited," said Margarita.

Danny, happy, helping, jumped into his father's light gray chariot and smartly kicked the motor over. "Come on, you maniacs. Hop in, everybody." He gunned the accelerator three times hard vrooom vrooom vroooooom. Silvestre held the front door open for Rosa and slid in after her. "Come on, gang."

Ramiro got in back, leaving the door open, saying, "Why don't we go in Jesus's car?"

"Because I want to drive," said Danny, gunning and snorting the motor like a great impatient metal bull. "OK. Free tickets everybody!" As long as Rosa was along, Danny got to use the car all he wanted.

Margarita turned toward the house.

"Hey, sis," called Danny, easing back.

"Come on, you ninny," said Rosa.

Margarita turned and impulsively sat in back, as far from Ramiro as she could get. Danny poured his soul into the trigger and blasted off like a nightmare of sighing jets. Hablame de tu corazon, sang Silvestre in his best seranade sonata, his lounging arm running along the seat top behind Rosa's head.

"Me?" sang out Danny, flaming out.

"You got some plan, hombre?" yelled Silvestre.

Rosa too was happy. Silvestre was happy. Danny was happy. Ramiro was -- Margarita felt vaguely uncomfortable. She didn't like it. She could take care of Danny and Rosa. She wasn't afraid of Ramiro. But the combination didn't feel right. Something, some vague premonition was gnawing at her.

"Que pasa, chica?" said Ramiro, speaking softly to her. She turned her head, looked at him, serious now, and turned again to look out the window. She didn't answer.

The car bounded over the ruts like a bucking bronco in second trying to kick off the woes of the world. Dan got such a big kick out of gunning it. "Lousy car!" he yelped. Nearly new. It bucked and bounced and dipped and swayed. Dan grinning like a mad monkey atop a berserk elephant. "Lousy gear!" At the boulevard he had to wait a lousy minute before he could shoot out across and swing left into the light traffic.

"Lousy day!" He chortled, the grinningest pilot of the western world.

"Lousy what?" said Silvestre. "Hey, Ramiro!"

"Lousy driver," said Ramiro drily. "Watch it."

"Hey, Ramiro, you woke up, man. I like, I sure do like being out every day like this," yelped Dan, the big man. "I -- man, look. No hands. See. Now Margarita, glum glum, she thinks her teachers are real great. She gets into a little scrape and she folds up. Know that? The lousy women's counselor calls her in, calls in all the Metsican girls and then she bawls them out. Bawls them out because the blondies picked on them. But they don't call the blondies in. No sir. Know what? They never call me in or bawl me out. What for? And Margarita didn't even do nothing either. The blondies, no, no, they never ever do nothing, no, never. They are pure gold. All they know is how to stab and smile real good."

It was partly true. Margarita had her own reasons for hating school, for being mistreated, but not Dan's reasons. She turned around at Ramiro who was watching the passing traffic. His legs were crossed casually, and she kept her own hands folded in her yellow lap. They took the green light easily, crossed Winchester, passed under the Santa Cruz overpass, crossed Bascom where the boulevard changed its name to San Carlos Street, and where the lanes singled and the stream of traffic thinned down still more.

Margarita had often thought of dropping out of school. It would be so easy. What was Maria, her former best chum, up to now? Maria often baby-sat, tired of it, then popped herself into a drive-in waitress job. Margarita liked drive-ins to eat goodies in, but not to work in, the fellows were too fresh. So she stayed on at school. She liked to study, but she didn't like the constant pressure, the friction, always having to be constantly defending herself. Dan didn't mind the fighting; he liked it; he was a scrapper. Why were the gueros so set against them? Because they were Mexican? Because their skins were darker? Because they spoke Spanish? That couldn't be enough reason. Could it? There were too many different kinds of Americans. Violence bred more violence. She didn't like that. Always arguing, insulting, fighting. Love bloomed so fragilely and you had to wait for it to happen. And fights came so easy. Like storms. Like storm troopers. Pretexts were worse than useless. Among her people she remembered a saying that a shorthaired mongrel would live longer in a fiery hell. The catch was, usually not very much longer. The longhaired silksmooth gueras, how she resented them. She did nothing to them. But they resented her. She was determined not to fight back. Not hatred, but sadness engulfed her. All they needed was energy, boredom, resentment, anger, envy, hatred, and they'd all turn out like her brother Dan with his overpowering need to constantly assert himself and his manhood, what their mother called machismo. Among Mexicans, she'd heard her teacher Miss Rodriguez say, are exactly the same proportions of docile to aggressive as in other cultural or national groups. That was another lie. There was more of everything in the Mexican character except money or love of money. More sadness, more joy, more love, more ferocity, more intensity, more softness, more intimacy, more warmth, more family, and more hatred.

Danny was bragging about a fight he'd got caught in at school. He laughed at the way he'd lied out of it at the principal's office, with the principal believing him and taking his side against some snots.

"You provoked them," said Margarita. "I saw you."

"So? They had it coming. What do you want me to do? I say to hell with justice. They lie. I lie. I lie ten times better. Right, Silvestre?"

"You might regret it," said Ramiro softly.

"Yeah?" laughed Danny. "Why?"

"What else have you got?"

"What else have they got?"

That wasn't papa Pepe's way. Pepe was sometimes furious with Daniel's taunting trouble, sometimes proud. Pepe was quiet but not deceitful, nor was he docile. He had his own troubles, but Daniel liked ferreting out trouble. Danny was cunning, like an animal. Danny did not wait to be provoked. His trick was to stand in the path of provocation, to ambush it.

"It sure is a free country, hah, ain't it?"

A car on their left shot past them. Dan pressed the accelerator suddenly, trying to keep his bumper up even. The other speeded up more. One of the passengers leaned his head out and spat at Dan who quickly put his window up. Margarita leaned forward and pressed Dan's shoulder. "Please, Dan! This is papa's car. Papa will --"

"Let's get 'em," said Silvestre.

But Papa wasn't the immediate problem. The immediate problem, which Ramiro alerted them to, was shaping up to an ominous trap: there were four motorcyclists weaving their way purposefully up behind them. It was a nice quiet peaceful San Jose Sunday afternoon, with families traveling peacefully and visiting friendly relations.

They were hemmed in, trapped front and back.

The four toughs in the front car were alert as straight soldiers. They cut in front of Danny and deliberately slowed down. They watched every swing of Dan's wheel. When Dan cut to the right, they cut right. When he tried to pass left, they'd stop him, or oncoming traffic did. The cyclists were now glued to their rear bumper, four superjawed blond giants with flashing blue lightning eyes and heavy gold swastikas thumping like guillotine blades against their shiny black leather jackets. Two cut out and swung around either side of their car. Then, with short heavy chains, they smashed the safety glass of the uprolled windows. Dan swung over sharply to the right but the cyclists, anticipating, pulled smartly back. Dan

110

braked and jumped out, followed by Silvestre and Ramiro.

The four front quadrupeds and the four tough spark plugs in back converged fast. Eight brave rebels, redblooded blooms of he-mens. Eight blond adrenalined young American American youth. Eight prancing mothers' sons. Eight freak aberrations of U.S.A.'s benign civilization, cancerous off-shoots of church, hope, home, hearth, state, school, deten-tion centers, and so on. Eight dragged, deranged nonconfor-mists magnificently pompadoured, minimally educated, and gyroscopically hairbrained.

All eight braves in their black tutus, turning off their sim-ulated brains, pounced fiercely in visceral unison upon the three defenders and pounded them to insensibility in less than a minute. Perfect timing. Running clocks. They wrenched Margarita and Rosa screaming out of the car and started drag-ging them to their rocket of doom when, as at a signal, they dropped them and bounded onto their magnificently souped-on superchargers. Vrrrrrrrrooom vrooooom. The last heroic thug spat exultantly. "I told youse bastards we'd get youse youse goddamn rotten dirty Mexican bastards." And off they roared with great gusto, with great barrelling bravura, into the glory of their own unspoiled Valhally sunset, their doped-up genes gestating vigorously in their shriveled testicles, their glowing swastikas ticking awesomely.

The American Patrol, the polite police squad car swung up just in the nick of time, as the gawking crowd surged, forming, turning everything back to day again, a neat Sunday afternoon. The first thing the first polite cop said, shaking his head, was, "When you Mexican kids going to learn to quit fighting among yourselves, eh?"

Margarita remained huddled on the curb, head bowed down, bruised, bleeding, and frightened. She was unable to stop her uncontrollable sobbing. What would papa do to her now?

18

Life is like a river, flowing relentlessly.

The nascent Guadalupe River of San Jose, starting its life as a vast hopeful network of tiny brooks and freshets high up among the rocky crevices of the Santa Cruz range, finding out what life was about, rushes down the hilly sides, gathers, then slowly peters out. It meanders north alongside Almaden Road all through the city of San Jose, a crooked charming chasm hidden behind rows of residential MJB boxes, beneath overhanging weeping willows, its IBM slopes at times cemented in, and limps past San Jose's SOC Airport. It then skirts Laurelwood Road, passes near the Southern Pacific's magnificently unguarded r. r. crossing at Lafayette Street, ambles past acres of broad, open tomato fields, flows past Agnews State Mental Hospital, trickles past sinking Alviso, past stinking garbage pits, past sunken Drawbridge, and finally disgorges itself into the enormously profitable salt flats abounding in and around the southern tip of San Francisco's Bay.

If the vast Santa Clara tomato fields, bursting green with red life, heavy with a quarter of a million round, hard fruit per acre, reaching easily to the moon and back, were aching to be picked; if they had not been well cared for, well cultivated, well planted, well manured, well weeded, and well irrigated, they were also somehow to some extent dependent upon thousands of miserable tomato pickers trying their best to keep up with nature's glut and at the same time trying to work their own way out of their misery. Every fruit identical, sweet, delicious, bugless, bulging with nutriments, hundreds of thousands of tomato-bearing plants had done their work well, impeccably, impersonally, perfectly, in this most ideal of all benign climes.

Next project on the board's agenda: why not turn the ant people into automatic pickers and save the cost of an internal

HOW TO PICK CANNING TOMATOES
--by the Agricultural Extension Service
of the University of California--
+
THE tomato harvest is very important
in California. Many people share the
income from it -- pickers, farmers,
truckers, cannery workers, can manufacturers, chemical manufacturers,
and many others.

machine? Every plant would by then be absolutely perfect. Every picker perfect too. No complainers. In marked contrast, in their own board meetings in the fields, all that the

A LITTLE "know-how" will make your
work easier and will help you to earn
more money.

miserable migrants had to worry about was their everlasting hunger, their basic insecurity, and their miserable worthless existence, where they plotted whether they really existed or not.

And in all that heady gardening, all the growers growing everything they could, mightily, greenbacks back to back, and all the glands of agricombines owned by holding companies holding their regular hoard meetings, engendering still more agriblobconglomerates up and down the agricoast, the ups and downs of the greedy agridollar coasters had also to be computed. Plant more. Make more. Raise more. Sell more. Eat less. Many happy combines, thank you. Sappy happy company heads. Paying off their collegiate kids. Threading pears to the moon. And all those lands were all owned by, controlled by, inflated by still vaster holders buried in the tickerape emporiums, far from the madding migrants. What golden crops could be sown. When they were to be planted. When to be rotated. Rotation is great. What projects. Plans encompassed even an unborn city upon these very sinking salt marshes

113

as part of the biggest master plan of all -- to fill in the whole
San Francisco Bay entirely.   Just leave a little trickle of a
stream locked in a cementlined tube under Main Street, where
the Golden Gate used to be. No more bay. No more cool wa-
ters. No more lapping waves. An enormous greed was growing, a greed that knew no bounds. Why should it? Wasn't
greed the greatest, the most powerful human emotion, after
killing? And who or what was powerful enough around to stop
it? Nothing. And so the growers and the corporations and the
holding companies and the combines grew bigger and happier
and tighter and fatter and wealthier and smarter and kindlier

> IN THIS leaflet, we offer suggestions
> that may be helpful to both new and ex-
> perienced tomato pickers.
> +
> WEAR COMFORTABLE clothes. Old
> ones are fine. A straw hat to shade your
> head. Some workers wear cloth or rub-
> ber gloves to protect their hands from
> tomato leaf stains.   Tomato juice will
> remove these stains from hands.

disposed to hypocritical charity drives. And why not? Everything paid, paid well, nay, paid handsomely.
    It was therefore only natural that the most bootlicking,
shortsighted, inhumane, egotistical, inchoate, despicable,
contemptuous, tawdry, and most deceptive trick on earth was
to exhume some lordly profit out of human misery.   And
among the most knowledgeable in-group, it was almost uni-
versally conceded that Fredrick C. (Combine) Turner managed neatly to turn this trick, antwise and otherwise, and also
to appear virtuous at it as well, with no excrementa showing,
without experiencing even the slightest tinge or nidge of inner
pain or shame. And Turner, in turn, all full of good inten-
tions on his way to hell, was all pure, pure-all. He was a
great sparkling symbol of California's grand wine and dine
club, eat and be merry, give 'em cake, me fustest with the
mustest, combining everything: land, water, taxes, corrup-
tion, population, levies, pickers. Turner, consistently one
of America's best ten-dressed men, his flaming ascot fluffed
boldly out of his scrawny neck, to show how nonconformist he
was when he felt like it, to hell with the kids, rated highly in
Fortune -- also in southern Texas -- as well as in Dun & Brad
-- even in the USSR -- and, of all places, last but not least,
in the BBR, the Bastards' & Brothers' Roasting. There sure
was nothing like saintliness for getting next to holiness and
godliness, the good lord knew, though few mortals knew, but

Turner also knew.

Meanwhile, however, back at the raunchy ranch, th e tempestuous tomatoes kept right on ripening and growing wildly, as though there were nothing more important in the world as their

> TAKE a (10) ten (10) minute cotton picking rest period midmorning & afternoon.
> YOU'LL pick just as many tomatoes
> AND you won't be so tired.
> +
> BRING two sandwishes with you.
> EAT one in the morning.
> AND one in the afternoon.
> A little food will give you more energy.
> THE grower will furnish drinking water.
> AND toilets near where you are picking.

ripening inexorably toward their only possible solution -- getting picked -- so some one could eat them.

And meanwhile corporate profits had also to be carefully nursed or else the whole whale could be beached. Then who would meet the payrolls? Did Gaspar de Portola, as he gazed grandly upon this lissome Bay for the first time, ever even once have to meet a payroll himself? Of course not. Sights are for sore eyes, not for business. Business is business. Business is for computers, for responsible managers, and for empire builders, not for daydreamers or stargazers or goody do-gooders. All Gaspar did was stumble by sheer accident, not through careful pre-planning, upon this grand body of holy water, which is now being inexorably filled in for the needs of forthcoming millions of future residents. It was not altogether a matter wholly of wages then. No indeed. Scru-pulously honest and enlightened corporation heads, the few that abounded, when they knew of it, bowed to the inexorable. Hawaii was near, the grandest land development of all time, for the great benefit of the few -- a richness of the elite, for the elite, and by the elite. To hell with the Pacific.

El Camino Real took its time slinking past Santa Clara's residential streets. Numerous motels on the boulevard rose up varying in stages of disrepair, from allure to hanky panky, filling their rooms at differing rates collecting from differing clientele. Migrants traveled from Texas to Idaho, ten thousand migrants stopping by in Santa Clara County every blessed year to pay their respects to the power of inverted green. Out where the noises of men and machines were muffled by the great green verdant country. Soon there would be tracts, and more tracts, and multi-family dwelling units, but right now there were only bugless plants growing greener. In

115

the distance, the longlined railroad train clanked elegantly down its track, boring a hole into the distant sky. The green sky sun beat down. Down, down, down, and the blasted redhot romantic tomatoes, begging to be plucked, sighed.

Alberto Fernandez and his crew had little to fear and less knowledge whatsoever of corporate intricacies. Indeed they just didn't give a good goddamn about such matters, thereby

SANTA   CLARA   COUNTY   TOMATOES
+

San Marzano	- for bland, dry sauces
Red Cherry	- tart
Ponderosa	- low-acid, large, meaty
Burpee Globe	- mild
Red & Yellow Pear	- pear-shaped
Pearson	- sweet
Sunray	- mild
Ace	- full flavor
VF 36	- bland
Big Boy	- large, tart
Jubilee	- mild
Earliana	- mild

repaying the corporations' indifference in kind, with a vengeance. They at least were alive, where the corporation heads were dead. Deadheads. The pickers only knew what they read in the papers, and since they never read the papers, they did not give a damn about anything. They'd learned to make contract for themselves, as individuals, leaving their families behind in Texas, thereby bypassing a good deal of the executive misery that befell the vast majority of migrating thousands in search of work, picking fruit, entrusting themselves to the chicaneries of unscrupulous crew leaders. Alberto's six stayed in one place as long as honest, legitimate work was offered them, not fake leads, no strike breaking, no waiting interminably until the fickle crops ripened, no waiting for the farmer's or grower's comfortable convenience who knew where their dinners were that evening. In any of these fraudulent situations, Alberto's six — having picked up two new members — simply moved on to the next picking town, section, county, or state, wherever new crops were ripening. They paid for their rooms with spot cash. Mr. Quill was delighted with clients like these, cash in hand, no questions asked, even if they were Mexicans. He also enjoyed giving the impression that there was no one more openminded toward the doctrine of the downtrodden than he, which was quite a big distance from the truth.

One arresting aspect of the whole complex matter was that Alberto and his happy crew really didn't mind working piece rate. They were fast, young, hard workers, and often earned far beyond the minimum rates established by federal law. At

HERE are some suggestions to increase
your income:
+
USUALLY you will pick from two rows, called a claim. Carry 4 to 6 empty boxes to your claim and scatter them along the rows. When you have filled all your boxes, carry a full box to the end of your claim and bring back more empties.

times, Alberto did find himself wondering what, if anything, was wrong with picking wild fruit. Or feeding your family. Or even living off the world. Was there something wrong with that? Fruit grew free and naturally in the tropics. Fruit grew free and wild, bananas, mangos, coconuts. At piece rate, at any rate, they didn't have to suffer a heavy, a boss breathing hard, breathing hot down their sodden necks. Alberto and his flying crew, proud, independent, and free men, knew that the father of the country was money, and the faster they picked, and the fatter the rich got, and the hotter they worked, the more crumbs they got, and the somewhat slightly better off they were. That was all right. They knew exactly what was coming to them, neither a pawn more nor a pfennig less. They couldn't have felt much better if they'd planted the crops personally them-selves and had to sweat out the bugs, and the irrigation, and the tax collectors and the county bounty. They were hired for their specialty, which was picking. Their profession was pick-ing crops. It was strong, exhausting, outdoor work. It helped them to live longer. It gave them access to nature's clean air. It purified their souls. It calmed their spirits. It gave them cleansing showers in nature's free wind, storm, and rains....

WHEN you pick up boxes to carry to the roadway, do not bend over and lift with your arm and back muscles. Squat down by the box, then straighten your legs as you lift the box. This is much easier on your back. Continue picking until you have finished your rows and all your boxes are stacked at the end of your claim. Chalk your picking number on each box so that the checker can keep track of the number of boxes you pick.

For the futures, all they had to do was to get better organized. Get a union going. Get the growers over a nice fat wine barrel. Make it unbearable for them. Then -- make them pay. What the work was really worth. Go on strike. What a laugh. With the governor, Howlin Mad Nolan, the fairhaired mortician of the great snurd combines. Ha ha. A factory in the field. All they wanted was the freedom to work just as long as they damn well felt like, like anybody else. They liked offering contract by their word. If for any good reason they felt they had to default, they wanted the freedom to give their responsible reason to back off -- whether it was sickness, injury, or just plain fishing. Like any factory worker. Like any businessman. A man knows when he can go on, or when he wants to go on. And he knows when he has had enough. The great insight that was escaping the intelligent growers was that it was within the real realm of possibility to treat a picker decently. It was right to treat them decently -- and it could be profitable too.

All a picker wanted was to be treated as a human being with skill and technique. Then if nothing else worked, to hell with them. Sock it to them hard with a strike. Strike, strike.

Alberto Fernandez felt that the best, the proudest, and the most exciting work was where a man could work for himself. Whether it was for his own store, a profession, a hair cutter, or leasing his stupendous skills plucking fruit, even at piecework -- provided he was free all the way to bargain for his compensation, to accept or refuse according to his feelings about the matter. A good way to avoid being cheated, or complaining. Cheating, shortchanging, holding back fair wages

LEARN to pick so that the stem will remain on the vine.
+
DO: A good way to pick is to pull steadily as you tip the tomato sideways, turning in a spinning motion at the same time. If the stem stays in the fruit, remove it by brushing sideways with the thumb. Do not jerk the vines in picking.
DON'T: If you lift the tomato, the stem will break.
DON'T: If you pull straight out, the branch may break.

for hard work fairly done, was not fair in any game. As an independent picker Alberto Fernandez and his free traveling pickers did not have to worry, did not have to disturb his deep inner recesses of his conscience, did not have to harbor any mental reservations, did not have to shuffle around like a ballerina making believe he was busy on any job to keep the boss from getting upset. None of that kind of stupid waste for him or them. Piecework, as long as it paid well, permitted him to get high pay for hard work well and honestly done. The cheating occurred where the rates were set so low that hard hard work resulted only in slightly better wages.

Alberto Fernandez, standing out there in the darkness of another endlessly stupid picking dawn, baring his soul to the superstudded starry universe out there, withdrew his organ and started pissing with enormous satisfaction and relief against the crumbling wall of the back corner of Mr. Ferdi nand Y. Turner's exclusive Western Grande compound, when he heard someone's irate approach.

It was, of all people, Mr. Quill himself, coming upon him in such a rush, waving his arms askew, in great alarumm. Where was the fire? "Wh wh wh wh what are you do do do you ghastly simply ghastly do you think you you you are do dodoing here, with with with you you you your -- ?" Sppppluttering.

"How de do," replied Alberto politely. Expertly shaking then replacing his organ, he then ran the zipper up. No strain. "Dare I surmise there is ah something ah amiss, Mr. Q. ?"

"Some a thing? Something uh yes uh something uj uj --"

"Oh. Perhaps because it is, ah, I am pissing."

"You you you uj uj --"

"But hombre you you you are how you say? sut-stutter."

"I don't I don't I have I don't --"

"In that case you are one very lucky hombre."

"You know where the bathroom is you pig."

"Ah. Now. Yes. I do so admit to having knowledge of such a stinkpot."

AHA! "Well, then!"

"Ah, yes. I see. Si si. Well well. I might therefore add, my fat dreary friend, that my compadre Silvestre is at this very moment undergoing an uncontrollable siege of diarrhea as a result of having consumed a packet of your rotten but very expensive hot dogs, and that he is at this very moment occupying the solitary throne of our community toilet, and sitting thereupon with a great deal of groaning pain, and that furthermore I could also have tapped politely upon your own door to ask if you would be kind enough to permit me the honor of utilizing your own private stall for just a minute or two myself, for as a matter of additional fact I do still feel another kind of urgent --"

"Never mind!" exploded Mr. Quill in no unmincing terms, rushing back into the wind.

In that bustling dawn, while Mr. Quill was still working off his all-but-unbearable annoyance caused by the destruction of No. 16's unexpected departure, several families, and among them the six men belonging to Alberto's roving band, finished

119

off their huevos rancheros for breakfast in various stages of
tension and apprehension within their respective squalor huts.
This group of six, meeting in the compound's courtyard at

> A GOOD tomato picker makes all his
> motions count. What this means is this:
> Start with one section of the plant and
> then pick around it so you don't waste
> time or motion.
> ALSO: Be sure to put the fine vines
> back as they were so that the partly
> ripe tomatoes will not sunburn.

dawn, tipped their sombreros to Mr. Quill's waddling gait,
and jammed into Jesus's waiting car. They had been picking
tomatoes for seven days running, excellent picking, in the
huge Agnews farm, and now they had but three more days
ahead of them before embarking on their next move.

The two younger men, Alberto Fernandez and Silvestre
Salazar, as yet unmarried at twenty-four, had lighter burdens.
Silvestre's eyes often sought Rosa's. If he could just stay a
little while longer -- now, would she have him? Could he have
her? He wasn't sure. He couldn't stay around to find out either. He could plan a comeback. She was young. Ripe and
ready. She wanted a husband. And she wanted romance too.
She was young and tender. And a little wild. "She's probably
all yours," said Alberto, "if you want to marry her." And
Silvestre guffawed. He was young too. He was too young for
marriage. He would wait. Alberto eyed Margarita himself
but backed off when he saw her eyes light up in Ramiro's presence. Ramiro would be a good guy to have in his crew. Too
bad they didn't have the room. How did Ramiro make it? How
did he get around? He was a real loner, that Ramiro. The
other four members of his crew, Juan and Francisco, Jesus

> YOU'LL pick more tomatoes each
> day if you pick with both hands.

and Santiago, all had families of their own waiting for their
return in south Texas at the end of the season.

Jesus at the wheel, the car moved out in darkness into the
broad royal highway, El Camino Real, and joined dawn's thin
traffic. It felt good to be going out there in California's crisp
dawn air, and to go to work at your own heart's desire....

Hey, said Santiago, the trouble is there are too many of
you greedy hijos de la chingada out there.

Hey, said Francisco, you bat. You go watch us all right.
And ho, Jesus, you got to watch that crazy wheel you loco.

Hey, man, said Alberto, if we could just make one good haul we can make twice as much this summer.

Hey, said Silvestre, you watch those muchachos give them grape growers hell over there in Delano.

Hiu, watch it, said Juan, you nearly make that stupid trock chop us up, hombre.

Jesus laughed. His late model sedan, less than two years old, obeyed all his commands instantly, smoothly, even the most frivolous. There was hardly any traffic on Lafayette. He

> KEEP your hands close together. Fill
> both hands with fruit, then move them
> together to the box. Carry the fruit to
> the box. DON'T THROW IT.

swung the car up the overpass. The Bayshore Freeway below carried a heavy stream of early morning traffic already moving thickly north and south. Jesus gunned the accelerator on the downslope just for the hell of it, for kicks, because it was downgrade, because he felt good, heading for the huge tomato field flanking the rail line. He touched the brake lightly while making the sharp right on Laurelwood Road, the deadend road bordering the tomato field.

At that same moment, the fast-paced smooth-flying Southern Pacific engine reached the same identical blind corner of Laurelwood and Lafayette at precisely the same instant in time.

The automobile exploded.

In that one single instant of violent impact, six lives were snuffed out. The iron law of impact, though both swift and terrifying, lasted for a mere moment, one hot flash.

Mr. Quill was very annoyed at having to lose some of his best and most prompt-paying customers. Now there would be

> KEEP the box close to where you are
> picking. You won't have so far to carry
> the fruit and you'll have more time for
> picking.

a period of confusion until the upset families were able to sort out and remove personal possessions and the like. In the meantime, he would have to place all their personal belongings in The Warehouse, along with all the other bricabrac.

When they heard about the accident, the Southern Pacific Board of Trained Directors said, we are most heartily sorry. And immediately dispatched the Engine to the repair yard.

The California Farm Bureau, representing every kind of

crop grower, very, very concerned, said, we are sorry.

The Great and Honorable Fruit Governor of California, Howlin Mad Nolan, said, yup, we shore air sorry. The Di Gestation Fruit Co also said, we are veddy soddy. The California Fruit Farmer Ass. Inc. said, we are most sorry. The

Drawbridge Courier
Wednesday Eighteen

Braceros OK'd to pick tomatoes
SAN FRANCISCO (UP)--The way was clear today for the emergency importation of 8,100 Mexican braceros to help harvest California's big tomato crop.
The U. S. Labor Departmentapproved the action Thursday after the California Employment Department said there were not enough domestic field hands to meet growers' needs.

Modesto Crap Growers Co said, eh we're sorry too. America's wealthiest man, over his breakfast coffee, said, I'm so sorry. The American Farm Bureau Fed said, we are very sorry. The National Grange said softly, we are sorry. The National Cotton Picking Council said, we are most deeply and humbly sorry. The National Beet Growers Associa also said they were sorry indeedy. The Amalgamated Sugar Guard was also extremely disturbed. The Diversified Growers of California extended their most cordial sympathies. Meanwhile, the National Farm Labor Users Committee solemnly intoned, as a kind of universal warning, broadcast:

When our whole yearly income depends on only a few days of summer harvest, the callous attitude of American labor is intolerable and necessitates the importation of foreign labor.

There. There it was. In cold, white blood. Though they had nothing to do directly with the train wreck either, they were obviously a little out of joint too.

The big-breasted, purple-feathered, horn-dimpled, large-mouthed, close-cropped, horse-maned corporation bigs in New York, -- whose compliant, obsequious, servile department heads never overlooked the inexorable laws of overhead and eating taxes -- knew all about the lazy Mexican migrant workers. They sighed briefly and shook their dignified temples, anticipating a brief public hullabaloo. Now their cor-

122

porate taxes would have to go toward helping pay for the up-bringing of an additional seventeen lazy offspring of the families involved. Carless families. So untidy. So they were both very sorry and also worried.

Finally, however, it was Mr. F. X. (F^{i}xit) Turner who brought the whole tragedy of the circumstance into sharpest focus. Mr. Turner, he said: "Why, that's terrible. How now how in helllllll am I going to get all the goddem prune pickers I need in all that hurry?"
A truly lamentable situation for a truly greedy man.
An even worse one for greedier growers.
For the tomatoes HAD to be and would be picked.
And the apricots, and the snap beans, and the pickles, and the squash, and the pumpkins, and the potatoes in sacks -- as well as the plump plump plums.
And the Guadalupe River kept right on flowing on, across the immensely profitable salt flats and on into the Bay.
Relentlessly.

19

Life is also a smart pet shop. It is so lifelike.

After leaving the buzzing bar, Manuel felt his head get dizzy inside. It felt fuzzy like. Like felt. He found himself standing in a small dark zoo, a jungle in miniature. Loneliness by itself was terrible enough. Inside the oven of the pet shop, the warm and oddly assorted odors of stale urine, the barks, the yips and squawks assailed his buzzing ears and his stuffy nose. Over and over again he kept asking himself: What Am I? Am I freak? Am I human? Am I man? Am I monkey? No fun drinking alone. He sorely missed his compañeros. What would Lupe have done had he gone along with them on their fatal last tomato ride -- and widowed her?

He wondered. And he wondered. And he shook his head.

Animals. Animal sequence. Animal sequences took turns swimming before his redrimmed eyes. The horse tropics of the square pisces. OK hijos de la chingada. Now, where do we go? What else is happen? Taking a long at one long freak freckled speck of a fish sucking water and wanting to spear him. OK. Or sending the big live turtlebacks on a fast buckspin. Slowly he counted. Slowly he counted twenty-two large coconuts. Large coconutsized graybacked trunklegged thicknecked bigshelled turtles all resigned to endless piddling inthe piddling pet shop's murky pool. Take away the underwater

124

rocks from the high seas that nurtured them, take them from the shores and ponds and lakes of their primordial ancestry lock them up in this square dismal gray muck to silt and sulk on as all life and vigor and thrill and joy drill slowly down dow down down down downdowdowdowdownthedrain.....

Manuel Gutierrez, trying to find himself.

Manuel Gutierrez, born in an iridescent paradise.

Deep in the southern tropics' most exciting paradise.

Raised on succulent fruit and nutritious corn.

Uneducated, excepted by instinct.

Ignored by ignominy.

The sharp instinct of the castoff.

Eyes dark. And Alive.

Possessor of a total of twenty-two hours of formal school-ing, plus some uncertain minutes. The puppies in the pet shop yelped on him. Playful puppies. Wiggly puppies. Tail-wagging puppies. Whining and dining puppies. Calling barking yapping and yipping puppies. Was he, Manuel Gutierrez, eh no better than a dog? For sale? Seeking out new masters with wet eyes? Children laughed and teased and poked them with play-ful fingers. Children trapped, too. They were all so lonely, All, all. Loneliness was an old sickness, not a happiness, no matter what the dogs said. Sixty plux six. And still you work. And work And work And work.

Manuel coughed.

He recalled groggily he'd caught his finger in the car door and injured his good picking hand. Stooping for tomatoes wasn't too bad. But reaching for fruit in the higher trees stretched and pained his sore ligament.

Stranded in the doorway of the pet shop, leaning against the back door stoop to cool his forehead, tired, drained, beat, exhausted, drained, drained, drained, Manuel thought of the hophead Chuck Pope telling him: you lousy dirty rotten nogood lazy mexicans all you think of is pot and mañana and mañana. That man could get himself killed. Lupe was going to get sore at him again. Cheese, cheap wine, hot shack, cool breeze - picking, thinking: the titled rich would always win. They had to. Swimming pools and banks. How could they lose? They knew how to live all right. Ignoring the blasts. Turning their backs on migrant misery. That was the way all right. Wouldn't he? Sure. Si si señor. Siphon off your energy your bloom your skull your years your blood your chill and mind and skill and keep it up until you drop you idiot. And what for. And yet they grew fat. They squeezed you. They adored you. Un-til only your metsican brain is squashed flat flat flat and they can drive it around any which way they want. And even make you like it. Like eating dung. They even let you sleep so you can fill your eyes again with rest to be able to go out and bet you can pick sweet again. They know just how much you can earn with your eagerness and your hunger and your drive and your need and your fear and your kids and they slip their iced highballs down down their smooth gullets without the slightest qualm as they sleekily grow sleeker and happier hey you rich fat sharlieboy yeh yeh sharliebrown you happiness too you big fat knowitall and of course and and and send their sassy fat little girls east to sleep in college dorms and when they want and while you contemplate and while you metsican kids and wonder how the hell you going to buy a pair of the cheapie s the best tennis shoes forthebuck and wonder but that isn't so bad because what is much worse is you wonder how are you going to keep them alive and in school while they grow if all you do is move around like a hulking gypsy animal all the time.

All the time. All the time from Teasdale to Groville. From Idahoho to Oreganoho. From Florida to Orangegrange. From Daytown to the prayrie to the ocean shit with foam and educated in the pet shop and now I am going to buy a house and this vicious cauliflowered circle but the gringos and the orregonians and the washingtonians know how and the goldbraids know how and the water sluicers know how just pill yourself up your own goldbraided bootstraps you punks wewewe didit didit didit why the hell oh say can't you see? or are you blind?

So.

Out of school early is it. So. Break out early. Help with the prune juicer in the flowering May for the heyday. Do not repeat do not send your tiny tims back for opener day on September morn. A very very good time can be had by all. It won't do any good to educate them no how. How can a bunch a iggorant Indians an Metsicans help the mighty USA anyway? The regular heroes got it all sewed up. John Wainscote. And his Regulars. The Roaring Squares. Regular Shooters. Great Shots. You see them in summery camps while you pick pick pick while your own kids grow up dumb without school. Adios mariquita linda. They even say it is your fault for being so lazy. Can't teach English. Se habla español.

He knew what the bosses would say.

He knew what the bosses would do.

They wouldn't give a good goddamn.

How to get the Metsican to do his dirty work in the yard and not complain? To agree with their evil design to come onto the clean land to climb up the clean trees and to go down the hedge rows and pick all the clean fresh pods and place the harvest all so tenderly in those nice clean boxes -- without complaining? You don't. Careful now. Now don't bruise it, otherwise the foreman will otherwise the foursquare greedy grower otherwise the stunted foremen otherwise the underpaid policeman otherwise don't. Don't don't don't. You don't get any otherwise the girls are in such sequence as to ask all over and over and over: WHAT AM I?

Am I rotting weed?

Am I no good?

Am I indeed a proud Mexican?

Am I indecent?

Am I Indian?

Or am I undemocratic?

Am I American citizen?

Am I -- ignorant?

A box. That's it. A box. And another. And another box. And a box. A man. A man. Is. A man is a boxer. A bb box filler. How many apricots you need to keep alive? Man alive. Woman alive. Family alive. How many little of those teeny dingdong orange cots can a idiot pick one a minute? One each second? In a clear row. Ladders to climb. Two thousand cots a hour. Uncanny. Can't count 'em. A picker earns two dollars for two thousand cots worth forty dollars on the market shelf. Uncanny. Uncanned. Count count count. J. Some body sure making something. Not the picker. Two dollars for the picker -- and thirty-eight dollars for somebody else. Hey.

And the picker the most important man. Sure -- but without the picker. . . . man. At least an equal man. Or a ginger-bread man? Uncanny. Somebody sure was coming out ahead. The planter. True, the picker didn't plant the pits. The trucker. The picker sure didn't truck 'em. The grocer. The picker only buys groceries. The advertiser. Pickers don't even read ads, let alone write 'em. A big fat thick spread giving lots of happy wellcooked middlemen and happier trades-men and happiest housewives always giving sharlie brown credit for their bangbang happiness. Happiness fellow chem-ists and happiness fellow turtles and happiness fellow super visors and so on and on while the picker through whose fingers funnel best best damned prunes and cots and horseradish in the land -- the bank clerk through whose hands funnel the real green -- never creeps up out of the turtle muck either.

Vegetables, a dime a dozen. Planks, and bare bulbs.

Am I vegetable?

Spiders. Adios arañas. Adios mi tierra linda. Hello you black widow. And so will all fairy tales come true if only you sit upon a sharp-pointed star. The braceros and the fruit pickers will soon all be gone, all gone, kicked out. All fruit will hereby be picked by machine picked canned conned dried filled folded cut stacked wrapped boxed foiled boiled shipped stored sold and deliciously dated by -- machine. Then -- what am I? Am I

a machine?

a hope blaster?

a bar oyster?
a cool ingrate?
a hots?
a blood banker?
a social shanker?
a mere pisser?
a ingrate?
a bug?
a slug?
a turtle dung dropper?

There had to be some decent answers. What am I then? So it's you in your blood man and so guzzle down another tall beaker of gall you all in your doony brine in your hot mine and eat it down and throw it up and pick your tools up and don't complain because we'll can your ass off welfare and because the bugs and the fat glue companies and the baby strollers and eventually your own sons and merchants and decent ddt manufacturers will all get up tight have got it sewed up fright and if you care to try you get the hell off our free land man and go on back to your own wet dreams nobody's forcing you to work your asses office is they. it's all free free aint't it. so yo are a metsicannorthandsouthamericano sowhat grub your partner grab the machine grab the picker grab the switch and bring on another forty thousand pickers for getting this goddem job done right for my forty million lilting acres of golden corn so we can pack another forty thousand dolls an hour into our swiss cheese nocount besides blast this USGovt for great gravy handouts for not planting so what are you kicking about. take some prunes and stuff em in your carcass and grow your own goddem green trees in the northpole some free land there. to the mountains to the prairies and the rocks and rills give me that made this country great four stories and more years ago you big bellyachers you howling stupid dogs you sitting on sharp rocks you too stupid to get up. and let us decent denizens citizens do our godgivenfreedomboring thing in peace. exploit return investment interest capital gains Oh God you hear?

We are leave you alone. You be leave us alone. Pain rain. Pale skies. Fair enough. Rain then. Agreed. Rain. A Greed. After the fair rains, it gives us great honor to maim as the next -- and so fellow zitizens onward and upward we are gathered here upon this great plain fore scoot and more years than we care to dismember our four fathers and seventeen mothers brought forth on this here continental divide a newer nation conceived in liberty and demaciated in the proudest tradition that since all men are basically created greedy pass a big belly laugh and that ain't all and that all the fruit of the elite by the elite shall sure be for the elite, while all rats, dogs, and cockroaches shall be kept locked out. Out of the prune patch.

So Manuel kept staring at the ugliest creatures in all the world, just sitting there in the middle of all them ugly turtles, just oggling there in the pot there in the pet shop doing nothing absolutely nothing, nada, not even thinking, nada. What am I then? Am I not a man? Or a turtle turner? Manuel couldn't answer himself. The only thing he thought he felt he might be able to do with any dignity at all was to throw up.

He did.

20

Dawn.

Outside, wrapped in still, cool air, lingered the soft, plush, pearly sheen of midsummer's blackest night. Within, Mr. Quill lay sleeping in his stuffy, scruffy little room.

His round, bearded, balding head lay buried beneath his greasy covers. With great difficulty he clambered up through thick layers of deep sleep trying to drag himself awake. The connectors seemed to be all plugged up. Either he was flying or he was crawling, or he was dreaming, or he was crashing down a crumbling headland. Maybe it was a roaring cataract.

The roaring came on louder and stronger.

His breath came in short, quick gasps. His throat felt throttled. In the darkness, not sure whether his eyes could really open, his groping, trembling hands gripped the thin cold iron bar of the bedstead, clutching it for dear life, terror stricken, as a drowning man might. Then he suddenly snapped awake. He realized, with great relief, breaking into a cold sweat, what the noisy explosions were.

It was the sound of a gunned car, its motor roaring.

He was fully awake. He turned his head. He heard the car moving. Now it was turning or backing. The shifting gear clicked and he clicked off the stick shifts in his corral. The motor's roar grew louder. Dropping his feet and searching for his slippers, he listened to the squidge of the tires along the gravel in the driveway just outside the thin wall of his miserable room. All in an instant. He raised himself on his skinny elbow and clambered up the skinny iron lamp bolted to the wall. But he knew -- even before the dim yellow glow bathed his twitching eyes -- he well knew that he was already too late, for the car was already dipping down at the curb, poised for flight. Another vagrant. Another moment, and the noise of the escaping artist vanished altogether. Another prune picker slipping his chain. What would Mr. Turner say now?

Mr. Quill, retaining his locked elbow position, as though holding a thin iron cocktail, contemplated the sad face of his cheap alarm clock as though it were trying to say something to him. Ten minutes to six, it said. Not even dawn yet.

How he could have..... but sleep was now impractical. He knew that. His sharp little mind whirred like a shiny computer. It clicked off the fourteen components of the twenty odd shacks in his charge, and he knew he'd soon have to face up to it. Oh, there would be depths to plumb when Mr. Turner came to.

A mean new thought: this new intrigue concerning Mr. T. created another painful new knot deep in the middle of Mr. Quill's fat round overwrought tummy. Accompanying the pain, in the cool night air, his bald pate gleamed sullenly under a fine patina of sweat. At least they didn't break his window with a brick this time. Swinging his thin unmuscled legsticks around in order to sit up, Mr. Quill held his throbbing head in his hands. He guessed he'd better shave this morning; he'd already skipped two days, and his stubble showed. Well, he knew what he had to do. And what he would do.

First. He would get dressed.

A morbid impulse shook his frame. Pants over shirt, shirt tucked in, limp sack corduroy jacket, a jacket as old as he, though not so old as Mr. T. -- ! Again, his breath sucked in quickly. The terror of catharsis was making him wince, making him wish he were miles away from all this. It almost made him wish for the quiet hum of eternal peace. Shuddering slightly at such a morbid impulse, he tossed the covers back over his only bed, snapped the light out, and stepped vigorously into the icy night air. The dull yellow street lamp overhead, jutting out at the highway, was still glowing full blast at the empty night. Its persistent and forlorn glow against the brackish gray of dawn announced to every passing traveler that here at long last was the famous Western Grande whose very squalor was in reality its most attractive feature.

At last...... Treachery at the check-off. In that... garish light, illuminated softly now as well by a tiny but growing wedge of the palest grapegreen dawn creeping down from the horizon, Mr. Quill ran his sleep-robbed eyes along the left-hand group of dark shacks constituting that section of his hostel complex. At the same time he checked out each automobile squatting in front of each occupied roost like some huge hulking caged drunk-sodden beast.

And then Mr. Quill knew. What he most feared. What he most avidly suspected. It was No. 16 after all that had skipped. The turncoat. Mr. Quill's neat ledger on every row and every room and every tenant in every poverty shack in the compound showed so many permanenties, so many overnighters, so many transients, and so many intransigents. The skip was a permie. Name. Rank. License Number. Well, it -- all that was in his office. Wife. Two brats. Unemployed. Underemployed. Unemployable. A discard. Human flotsam. Sometime fruit tickler. Alltime fruit eater. Mr. Quill knew even better than Mr. Turner what the odds were of ever catching up with this odd meatball, that the odds, even if they happened to stay right here, were too slim in San Jose let alone in Drawbridge, way too slim even if caught, and if caught next to impossible to prosecute because of all those miserable bleeding heart judges. It was all so unjust. Justice --! So who would get gaffed. He. Quill. As usual.

Keeping in trim. A hard job, keeping track of all this miserable truck. Mr. Quill was ever at the point of sweeping the whole blasted race off the globe. He knew he deserved better treatment from both ends, as his mother used to say. But he'd never been able to do anything about it. Mr. Turner kept tinkering with the plans all year round, having the compound westernized, to keep his senile dream aglow, a grand slam westernized villa all dollared up for hilarious tourists. During the spring and summer months it was especially difficult for Quill to keep humanity from overtaking him. What was that nut planning to do? Show off starving migrants to fat tourists? People were always taking advantage of him.

At times Mr. Quill was amused. What a jolt, he thought. Turner could have his crackerberries and eat too. The third classiest joint of the century and he wanted it built up from scratch. And in the middle of all those garbage dumps. Big Brassy Futures. Free listing on the Industrials. Rails and Utilities go down. Well, didn't Dewlapp and Backard also get their phenomenal start in the Bay Area? And D D & T? Not to mention dozens of other monumental successes. Money was growing all over the place. Big Flashy Travelers. The dingiest slum in all the west, the biggest Western Grande west of the Rio Grande. In Drawbridge, of Santa Clara. The wealthiest prune county in the U. S. More like a decrepit ant trap. But even as a hobby he had to hand it to that dummy old money conservationist. Old Chief Midas Rubler, who not only made everything but everyone pay. Inner doubts? Yes, he had some inner doubts. Nevertheless, Mr. Quill himself got some pretty fluffy fantasies out of it all. A beautiful bathroom for himself, an offbeat hall, real western mail, country fresh meals, cowboy boots, a conventional saddle, old woodside barn drippings, musty candelabras, splattered spittoons, miles of stiles, wild boas, rustic rattlers, antiqued bricabrac, and an occasional treat, like brandied hot dogs. Even if it should never pan out, Mr. Turner still had his mitts on a pretty husky chunk of good land. A giant game of monopoly, Turner's taking every turn himself, tilting to his heart's content, pushing humans around for markers. How could he lose. And the jail burned down. Turner's avaricious shrewdness had no known limits, like the sky, past the moon. His greed was so dense, so intense, and so thick he simply couldn't see not even the tiniest nidge of a connection between his fat larders, his obese holdings, his overextended realestatic holdings and the puking misery of the hundreds and thousands of the fruit pickers his establishment exploited so happily. But that was because he had so many other idealistic concerns. It wouldn't be long before he had the Drawbridge mayoralty stitched to his lapel too. Then -- U. S. Senator? Perhaps no, not yet. It was still too hard to dislodge that hardcore softshoe sludge. The legistlature in Sacramento? Perhaps. Turner's ambitions were so oblique that he himself didn't know, outside of still more money, what he really wanted. Maybe the Governorship? Not with Howlin Mad Nolan still running a pretty tight ship. Unless he slipped. Ah, then, His Honor, The Right Honorable Governor of These United States.......

And still the travelers came. Always weary. The occasional unwary traveler, too tired or too indifferent to hunt any further, would stumble into this moribund corral for an exhausting night's leap, listening to the bandidos howling in the willows, the coyotes, and the lapping of the distant minehaha water of the daily diminishing Bay, the grandest humid toilet in twenty centuries. Most of the traveling trade was compost of transients moving to and fro from the fruit orchards. The dregs. The scum. All they were worth, as Mr. Trueheart Turner never tired of trumpeting, was -- Well, did they -- They never had to pad a payroll. The miscreants. The pit spitters. Sometimes whole families came by in their truly astounding clunkers, the Joads all over again, in a ridiculous thirty-year re-run. Stuffing themselves into one single room. Eighteen headknockers in a palatial one-room square. Well, it had more room than inside a car. Merchants of misery. Pa, ma, son, son, son, dau, dau, grandson, son, son. All jammed together. Happy togetherness. Eight to a mattress.

Toe to toe. And Christmas only nineteen light years away.

Mr. Quill didn't mind. His practiced eye distinguished the fishy-eyed from the shifty-eyed. He had grown accustomed to judging the human fleet that floated past or sloshed into his establishment, shiftless from the word go, separating the sleazy from the disreputable, the shills from the scared, the parasites from the true vagabonds. Many of the migrants passing through preferred their own tents out in the fields, or their cardboard lean-tos or simply under the stars in a rolled-up blanket. Round pegs pulling into the square slots of the Western Grande. Took all kinds all right. Darkhaired, blackeyed Mexicans, timid Mexicans, brash, drinking Mexicans. Yellowhaired peanut pickers from Kentucky. Curlyeared tomato pickers from eastern Navaho. Smart Yankis from southern Rhodesia. Snappy-eyed creoles from loose New Orleans. Pollocks, Indians, Eyetalians, Spics, Micks, Nicks, Portowaps and Rototundios. All kinds all right. Some gruff. Some kind. He watched them as they entered and sized them up. Most of them paid their bills, didn't steal too many figs, didn't muck off. Some of the steadier workers he got to know pretty well, letting them a day or two on the cuff, sometimes a week, c onfident they'd pay up. That was his special skill. That way he kept the ledger pretty for his sour boss. Hi, Mr. Turn -- burrrr, but right now, Mr. Quill was facing a real torment.

Across the darkness: across the sleeping continent and into the treelit darkness, Mr. Quill stepped through No. 16's open door. He flicked the switch. His nose twitched Dantesquely. He found exactly what he imagined he would find. The room was almost in total shambles. The bed stripped. The mattress ripped. The extra mattress on the floor soaked with rum and urine. These people went a mite too far. The bastards gone gone and pulled out all the bureau drawers and stomped them to splinters. What made them do that? That any way to treat a respectable migrant shack? That any way to grow up to be a responsible and decent law-abiding citizen? They should be charged double income tax. No wonder they couldn't find decent jobs.

Tears of rage welled and conmingled with the thrill of desperation. A sense of utterly uncontrollable destruction shuddered through his pudgy frame, causing his paunch to quiver jellylike. Then he experienced a pure reverse thrill, as though wafting through hell itself. wanting to destroy more, to tear the whole plant down, walls, shingles, paintings, drapes, planks, boards, the whole -- !

With great difficulty, he quelled the revolting tremor.

Then, confident that his sanity was returning, he reassured himself. His quick little mind calculated the costs, what, if anything, he would report to Mr. T. , and what would have to

134

come out of his own threadbare pocket.

Love thy neighbor. A good one. Mr. Quill had long before
given up hating his fights with Mr. T. The fact of its being an
uneven struggle never bothered him. As it was in the beginning so it was in the end. Mr. Quill knew he had to lose. The
fact of being engaged in a hopeless struggle with such a far
superior adversary actually helped give some small mean
meaning to his terribly shrunken spirit. He enjoyed the unten-
able position as a chess master might, caught, fraught in a
game full of devious traps, before shooting himself, filling
his days and horrors with purposeful despair. Mr. Quill's
fertile imagination savored scores of possibilities of avenging
himself, or repaying all the humilities he'd suffered and large
psychic damages. But in the end they always seemed too
bland.

Sociability. Mr. Turner turned up most disconcertingly in
Mr. Quill's office.
"How are you, ah, erh, Morton?"
"Fine, Mr. Turner. "
Mr. Turner then sat down at the oldfashioned rolltop, and
started looking over the registration record. Mr. Quill gave
him a short glass of cheap pink wine which Mr. T. tossed down
like a quick aperatif. Then from his inner pocket, he absent-
mindedly pulled out a flat pint of the best imported scotch
whiskey available anywhere in the world and drained it down
to the button gluggglug, all by himself, while looking over the
records, saying hmmm hmm all the while, while Mr. Quill
stood there helplessly looking respectfully, his round eyes
going gluggglug, his mouth salivating. What a marvelous
thing it must be to be so rotten filthy and rich!
"Good man, " was Mr. Turner's invariable comment,
meaning the bottle contents were good, man. After he left,
all Quill got were three drops drained out of the precious
bottle and a good long sniff. It was much worse than nothing
at all.

How marvelous, then, Mr. Q. 's suiting Mr. T. to a B.
The devilish side of Mr. Turner Mr. Quill found constantly
baffling. Their relationship came close to master/ subject
perfect. Nothing overt. The aggressor versus the trans-
gressed. The dog versus the bun. The doer versus the done
to. The exploiter versus the exploitee. A perfect match.
Would Mr. Q. ever have the nerve to ask for his raise? Of
course not. For shame, Mr. Q. Smile on, Mr. T. Need
thus fulfilled need. Two impartial miseries squatting on one
absolute happiness -- the misery of others.

With the help of another raw sniff from the empty bottle of pure scotch, Mr. Q. shoved the rising gorge of rage back into his smoldering craw. It was pure hell. Smile on, Mr. T. Back to the repairs, Mr. Q.

21

What a very lucky thing that her headache should vanish just like that, just in time, how very lucky, before her very first visitor arrived.

Jean Angelica Turner wasn't planning a very big bash, just her usual monthly very social sans souci gathering, just the usual twenty or so ladies, each of whom (with only an occa-sional exception) (such as some special wit of her own, as an artist, a novelist, or a particularly successful charmer) was either a leader herself in the community or, even better, married to one.

Mrs. Turner's plump, placid, easygoing nature matched her normally, homely little figure. Her tailored light green velvet dress sported a white organdy ruffled collar which, with the help of a tight corset, helped her look slim as a fresh snap bean. She never would have gravitated to any position of power via the Darwinian route of natural selection -- if, indeed, she would have allowed the utterance of such a blas-phemous remark in her presence. It was so untidy.

Under other circumstances, Jean Turner would simply have either folded up or else been glossed over by other more dynamic, more athletic, more beautiful, or more purpose-ful ladies. But not more resourceful. No. Nor more deter-mined. No. She found it helped even to fake her helplessness. She fooled everyone. She was the quiet one who held the more aggressive natural leaders in check, which is about as powerful as any one can really hope to get. Her calm, quiet, friendly cover gave no hint of the frigid hatred she'd distilled for the swill of mankind, which to her included most of the race. She was pretty sure this bitterness of hers caused most of her migraines, but it sure was worth it.

Besides being a member of several local ladies' clubs, she was also an upper drawer officer, because of her specious influence, of the Drawbridge Country Club. She always turned down higher honors. She tolerated these outside frivolities only to be able to keep her false image up and also to be in a position to offer her coveted invitation to a new prospect for her own inner ring, whenever such a coveted opening should occur.

She was in all things an easygoing woman, one who wouldn't be noticed in any gathering, either way. All her hatred was healthily internalized. She twitted and twittered, fooling everyone with her simpering bit, putting them on with the mistaken belief that she was simpleminded, fatuous, shallow, and inconsequential. A little on the plump side for her short size, she had a quiet little voice that a listener had to strain to hear. The listener strained. She wouldn't. As a young woman she had yearned to be an actress, and a little obstacle -- an utter lack of talent -- caused her to say no to everything and everyone. Her thrust toward an ecstatic acting career was therefore an utter loss except for having met her precious Frederick, who himself had also been temporarily hooked, surviving now in only a few Charley Tempe trailers. Their common initial mistakes thereby activated a union that could only have been contemptuously plotted by the Oolies, in disastrous consequence for the whole human race.

Jean Turner turned all these shortcomings, misconstrued as insignificant by inferiors, to subtle and powerful advantage. An example. It thrilled her to discover that she actually did possess a marvelously deft ability to act and to be marvelously deceptive, despite all the experts' scornful doubts to the contrary. That was her most important initial self-discovery. She could test this ability at will. She could be absolutely miserable within, and by feigning her smile, her tinkle of laughter, and her easygoing nature, she could easily deliver a Sunday punch to an unsuspecting antagonist.

It took her a while, a few empty years of fooling around, following precious Frederick around, catching on to his own wily ways and loose purposes, a kind of meaningless existence as a sort of female consort, just piling up money, until it occurred to her she actually had a wit of her own. Subtle, but nevertheless a wit. She then polished her wiles. The world was made up of leaders, in the minority to be sure, while sheep were always being publicized simply because they happened to make up the great majority. Majorities! What possible importance were they! The poor dears. Poor people always have to have someone responsible to lead them around, to their work, to their plates, to their houses, to their learning. She gradually evolved her one great overwheening ambition: her responsibility to all of nature. Otherwise the whole system, and therefore the whole future of the universe, would collapse. And as it dawned on her that she was, thankfully, one of nature's natural aristocrats, a leader of the elites, for the elites, and by the elites, she experienced an almost overpowering sense of humility toward her own base passions. She would follow her conscience religiously. She would follow her own Divine Inspiration. She would follow her Inner Eye. She would take humbly and gratefully whatever Life Force granted her. And so it was coming to pass that she, in all her simple humility, in her quiet, insipid, stupid way, was able to help so many, poor, helpless, defenceless, unfortunate, undeserving, underprivileged human beings. She even took to wondering whether they would name a university after her, the first exciting one named for a Woman.

"How nice of you."

"Really --"

"What a nice breeze blowing away from us."

"Really, I was going to call you first."

"A shame it had to rain so much."

"Yes, isn't it lovely."

"My husband doesn't seem to think so."

"Oh?"

The inner courtyard before the great mansion was filled with cars, all shiny, all gleaming, all sunny, all new. Some even had to park off the entry driveway, on the shoulder, coming in. Small clucks of ladies clustered on the bright yellow-green lawn, which had been watered before dawn by the gardeners so it wouldn't be too wet this afternoon. They all stood happy in their soft pink puppy dresses, in their elegant little white hats and black gloves, so happy to have such good fortune as to be present in and actually a member of Mrs. Turner's soiree in the afternoon. Yes, this was her group, her kind, and it thrilled her to think of herself as being a new kind of missionary among these frail, delicate, modern American ladies. For if she could bring these lovelies around to be her biddies, then she had a fair chance of becoming singled out as a great benefactor, a truly great prognosticator, in place of horrid creatures like that zany Margaret Zanger with her filthy mind and her impeccably filthy birth control business. Monstrous. Every birth-control abortionist should be casterated on the spot.

Past the huge, heavy oak front doors, dropping their coats and things easily on the foyer table, they navigated the thick, ankle-deep important rug, and passed out into the sleek Frenchdoored saloon. From within, they were able to look out upon a splendid view of the broad expanse of elegant lawn outside, as big as a continental golf course, flanked by enormous elms, oaks, cypress, and eucalyptus, not to mention an occasional redwood, and then the huge magnificent San Francisco Bay beyond, with its picturesque San Mateo Bridge marching smartly right across it.

"What delicate canapes. "

"I wonder which delicatessen she uses?"

"I shouldn't wonder. "

"I wonder what they do on their day off?"

"The pickers?"

"What a frightful ruffle. "

"No, the gardeners. "

The theme for the day -- my word, what was it? -- was about to be presented. There had to be so much implementation. Mrs. Turner, at last, was ready to test her newest idea: Working Together. What a beauty-filled throught. Operation Bootstraps was another excellent phrase, but she'd heard some other vulgar country had gotten ahold of it. In her rounds she had noted an astonishing thing. She noted that the poorer the family the more children theỹ procreated.

Now that struck her as decidedly queer.

Just the reverse of what it should be. No wonder there were so many, many more poor creatures than her kind. But Mrs. Turner was, if nothing else, turned on by challenges. And if honesty was a challenge, she was perfectly willing to face it, if not entirely agree with it. If she was going to oppose M. Zanger's crude immoral prostitutionalism she, Jean Turner, was going to have to come up with something even better than sex, more attractive, and if need be more sinful. The idea for her revolting thought came to her from reading carefully what the Russians were up to. They too were of course highly immoral also but there was one thing you sure couldn't take away from them -- they sure had some good ideas some of the time. This was a dilly: she was going to propose a Day School Center for Indolent Mothers, the DSCIM. The very idea of it staggered the hell out of her. Enabling legislation would have to be passed and so on to force the lazy ones, but she would work on Frederick later. The thing was to lay the groundwork. Get the ball rolling.

"What kind of woman is she?"

"She collects pottery. "

"She's a saint. "

140

"I wouldn't want to be mummified. "

"Such a beautiful thought. "

"She's an angel. "

Mrs. Turner, however, wasn't fooling either. She knew what they all thought of her. It was going to take a little time, a little work. She would go underground, to borrow a term from the enemy. Seeing healthy, vigorous, alert young women sitting around on their duffs doing absolutely nothing all day, freshening up only for their boyfriends or husbands at night, while her taxes kept mounting to pay off all those public welfare checks, stretched Mrs. Turner's tummy knots taut.

What finally fried her was the thought that by offering such wayward ladies honest jobs, and offering them a way of taking care of their vagrant accidental dropoffs by day, she would be BUILDING Their Moral Fiber, and at the same time help slow down the outflow of public monies that Aid to Dependent Children, as well as Aid to the Blind, drained from her and from other similar honest fortune-accumulating citizens. Maybe those loose creatures would also stop having so many illegitimate offspring. Or at least slow down some. There would be plenty of discussion from her, but no challenges, no referendum, no chairman, no veto. Just advice. And then the vote. That was it. That was best. That was efficient. That was her way. And the vote, to be valid had, of course, to go her way.

"Who can afford three cars these days. "

"We've had to cut down another forty acres of pears. "

"No place to have my pearls restrung decently. "

"Miami is simply going to pot. "

"No wonder the pickers scream. "

"I never did like table grapes anyway. "

Operation Bookstraps. Such a succulent idea. Pick yourself up by your own strings. Help the indigents pick the fleas off themselves. Give them a chance to get off your back and off welfare. That Gutierrez woman was one strong and healthy example, for example. But her husband supported her, so no problem there. Unless he left her, or got himself killed. Pride was a usury you can either afford or not afford. Shameless pride could easily upset everything. Those timid mummies have no business showing stupid signs of discontent.

The pickers were all screaming for double wages again, or triple, or whatever. Poor Frederick. He was doing his very best to keep the whole operation going so it wouldn't collapse bang like a big circus tent. And what did he get. Complaints. What was going on? Pure socialism. After all these lovely, beautiful years, the socialists were finally getting their way throug unions and strikes. Those Mexicans and all those lazy ignorant migrant workers. Bunch of basically lazy slobs. She and Fred had spent many, zany, hard, lean years putting their trees down and orchards up, investing, risking, planting, reinvesting, infesting, fighting off the bugs, the banks, and fixing the books. Shame. Just because she and Fred finally made good, and now owned a huge air-conditioned traveling motel room, plus a limimousine or so plus thirty or forty smaller appliances, was no reason to carp. Envy. They had worked and they had no envy of anyone else. Malice. They had started with nothing, only their brains and their hands and their skin and their ideas and a little capital and a few hundred shiftless worthless Mexican migrant braceros. Greed. Fred had worked hard for their better-than-average income. Jealousy. People have no right to force their corrupt idea of democracy on others, or their rotten morality, or whatever. Immoral. They were the ones who were being robbed of their God--given right, who needed protection to use their own wealth as they saw fits. They were being intimidated by incompotent, immoral, lethargic slaves. That's exactly what they were. Slaves. It wasn't right. It just wasn't right. And she prayed fervently day after day that they could have just one Supreme Court Justice who would take their side just once, once in a while. Why don't those pickers get off their duggs? A bunch of lazy undeodorized do-nothing sleeping mañana migrants. Give them extra money, a small wage hike or a little something like used clothing, and what do they do? Instead of buying something necessary such as a new iron or curtains, they splurge it on wine or a TV or a good time. Instead of practicing responsibility and working hard and scheming as she and Fred had done -- though of course that was when there was more land around -- why, they just sang around their campfires and simply had fun. Oh she knew what they thought of Fred. Oh they didn't fool her. Oh not one bit. Oh she knew all right. She knew very well that they called him The Green Worm behind his back. She even knew it in Spanish, El Gusano Verde. How vulgar. Oh she knew her Spanish. But they didn't know one thing. They didn't know she knew. They also didn't know, out of their ignorance, how hard he had started out as a young man with a bucket a brush, a sponge and some newspapers tucked under his arms, and how he went free from house to house, knocking and banging and betting and banking on work, or just food.

"Ma'm, could I wash your undies?"

"Sahib, could I have your weeds?"

"Sir, could I polish your brass?"

Yes. That was how Fred started. Nobody knew that. That showed how fearless and how hardworking he was. Of course when her papa died and she got her inheritance back, then they really began to really live, for the first time. That was no reason under God's holy sun why these selfish shortsighted fruit pickers couldn't do the same if they would just learn a little hokey English and laugh a lot and get busy and go out and do some honest work and quit crabbing about poor working conditions and moaning over a few miserable pennies per basket. Envy was a bid, a win, a bad lot, worse than termites, eating, eating, eating into one.

"I never dreamed Cuernavaca was like that."

"The horn of the cow."

"Nor I."

"Just like the States."

"Yes, the Service --"

"Acapulco has gotten so spoiled."

"I get seasick everytime I fly the Pacific."

"You must be kidding."

"No, I --"

A beautiful morning indeed. A beautiful meeting. First they hummed her favorite hymn. It was a little sticky with some of the Catholic ladies. She let them think they were getting away with just moving their lips. Mrs. Turner had much bigger issues afoot than mere religion or conversion. Now she gaily introduced her piece de resistance, the out-of-town professional woman speaker, an exciting nomad who knew just how to light the proper sparks on any issue, either pro or con. A real pro. A simply marvelous woman. Flashing eyes and vibrating hips. If a woman ever ran for U.S. President, this would be the type to run. Just marvelous. Her eloquent topic was: "And If A Woman Can Be A Mother, Why Can't She Be A President?" This marvel of a speaker, this enigma, this charisma in female clothing, this eloquently lipsticked bubbly mouth warned her listeners of the impending doom. What impending doom? That their most precious motto, A Portfolio of Trusts, was at that very moment in dire danger of being legislated out of existence, or of being rudely investigated by some radical Senators in the Subcommittee on Migratory -- "And you MY DEARS --" she skareamed, "had sure bitter git off your duffs and get some ropes around some necks or write them something --" in clear bell-like tones.

All the ladies duly voted they would do something. They also voted unanimously in favor of launching Mrs. Turner's pet projectile, the study to investigate the question of initiating the possibility of underwriting the DSCIM, the Dandy Scrumptious Center for Indifferent Mamas. Then, her chief mission accomplished, she turned the girls loose on the goodies.

Afterwards, when everyone left, Jean Turner's head started to ache something awful again. She would simply have to try a new doctor. That's all there was to it. But where? Her present one, Dr. Thilmud Baledaranakainukius, was really just like all the rest, despite his unusual background and his Honorary Degree. He just didn't seem to care about her or her problems any more. He just wanted her to write checks. But where could she find another she didn't know who could care as much for her and more?

For starters, she tore off her ruffled collar and began crying, softly at first.

22

Dawn.

Outside the row of gracefully splintered, delicately antiquated, crumbling migrants' shacks of Drawbridge, and inside Mr. Turner's outrageous Western Grande, the cool sleek bleakness of Mr. Turner's night started relinquishing its fervent grip on the fertile land. This incredible fertility, one of America's most brilliant horticultural contributions to all humankind, is one America can well be proud of. A fantasy, but nevertheless a genuine contribution.

The only thing left needed to be weeded out was — greed.

Santa Clara Valley, fronting San Francisco's ever-diminishing Bay, is a lush paradise where mankind is gorged, where want dares not show its ugly face, where babies proliferate, and rains pour beautifully. Contained within this lushest of all plush valleys are 10,000 acres of gorgeous prunes, 6,000 acres of peachy apricots, 4,000 acres of clinging pears, another 4,000 acres of black walnuts, more than 1,000 acres each of bright red cherries and succulent purpling grapes, all of that and more, plus an additional assorted 17,000 acres of snapping fresh vegetables, all spread around for miles and miles in every direction of the County, from Palo Alto in the north, down through Mountain View, Los Altos, Sunnyvale, Santa Clara, Alviso, Drawbridge, San Jose, Morgan Hill,

Los Gatos and Saratoga, Coyote, all the way to Gilroy in the southern part of the County. All this delicious deciduous fruit, all these abundant crops ripen every year right on schedule, inexorably, awaiting no man, ready to be plucked, enrichening everyone. Except the pickers.

The pickers slept.

Manuelito awakened.

A slim sliver of pale light reached him tentatively through the uncurtained, partly cardboarded window across the shack's single room where they all slept. Papa slept. Mama too was deep in sleep, as was Mariquita, and baby Cati. He got up quietly in his tattered pajamas, pattered barefooted across the bare wooden floor to the dark door and slowly pried it open. He screwed his dark little Indian features into an intense scowl. He peered out into the dim night glow. His mind slowly blazed with the barest of grand possibilities. He inhaled the pungent humidity of the fresh outdoors. He felt the wet air. He touched the bark of the dark friendly trees and turned into bark. The moist earth, swelling, awakened the sap rising slowly within his veins, from fifty million years back. Despite the cold, he crept about, stealthy as a cat, taut, poised, touching everything, changing back and forth into dirt, cleansing himself with earth.

He listened for his friends the bugs.

He was on a hunt, out, far away, alone. Powerful primordial urges welled up within his little insides. His tiny powerful perfect lungs expanded deeply and joyously. His keen nut-brown eyes stared with great care through the black swirling newday mist for the day's news, his ears strained, unable to fathom the call. He tried to respond, without being conscious of the profound instincts gutting his tiny body, playing with his brand new set of nerves. The fat, sturdy, healthy plum trees stood gaunt, taut, and bushy, stretching away in long, well-cared-for rows, the very best trees that science and education and horticulturists and capital management and money could buy. Good buy.

Manuelito stood alone, shivering in godtime, all alone.

He re-entered his sparse shack, his warm home. Everyone was still asleep, even the baby. He fished his mended and remended little brown sweater out of the cardboard box on the floor and pulled it on over his pajamas. Sitting on the floor, he put on his socks and laced his torn tennis shoes. Now he was able to stand the dawny shivers better. That was better. He pulled the door shut. The air was even sweeter. Long fingers of dull light began peeling away the overhanging darkness. The air's delicate flavor tasted like good, clean food, a clean pure smell coming up from the sweetly manured earth, a genuine sweetness he would never forget, and which the memories of countless thousands of his ancestors reminded him of. Tremors of hidden excitement shivered through his perfectly calciumed, perfectly functioning, sturdy little bones that so soon were destined to crumble from malnutrition.

He jogged along, around, and behind the lowly splintered shambles that was his home, on the lookout for something to do. He kicked a clumsy clod of earth, crumpled it with his heel for being in his way, enjoying the way it crunched flat. He bent down, picked up a rock that was smooth on one side and rough and jagged on the other, and then dropped it. Birds were twittering at him, joining him in his silent world. Worms wiggled out of sight. Sure he could fly. If he wanted to. Then he forgot about flying for the hose. He picked up the nozzle, went back, hooked up the other end and turned the faucet on just a little. So mama wouldn't hear. He squatted with the nozzle in front of a scrawny weed. He stood up again, dropped his pants, squatted again, and grunted hard. The caca came out, squeezing real good. He cleansed himself with a handful of dry grass. The water was a long time coming. He watched a ray of sunlight penetrating the intertwining branches, playing patterns across the dirty brown weathered siding of the shack. His eye followed the moving, slowly changing silhouettes, dark spidery shapes. He moved his head in silent nodding rhythm, a rhythm steeped in deeper origins than he could ever know, no matter how great his intellect, back before the crudeness of time. Back before the possibility or even the probability of his existence was actuated.

He got up finally, pulled his pajama pants up again, and went again to the faucet. He turned the handle up full force a moment, making the water bloat the hose suddenly, then shut it quickly. A fierce spurt emerged. He squatted and watered his caca, watching it melt away and join the good earth. He watered the scrawny plant. A plant gets plenty thirsty, needed plenty of water. Papa always told him that. He stood up, letting the hose drain to one side. His narrow almond slits studied the jewellike sparkles of dawn's sun clinging to the thin stream as it fell into the dust. He studied the patterned splatters of mud he'd made, fascinated. An artist in mud.

He moved on.

Carefully he watered another tall, spiky, bedraggled weed whose scraggly issue of worthless pods was still motherly hanging on -- having managed somehow to get this far through stern reality without the slightest nudge of help from anyone -- its seeds all set to be launched again onto the hard, barren, beaten, dry, dusty, friendless, waterless soil, in order to begin their fierce meaningless struggle for dull existence all over again. The world wasn't that full of greedy mongers yet.

He moved on.

Squinting into the borning sun, Manuelito looked straight at the flickering peaks of the nearby friendly Diablo range. They were so close he could reach out and grab a fistful of mounds. He smiled at the possibility. His perfect little teeth gleamed white, burnished like the morning star, and full of cavities. He would become an aged man well before his youth was over.

He spotted an empty plastic bottle on its side and went over to look it over. He filled it with water. It got too heavy. He plopped it down. He watched carefully as water sluiced luxuriantly over its side. Lifegiving water. Water, water. He stood up. Agua agua. He looked at it intently. Agua agua. Then he gave the turgid bottle a hard kick, spinning it, spraying it in every direction. He dribbled more water over it for good measure. He looked around. The giant hangem oak tree got a little water too, though it would evaporate in the heat of day, long before it got down to the roots to do any good. He stood up. He jogged over to an upright four-by-four redwood beam imbedded upright in the ground, part of an old discarded hitching post, and watered that. He watched its light tan color turn dark umber as the water stained it dark and rich as coffee grounds, dark as his own sunburnt brown skin. He hosed two more hitching posts for good measure, at ease. There. That was it. He shut the faucet off and tossed the hose down.

He turned east, facing the godlike sun.

A part of the universe was invested in him now. He turned to take another stance. Spotting a stick half buried in earth, he pried it out. Hosts of bugs scurred away in all directions. He captured an earwig, its pair of vicious-looking curved pincers pointing back toward each other, and brushed it with the stick. He picked up a round stone and crushed the earwig. He studied its brown juices intently for a minute. Had he known that beyond, in all ten thousand sprawling acres of plum trees, that not one single efficient earwig survived, thanks to the sweetest poisons ever made, he might have spared his splattered brown friend. That same DDT was also in his bones.

He turned around, again.

Looking up, he saw his little sister Mariquita standing in the dark doorway, roundfaced, blinking. Standing in her frayed little red nightgown, blinking and smiling.

He smiled back.

All nature was theirs, and all the past, and all the future.
She stepped out.
Bang, bang, she said, killing him.
Bang, bang, he replied, killing her in return.
At that moment, instead of crossing over the beautiful divide, instead of being grateful for another bountiful day of thanks gracing tne superabundant land, they might have been

148

the two happiest, luckiest, and wealthiest American kids in all the world.

Instead they said, bang, bang.

23

Manuel and Lupe were asleep inside their tent, oblivious to the stealth of the approaching sun's rise. Outside, dissipating the cool night, the sun vaulted the high Sierras, the Diablo Mountains, the Santa Cruz Mountains, the Gabilan Range, and reached out for the vast seagreen sheen of the bleak Pacific's rump running west around the globe.

The sun lit the plains. It glimmered upon broad clumps of awakening green orchards. Leaves started shimmering expectantly in dawn's early mist. The sun steamed the soil humid to create still more priceless humus, adding still another morning's richness to the world's wealth. The sun was the power. The sun was the source. The Aztec Sun. Forever and ever, as the Aztecs knew and as the Egyptians worshipped, the Sun was the beginning, the be-all, the only, and would also be the end of the earth. Its rays shone upon the slanting sides of dozens of drab gray tents pitched along the edges of fields, near dry brooks, among ravines, and alongside wild trees.

Inside their tent, Manuel and Lupe stirred.

The strawberries were ripe again. Oh hallelujah!

The largest strawberry fields in the world and the pay-off was once more at hand. Bankers rubbed their hands in high glee. Some body planned them. Somebody bought and cleared the land. Somebody measured and powdered and strung and seeded and spaced and gambled and sectioned and timed and hired and capped and fired and irrigated and weeded them. In a word: capital.

Capital had done its marvelling work well. Again.

Now it was the picking pickers' turn to put their shoulders to the wheel and turn the stitch in nine into the biggest squeaky wheel in sight, and then give thanks to the almighty copu cornu - copulating dollar. The only force that was stronger than the $un. Why worry, $enator? Wheels. $. $. $. $. The $enator from Drawbridge, a real blooper, wildly proclaimed $toop-Over Play on $trawberry Day. They even got Al Capp on a Special Cartoon. Oh how the $enator's hard heart beat fast fast for the plight of the pure, the tenderly exposed, the sensitively dislocated, the cringing strawberry plants hiding from the terrible wrath of the sun's approaching heat. And light.

Roberto Morales was the sun's special son. He basked in the glory of shining light. His enormous crews, and the children of his crews, were strewn all over the huge acreage. The Pharaohs would have been proud of him. Roberto Morales, chief of the biggest picking crews in all the west, in all the world for that matter, but he didn't care about that kind of record. All he cared about, like a Latin Turner, was money. He had laughter built in to spare. Why shouldn't he? In league with the devil. And why not? He didn't have to stoop to pick . Why should he? He was too fat around the middle. Why shouldn't he? He picked wretches for crews. Half-starving wretches made the best pickers. A truly confident man. As crew leader he had every kind of resourceful shakedown in the book under control, for meals, for bringing scurvy crews in, for working hard, for working hand-in-hand with the smart, well-run, clean-shaved, efficient, neatly balanced Slylines Scramberry & Land Co Inc. For arranging squeaky busses to those too poor to have their own transport tatoo. And last but never least, -- his Own Personal Loan Finance Co.

His crews cleaned up a thousand acres of cherries in Santa Clara, and worked on some of the six thousand acres of apricots. Not to forget the endless prunes. Crisp paks of cellophaned prunes could now be stacked high and gleaming on supermarket shelves all over the U.S. Beaming. And now -- the stromberries. A drunkard or a fool might fight a Roberto Morales. But not Manuel Gutierrez. Roberto Morales forgave everyone everything eventually, smiling, because everything paid so well, knowing that sooner or later hunger, the greatest master of all, drove the worst ones into his maw.

Manuel's eyes clicked open inside the blackness of the tent. He saw nothing. Three days' steady picking. And another night's nervous sleep. His mind suddenly awakened fully, as though snapped on by a switch. His body ached from the previous day's picking, aches that were drugged partially but not entirely wiped out by the relieving draughts of wine he took before falling asleep. All his muscles were stiff. The tiredness would wear off. He would just walk around a little and stretch his legs. He knew he would get his strength back, to go at it again for another straight eight, ten, twelve hours' picking.

Lupe, still sleeping, was breathing deeply. Baby Cati, her plump round little body wedged between them on the ground, was also asleep. So were Manuelito and Mariquita, on their lumpy pads. Manuel was proud of his neat little family. He worried over Lupe's constant worrying about their constant scurrying about, their never seeming to get ahead. He could not answer. He did not know the answers. He was strong and healthy, wasn't he. She worried too much. That was woman for you. Wasn't he healthy and strong? "But what will I do if something happens to you, Manuel?" Do? How did he know? Why must she worry so? She had nothing to worry about. They slept. They traveled. Oh yes, sure, they sure traveled all right. But wasn't he healthy and strong? That was the only answer he had. The only answer he could have, -- for he had no future.

The cotton pad they slept on was shaped by sharp clots of painful earth and rocks beneath them which they were too tired to do anything about. Stupid dogs knew how to get off sharp rocks, as California's great golden Governor (Howlin Mad) Nolan astutely pointed out, from his own movie-making days, because they are lively and full of energy. But dog-tired human beings somehow had a much harder time coping with such a simple problem as how to sleep on lumpy clods of earth at night when you put your bedding out in the dark. Oh yes, the gueros do like to go camping, but somehow that didn't seem like the same thing. And Lupe was beyond comprehension as to how anyone could like going camping. The tarp shielded the moisture but not the cold from below. Manuel wished he could sleep more. It was no use. He lifted himself carefully on one elbow so as not to waken the others. The children's innocence let them sleep deeply. The sleep he was losing would haunt him late in the day, like an uppercut. He knew that. Wine would relax him. He was already looking forward to it. Wine would also bring along with it an overpowering urge to simply pass out on the works, in the rows, on the ground, or in the Sun and bake, if he made it that far.

They were getting along nicely -- The Sun and He.

In summer everything ripened at once. It was imperative to get in all the outside work possible. It was good to have so much work available. He wished it would never run out. He would like to pick fruit all year round, if only they'd invent year-round trees so as to make the word steady. For when he worked he could feed his whole family handily.

His clothing lay folded in a small mound at his feet. He inched, while seated, into his trousers. He pulled on his cotton shirt. He tied his laces and crept through the tent flap out into the dim gray world of earth and mist and plants and mixed smells of clean fresh air and frying cooking. Other tents, other families were beginning to stir. He took the dirt path to the outhouse fifty yards away and followed three companions already ahead of him. He joined the waiting line in the mist.

"Ola, compadre!"

"Ola. Acapulco was never like this, eh."

"You muss be kidding."

"No, I --"

"I tell you, I shore miss the pulque."

"What a question, eh."

"What a vacation, eh."

"What a dreamer, eh."

"How was it?"

Painfully holding his water back, he watched the gray shapes milling back and forth in the dirt ruts among the plants. At last it was his turn to enter the filthy latrine. Pulling the squeaky door shut after him, he held his breath and sat on the wooden dung seat. The shack was filthy. When he couldn't hold his breath against the powerful stench any longer, he breathed in. His lungs accepted, but his mind revolted. The buzzing drone of giant flies filled the foul air. Roberto Morales had given them all free advice more than once: "It does not matter in the least where you shit, my brothers. Do not step in it, that is all. You ever see a dog step into his own shit? Piss where you are, hombre...." Roberto liked making dirty plebian jokes, his goldcapped front teeth glistening.

Long slender fingers of soft white light filtered down from the misty hills to delicately caress the endless hundreds of thousands of priceless strawberry plants. Gossamer mists floated upward, as they had for millions of years before man arrived with all his wealth and cunning and prestige and plans and plantings. Outside in the clean air once more, Manuel breathed in the soft sweet perfume of humid earth in joy and relief. Misery and delight conmingled every morning and all through the day, every day, as though in some artificial setting. But it was really real. The hot orange ball popping above the mountain tops was real too, warning them all that another terrifyingly hot day was on its way. Again. The Sun would rise. Again. And the Sun would rule. Again.

Within the tent, Lupe finished dressing the children. Mariquita and Manuelito, old and wise for their years, stepped over

153

each other to avoid the center pole. Three cardboard boxes of
their personal clothing pressed against the far sloping side of
the tent, out of the way. Manuel rolled the cotton bedding back
into a fat roll, and also put it out of the way. Manuelito teased
Mariquita, pulling her dress, making her yell. "Enough!"
cried Lupe, cuffing his ear. "We cannot have such screeching
in here." Then she mothered and murmured to him, kissing
his temple. "I'm hungry, momi," he said. "I know, sweet.
I know."

Manuel brought back a pail of water from the sloppy, muddy
country faucet. Lupe fried six eggs on their little goslin stove
outside, three eggs in each of the two small frying pans, floating them in their own miserable oily pool. She stirred them
about until they were cooked hard. No time for fancy treats.
They sat on the ground, and gulped their breakfast, without
pleasure, in a hurry, in sight of other families equally occupied. Some of their fellow workers were already moving down
the lines to their day's work. Manuel fetched two more pails of
water, and helped Lupe clean up. They threw the dirty water
behind some thirsty strawberry plants. Lupe wrapped a mound

> pickers, here now, here
> here are some some suggestions
> some suggestions
> to increase your fantsi fants fantastic income

of tortillas in a cotton towel for their lunch. Manuel could see
how tired Lupe was. She was unhappy; sad, mad, tired, nervous, and fretful. And the day had not even started yet. Manuelito clung to her skirt. Manuel was willing to put an end to
this endless moving about. But how? How could he? He once
saw three tiny children suffering from great heat from fever
and from dehydration in San Joaquin Valley, locked inside a

> brint two   bring two
> bring tooo   sandwiches which you

hot car, a sunbroiled car, untended, while their parents
picked the melons. He had seen grown men faint in the rows.
He had experienced thirst so terrible it drove him to the edge
of madness. He had seen men and women too, squatting and
urinating in their clothing, letting it dry in the day's heat rather than stop their picking, for fear their bosses would fire
them or not rehire them. He knew that wasn't right. But what
could he ever say? It wasn't human or decent. What could he
do? Who would take their side? What they didn't know was
how to make their wants known and respected, and still not get
severely penalized. The uneven contest, year after year after

year, against the stink and the wretched man-made hunger and the sharp-pointed rocks the growers placed under their backs never ended.

And Manuel was afraid of union organizers most of all because -- the bosses, the landowners, and the growers hated them so much.

"You know what, mamacita? What a dream I had. I dream we are -- rich. Rich! I buy you everything, everything you ever want. First, a hose. Then a house. Then curtains. Drapes. And a rug for Cati to crawl on. Then a wading pool for the kids, and a trailer, and, and --"

"It seems a lie, but all I want is a magazine I can read in Spanish."

He couldn't even give her a magazine in Spanish, fresh from Mexico, because they were either too hard to locate, or all gone, or took too much time to track down in strange California towns. What kind of living was this? Gypsies. What of future did they have? Slipstream. If not for themselves, for their children then? None. And what kind of past did they have? None also. Their past had been sniped away from them. What of his fathers and all his fathers' fathers? Eaten up alive by revolution, scourged by hunger in that other motherland, emaciated by famine, shrunken by need, ground into dust, and despised by fate. Here at least, here in California's paradise, he could pick to heart's content in summer in the glut that was planted. At least he was able to work all he wanted to, in summer, to eat all he wanted to, to feed his family, and for that he

```
eat one d d d        every
one one delicacy  morning
eat one pastrami            every
wash it down with --
```

was grateful, like an animal. But even that had its price. They lived like the animals. No, worse than the animals. Peor que los animales. No refrigeration. What beast lived in its own filth? No food. No conveniences. No cleanliness. No quiet private kitchen. Above all no privacy, no hiding, no place to rest alone in. No place to relax and stretch his feet out good in. No clean bathroom. No yard for the children, no plans, nothing but a hand-to-mouth existence, frying fat in summer, lean and hungry in fall, and every conceivable kind of clammy hunger threat in winter's rainy days skirting this side of death. But where else could they go? They had to get to where the

```
a little foot    will go along
a little fool    long
a little food    way....
```

fruit picking was, begging Roberto Morales to take them, where the bosses beckoned, where the picking paid. They had to lose as little time as possible getting there next to those tart little berries. He didn't like the look of Lupe's face, shaded against the early morning Sun. The all-powerful Sun. Their Aztec Sun -- robbed by California -- shot down --

She was quiet now, contained, resolved, controlled, picking steadily. Perspiration tracked little rivulets in the dust on her smoothround face. Oh, where they -- tears! Dirty, torn clothing made no difference to him. But he didn't like seeing her wear her clothing torn, streaked, and dusty too. She would stop and gasp in the row, as though for air, and then she would stop and stoop again to pick furiously again, filling her basket almost as fast as anyone else. She pulled the baby along, on her petate mat on the ground. Manuelito and Mariquita either played or picked. Lupe's long skirt dragged in the dirt where she stooped. Then she would stop to pray. As though it were all part of a bad dream. As though she were in some enormous cathedral, with the soft light blue and purple streams of quiet light coming down and cooling her fevered forehead.

"All right, all right everybody. Back to work!" cried Roberto Morales, wriggling his horny hoof and plaited tail, fuming, snorting, crabbing, scratching, grumbling, chewing.

"Why? What's the matter?" said Manuel, standing up.

"What's the idea bringing your tribe and not working -- say, your old lady pregnant? That her fainting all the time?"

Fainting? Manuel looked down the row at her. She was looking up, making rapid signs to Manuel to get back to work. She had merely been praying....

"All right, all right everybody," shouted Roberto. "Back to work. You all have the right to work, so back to it." Another of his poor camaraderie jokes.

Lupe saw Manuel's jaw set and fists clenched. Don't fight please, corazon, she whispered to herself. They will only run us off. The luscious red strawberries, so well hidden behind their green leaves, piled and mounted, stacked into bigger mounds and then into giant mountains of berries, higher

> the cool fresh strawberries parted
> four ways sprinkled with sugar and
> bathed in dripping sweat dipped in
> cool sweet whipping cream taste
> so very very very good....

than the sun, shutting out the Gabilan Range. The salt from her sweat was on her tongue and she thought of the cleanbathed townsladies looking her over furtively in the market out of the

156

corners of their innocent eye makeup, making her feel like some kind of freak, indecent and unclean. Because she stank? Could they smell the urine? Like helpless fish trapped in tanks, writhing and helpless, like trapped turtles in a rocky pool, screaming brotherhood, gulping for air, and pushed in crowded and squashed, manipulated and manhandled, torn and separated, were they, the poor, always to be so humiliated and stared at? Was this living at its best? Was this what life was for? Oh, how she longed to get back to their shack in Drawbridge....

And she thought of the Anglos going to the forests laughing, camping for fun, for play. To have a cookout on a stove near the crop picking grounds was something else again. Something rotten. The pickers started at dawn and picked and stooped and picked all day, as long as daylight lasted, picking all they could for their life, for the growers, the bosses, for Roberto Morales, for themselves last of all, for the peanut pennies that piled up into painful dollars slowly, forbe rries and more berries, grabbing a quick meal at night. Then, after a long

> oh, all right
> just one more spoon
> > just one   more
> > they are so delish

hard exhausting tired muscle-pulling dizzying day, then lying back on the lumpy pad, again to rest, to rest like a beast, and again to rise, again to pick, again to turn in another crushing day, stooping and picking and plucking and picking again and again the day following and another day following until finally

> ohhh it's so maaaarvelous to have
> your breakfast
> berries in bed
> so   sweet   mmmmmm   and   succulent --

this field too was also at last picked sweet clean again. And the $enator was tickled pink again that all his friends the grower$ were plea$ed they got through another hot summer of all that cool cash banked up again. And then to turn over another field and plow another man and bury another soul and stoop another day another year another lifetime while --

> the grower will fill
> the grower will
> > furnish
> > clean drinking water

DIS --

```
DIS
DISCARD
DISCARD ALL   BERRIES
THAT   ARE   OVERRIPE   OR
SHRIVELED   DISCARD
ALL   BERRIES   THAT   ARE
STOP   FROZEN   OR   POOR
IN   COLOR   STOP   DISCARD
ALL   BERRIES   THAT   ARE
BUGGED   OR   BIRDPECKED
STOOP   DISCARD   DIS   DIS
DIS
```

          and toilets too
          the smartest, the latest thing
          in sweetsmelling flushing
          toiletdom   in many a day --

And so to stop.
And stoop and pull and pluck and spoon.
Again and again.
And bay at the moon.

24

Lupe, back in her Drawbridge dreamshack, mopping the torn, worn,splintered wooden floor, thought: you step outside-- you hear birds at work and insects at dusk, and you watch the columns of endlessly milling ants going up the sides of the garbage cans at all hours, never tiring, and you think that here in the middle of Drawbridge, here in the middle of all the magic that is supposed to be California, that you are instead in some grotesque jail, you have to watch the sky, watch out for passing jets, see that they don't drop a motor on you and kill you, or the trees their leaves, or the dogs their dirt, and you watch that the cats don't kill baby birds in their nests for the fun of it, and the birds don't eat up your centipedes, and the centipedes don't eat up your children. It was puzzling. All nature was so filthy rotten.

Except her poor little avocado plant. It was more than a foot tall now, thin, slender, and strong -- reminding her of Margarita's slim fragile beauty -- and yet she had no place where she could safely plant it, with care and love and confidence, no spot of land on earth she could call her own. The treelet would die before it had a chance to live.

"We need more fingers, corazon. " No, that couldn't be it.
"We need more frijoles, corazon. " Beans.
Lupe's recurrent daytime nightmares kept tormenting her.

Ants and roaches and earwigs and hundreds of mice scurrying around her, from under the house, cockroaches getting inside the coffee pot, fighting small wars over luscious scraps of fresh ripe garbage. Burrowing into the soft cool mother earth. Poison sprays would stop them -- they sprayed. The despicable bugs with their baleful looks disappeared. But they came back again a little later, starting all over, in bigger droves, as big as horses, bigger and more ferocious and more daring. They needed newer and more powerful insecticides because the coked roaches kept on getting bigger, fattening on the poison, and her children kept getting smaller as though they weren't getting enough food. It drove her mad. Many times at night, Manuel had to wake her out of her turbulent sleep when she started in moaning or screaming. Had she known that Fred Turner had to do the same for his wife Jean, Lupe might have felt better.

What a mess her hair was in. How could she ever comb it? It wasn't often she felt so depressed. Washing the baby's pañales, steamy water, sloshing, squidging, squeezing, one window pane cracked, another broken, cardboard, row of bricabrac, two avocado trees, one empty pit, one dried chile plant, shriveled black little chiles once so fair and plump and green now so bare and gaunt, and little paper cutouts from Manuelito's drawings. A Christmas scene. And some rocks she'd picked up at the beach, an old ashtray....

She knew she was simply being nervous. Or bitter. In her bitter moments she sometimes lost her selfcontrol. She gave thanks, gracias a dios, that this time it was only her period that was making her so tense and nervous.

"Frijoles, mujer!" He knew how to make her smile. "Where are my blessed frijoles, woman?" Manuel could not keep his stomach full without beans. She knew so many intricate ways to cook the delectable bean. Boiling and softening them, she could fry, mash, smash, and then refry them. She mixed them with rice to make delicious morisqueta. Tacos were marvelous with their fine heart of chopped meat, topped with a fiery smiling chile sauce. Cheese-melting enchiladas, and frijoles refritos. Chiles rellenos, long hot green chile peppers filled with sardine, dipped in egg batter and fried along with frijoles refritos. Everything went better with beans. And there was always maiz. Beans from the moon and corn from the golden sun. Corn for thick plump tamales, corn for tortillas --

"What are we having tonight, corazon?" She would try to shut off her anxieties by thinking of things that could go wrong. What would she do if something happened to her Manuel? Suppose he got sick? Well that, even that wouldn't be the worst. They'd always managed sickness. But -- hurt? Or -- worse?

Well, she was strong. She could work herself. She could always find something. But -- the children? Here was Manuelito already six and she still couldn't get him into kindergarten, they moved around so much.

She sat, licking the end of the thread, trying to sew the long tear in Cati's playsuit, given to her by Olive Pope. And what was all this struggling for? Suppose Mr. Turner sold his land? Or his business? Or simply went to Mexico to retire? Or stopped giving Manuel work for any number of unforeseeable reasons? What would they do? Travel north to Oregon and Washington again? Was it only that she wanted to have more? Was it a sin to want more? Wasn't it a sin not to have enough to live decently? When you saw everyone around you, and you wanted what they had, was that sinful? What what sin, dear God? Padre, is it immortal sin that I shall have to carry to my grave on my dying day to wish to see that evil old Mr. Turner hanging from the Hangman's Tree in place of the straw dummy? The very evilness of the thought made her shudder.

"Manuelito, ven acá!" She could work. She had already worked. The strawberries, true, were too hard for her. She did better in the prunes. She saw other families, living in their own homes nearby, go out to the prunes for a few days or weeks, pick all they could or wanted to, get paid, and go home each night. She could see that. That wasn't too bad. And as part-time extra work, for extra income, it was fine. But she also had to take care of her own children. When the children were bigger, like Serafina's, then they surely would be able to earn more. Lupe vowed to herself that she would spark ambition in her own children, somehow. She would have to. The next, the most immediate problem was how to get Manuelito into school this next fall. If they had to move again, there would be no chance to get him started. May dear God --

She saw that Margarita also suffered. Such a young girl, and already so much a woman. Lupe's motherly heart went out to her. A woman didn't need a profession; only had to get herself a good man. Margarita was getting an education; she studied hard. Still, she was unhappy. Why was Pepe so strict with her? Was her heart struck? Margarita would know how to raise her own children. She was serious. Had she known what love was? Had she fallen in love with Ramiro? Would Ramiro come back? For two weeks now he'd been gone; it was sad, a sadness no tears could wash away. But she was young. She still had plenty more years to grow sadder by.

Picking fruit was only a part-time evil. The insecurity was the worst of it. It was evil to get trapped, to be on tap, to be used like a faucet, turned on and off when beckoned, instead of being fed T-bones every blessed day. The picking part of it was healthy enough; the meager pay and the insecurity were the evil.

"Mamacita!" Then, after she had convinced herself and had convicted the system, Manuel came home with absolutely wonderful news: "Mamacita! You must guess, guess -- !" Mr. Schroeder had actually offered him a job, him of all workers, to work part-time in his nursery. Part-time through the winter, and maybe full-time by spring. Mr. Schroeder couldn't afford another full-time worker just yet, but it was steady work. "Permanent and steady work mamacita, and for a year!" Manuel could easily pick up extra odd jobs in his leftover time. But now, now they had a base that would let them stay put in one place. They might even rent a house, a poor one of course, but their own house. Maybe they could even get a credit card. Lupe burst into tears.

"Caramba, mujer, why are you crying? You are not happy with such wonderful news?"

"Si, si, si, of course, corazon --" She sobbed uncontrollably, out of sheer joy. "You ah you are not fooling me, you, Manuel?" They were happy tears. The first happy tears she'd shed in she didn't know how long. They felt so good. So clean. Did that also mean. . . . that they might start Manuelito in school next. . . . next month? Soon?

"Si, si, mi corazon. Of course."

She had so much to be grateful to America for, so grateful now, so many happy tears. And maybe now, dear God, ay dios -- perhaps, maybe now she would also be able to plant her very own little Mexican avocado tree in a permanent spot too, her very own tree!

25

The pseudo-shops in the Western Grande were slowly shaping up.

The Barber Shop, No. 9, finally got its stupid striped pole. Later on, in next year's budget perhaps, Mr. Quill might be able to get a motorized pole. The one hitch that Mr. Turner was sticky on however was authenticity. "Whoever heard of a goddem motorized bab bab bab barber's pole in the Old West?" Turner snorted softly, making old Quill pop.

No. 7, the Post Office, had a pair of small barrel windows on one side of the entrance. One said, STEMPS, the other GEN*DELIV. No. 2 was a lawyer's office, G. H. HILLERY EsqATTny@LAW. No. 11, called The Hungary Carafe, meaning cafe, was due to be repainted brown. There was also, and Mr. Quill was especially entranced with No. 5, The Wheel of Fortune, for he secretly considered himself the true incarnation of a great gambler, keeping the bats ready, watching out for crooks with sharpies and awkward dies, never changing the system, keeping the whole thing spinning, wow, well, winning with Phyllis Ferguson at his side, another fantasy. There was also a bank, a jail, an abortionist's office, a sheriff's hangout, another saloon, and all filthy. The Village Stores, more practically, was an actual running business.

In addition, each room had its own private hitching post out

in front, adding greatly to the colorfulness and authenticity of
the whole shebang. Also, these hitching posts happened to
serve another most colorful though somewhat sinister but also
very practical purpose of chaining a car's bumper whenever
Mr. Quill felt a need to do so for back rent, money owed, food,
or just general discipline.

The Village Stores was not actually a rentable room (though
prior to its conversion it so had been once) but a real gooney
country grocery store with salami smells which Mr. Quill
operated during the lesser busy hours from midmorning to
midafternoon. Besides being very sincere about getting all the
authenticity he could jam into the stupendous place, Mr. Quill
was not above garnering a loose penny or two with his own
greedy little paws. It had taken some doing to get Mr. Turner's approval. Mr. Quill couldn't have hidden all the prosti-
tutional possibilities from Mr. Turner's sharp eyes of course.
But two counts -- the Authenticity kick, plus the added incentive of keeping the clients contented while cooped in waiting for
the prunes to ripen for plucking -- turned the trick. The rubber
bands holding up his long shirt sleeves also helped. Mr. Quick
Kill Quill wasn't exactly losing all his marbles.

The house hours were rigorously posted:

---

11 to 1 daily E X C E P T Monday

Those clients who found themselves inconveniently forced
to stay behind or beyond the usual delayed stage stop, irritated
either by the service or the cash custom at the nearby Sureway
Supermarket, cussing, such clients were pleasantly surprised
to discover they could buy milk for the children, boxes of
crackers, cans of conveniently cooked beans whose lids could
be cracked and contents drained, if need be, straight into one's
mouth, consumed cold, or Norweigian sardines, for the usual
usurer's overcharge over their actual fair cost. Convenience
and credit were the critical factors in Mr. Quill's modest but
highly successful little operation.

There was one additional very private, nonpublic, and very
practical building set back behind the other buildings, alone,
in an unused section of the property.

This was The Warehouse.

The Warehouse loomed behind The Village Stores. To one
side of The Warehouse grew the ancient oak tree from which
the effigy of Black Bart hung limp, swaying in whatever breeze
happened by. The Warehouse wasn't a room, but a large gray
building. Herein were stored many oddball kinds of dilapidated
goods and worthless sundries, boxed and crated -- trunks,
valises, overnight suitcases, diplomats' pouches, a smatter-

ing of cracked baby cribs, play pens, and strollers. More than anything else there were dozens of cardboard boxes of every conceivable size and shape, usually bulging, usually split at the corners, most of them bound in heavy cord, string, or rope. These boxes were the prizes of war. They were the ransoms of defectors, of that unspeakable refuse who refused or, much more likely, were unable to pay the wherewithal for the debts they mounted steadily for the rentals plus the victuals from the Village Stores. This acquisitiveness in a way was a hangover from Mr. Turner's earlier vigilante days when hangings and hangovers were far more common and when scrounging was a basic activity, perhaps the vital ingredient for survival in those stringent days.

Despite the emotional jelly beneath his inellectual blubber, Mr. Quill had no ancient Aztec superstitions to unravel from his own inner images. The place was a mess again. What would Mr. Turner do? Mr. Turner, all sinew and cold nerve, was pure predator. Torn bits of paper were lying all around the yard outside, like some damn litterville. On top of everything else he had the careless kids to worry about. Inside his gray little office-bedroom, he held his stomach in a second, fat and panicky, and tried to listen to the radio. Then he jumped, hearing some shots ring out. It wasn't the radio. Some cops? Some cops stopped by and pulled up to his office window. They were grinning.

"Any trouble today, Mr. Quill?" they asked, very friendly.

"No, no," he said quickly, shaking his head, trembling. Hadn't they heard the shots? Not a sign of a rifleman anywhere. Kids yelling, cars honking, mothers screaming, motors roaring, everything as normal as it could be. "No. Thanks a lot."

The nice, young, clean-cut friendly cops smiled and pulled out again, just like on TV, saying, "Well, Mr. Quull, just give us a buzz if you have any more trouble."

Hadn't they heard the shots? Was it only his imagination? Was he going nuts? He walked around in back of his hut, and there it was. Another mess. Paint splattered all over. At first he thought it was some crazy abstract painting with crazy lettering. He had to tilt his pudgy head to make sense out of some of the signs:

and:

and:

and:

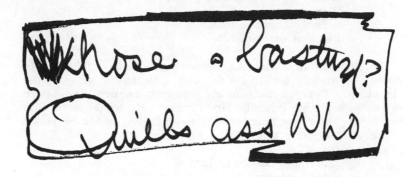

He tried to tell from the handwriting whether the same person could have written them all. From the spelling he couldn't deduce whether this was the work of men, or their children. They were all equally illiterate. He'd have to hose it off. Then he discovered the hose was cut into several chunks. The water running out of the outside faucet created a small pond. Bricks, garbage, boxes, torn paper, dogshit, dirt, filth, banana peels, dead cockroaches, feathers, string, beer can rings, and one broken toilet seat were all dumped into his neat little backyard as though it were a miniature garbage dump. In the most fashionable part of town, the stench from the nearby grand garbage dumps was still faintly noticeable. Mr. Quill's round little nose curled indelicately. Another brick came whirring through the air. He whirled, saw nothing, not even the brick. But he heard the crunch. He was still hearing things. He heard the roars of leatherjacketed motorcycle clowns, but couldn't see them, and raucous laughter. In the distance a train blew off its long whistle. Why couldn't these pests leave him alone? Scum. That's what they were. Dirty.... his radio was on, and other radios in the compound were blaring louder. Thoughts jumbled crazily around beneath his bald pate. A perfect slob, all the wet dreams of a degenerate intellectual, no saving grace, a parasite non pareil, he tried guessing what Mr. Turner would do in his place. He went back inside his own dark dirty cave, dreaming of the time he would set up his own orchid orchard with a whip for the pikers. The music stopped and a familiar voice came on the air - - Rat Barfy! Mr. Quill pulled in his imitation blubber to lend attention to his favorite oats common tator:

"GOOD EVENING! --"

> .... the parallel of the figs
> is really for the birds because
> I am as one of them.
> If they're too stupid to get orf
> those sharp rocks, I say
> horsefeathers to 'em.
> Let 'em eat bamboo. ....

Ah, the savant of savants. "Send moah money, folks." He would, he would. Quill, the fat slob. He heard screams in his sleep. Every human foible wrapped up in Mr. Turner :wise, benevolent, friendly Mr. Turner. He would never be like him. The young people today were finding haven in rotten .... hey, Rat Barfy was talking again:

> .... finding haven in that
> rotten precept
> that anyone can do anything
> they want
> provided they don't hurt
> anyone. Now ain't that the
> most asinine
> philosophy you've ever sucked
> into your earpipes?
> Only a jerk --

Mr. Quill sat up with a jerk. He'd dozed. The music was playing. He heard another brick slam against the wall. He decided to ignore it this time.

Mr. Turner had passed by The Western Grande only the day before Mr. Quill's heartrending discovery of No. 16's dismaying defoliation. Mr. Quill did not know that Mr. Turner had a small raise in the works for him, as it was Mr. Turner's genius to squirt in exactly the right number of drops of oil at exactly the right moment to rule out any squeaks in his tight organization. Tight was right. Mr. Quill's slovenliness was working in his favor.

First, however, an introspection. After careful deliberation, he decided he would become a modern vigilante himself. He henceforth would, figuratively squeaking, string up all the varmints that dared cross him. He resolved (1) to no longer give the slightest wisp of a benefit of any doubt to ANYONE marching throug the Western's grande portals. And (2) to sharpen his outlook for hypocritical sharpies. That meant tightening up on at least five or six families now in residence. The Gutierrez's were still in hock, though coming around, but still in hock. Some new crews were all caught up but bore watching. The Popes and the Jonsons were falling more and

168

more behind, without even mentioning Mrs. Ferguson whose shamelessness took such open advantage of his sexual fright of her. Mr. Quill was determined to see the gleam of green before letting one solitary single more parasite get anything more out of him. No. Sir. Ree. Mr. Turner was infernally right. Business W A S business. Not monkey business. Mr. Quill was getting mighty, mighty, mighty fed up.

He would strike back.

He went out, determined to find some part of the day to his liking, so as to polarize his annoyance. It was warm and sunny out, which put him in a foul mood. He was most often mean and surly on the nicest, brightest days. The birds chirped happily, annoying him with their infernal screeching. The central court was soon overflowing with the raucous squeals and screams and gyrations of destructive little monsters at play, interspersed with the equally raucous screams of their equally hairbrained dams.

Not a quarter of ten, and out of the corner of his eye he caught Mrs. Jonson's impudent stance before her door, as though she owned it, as though she had some genuine business to transact. Arms folded fatly like some hot Arab. As though she had absolutely not a thing to do. Which of course she had not. But he wasn't fooled. Not him. He knew very well what that stance meant.

Milk.

She was in dire need of milk. His milk. Her mother's milk. She was in even direr need of brains, too, but then there wasn't a meat shop in the whole country that could give her the kind she needed. Maybe at Stanford -- no; Quill decided to duck back into his dark moldy little cubicle. He buried his shiny pate in the ledger which he knew by heart, from the newest arrival to the oldest larcenist. He grew more and more furious by the minute. And finally even with Mr. Turner himself, without even knowing just how to finger the great man, whose tintyped image kept cynically staring at him from the wall. Showing Mr. Turner in all his sartorial splendor, dentures showing, fluffed out yellow ascot at the neck, his nerveless hand on the hawser hanging Black Bart up by the neck on the old oak hangem tree. That was the part for him all right. Just the part.

The waiting finally got him. Grabbing the giant ring of keys down from its meat hook, he re-entered the world of light out doors. He walked casually. He nodded curtly. Mrs. Jonson started waddling furiously over to The Stores.

The day had begun.

26

Drawbridge Courier
August Twenty-Six

Area prune packing
workers go on strike

PALO ALTO (AP)--Nearly 1,000 dried prune packers, from Sunnyvale to Hollister, walked off their jobs this morning.

The strike was called Thursday night by George Lumpitall, President of the ILWU Warehouseman's Local 11, after negotiations broke down, and they said they just didn't give a damn any more.

Four packing houses are affected by the strike. They are: Del Poniente in Sunnyvale; California Canners & Growers in San Jose; and Moonriver and Mayrain, who have several plants running from San Jose to Hollister.

Despite the strike, there will be no fruit spoilage, according to Robert R. Smudiniuri, the spokesman for Moonriver. He said the dehydrator sections of the packing plants will not be affected by the strike. Once fruit is dried, he added, whistling in the dark, it can be stored indefinitely. So can money.

*

27

Welfare roll red tape
bars prune pickers

SAN JOSE (UP) -- State and Santa
Clara County officials were at logger-
heads hacking away today at red tape
which has kept farm labor officials from
using hundreds of wellfed welfare recipients to harvest the county's desperate
need to pluck the new prune crop for the
relief of the harassed land companies.

The Board complained that the prune
crop was going unharvested because
there is no one to pick it, yet there are
1,500 men in the county who are unemployed.

"Why can't welfare people be artifi -
cially taken off welfare rolls and put to
work?" The County Board of Supervisors Board Chairman (who recently
lost his seat, his shirt, and his wiglet
in last week's election) asked of the
Welfare Director Fredrick Sharpedge.

"There is no sense in these welfare
people receiving, that is, what amounts
to being paid for doing nothing when
there is work to be done to be done, i.e.
to keep the plums from rotting in our
poor orchards, and driving our poor
growers to Agnews," (Agnews being the
local state mental institution nearby)
said still another Supervisor, Ralph
Merchuriochromatome, whose seat also
is ominously coming up next.

*

171

28

Farm labor desk set up
to save rotting crop

SANTA CLARA (AP) -- The State
Farm Labor Office today set up a desk
in the Santa Clara County Welfare Building to directly recruit pickers of the
county's prune crop, which is in dire
danger of not being completely picked,
thereby putting the poor prune growers
in a powerful, crushing bind.

Thus ended nearly two weeks of con-
troversy over hiring welfare recipients
to pick the prickly prune crop.

County Jail Inmates were used for
the first time today too as officials
attempted to help ravaged farmers sal-
vage their magnificent prune crop.

Prunes are Santa Clara County's
second most valuable crop, having a
$10,000,000 value last year.

It was only last week when the Welfare Director, Fredrick Sharpedge
replied, "Shit," as he refused to let the
Farm Labor Office set up a recruiting
prune-licking booth in the welfare building, saying recruiting plump plum
pickers was not his responsibility.

The next day, an angry Board of
Supervisors, all of whose seats are
soon coming up for re-election as a
result of a recall, ordered the Welfare
Board boss to give space to the Farm
Labor Office for the illicit recruitment,
legal or no. The prune growers were
apparently going all out to get all the
help possible to get their prunes plucked,
to calling out the National Guard if
necessary, swore the Super Trooper.

*

29

Come off it, Schroeder. You know goddem well what I'm saying. Come on, you know the score. You got a beautiful little
thing going for you, that dandy little nursery of yours. Efficient. You don't have those damned miserable pickers hanging
from your neck.
You want some plants.
Everybody calls me El Gusano Verde, the sons a bitches. I
know that. Well, I give as good as I get. Anything else new?
Take those college clucks — they gripe because I drive a hard,
hard bargain, no bazaar, not a band wagon. This is no circus.
If I didn't, if these thousands of acres weren't in good hands,
those pickers out there would be starving in some desert. I
give them work. I keep them alive. Do I force them to work?
I don't. They're free to go starve wherever the hell they like.
More plum saplings, Fred? Cherries?
Now see here, Schroeder. I want you to help me get all the
corn I mean prune pickers you can. Round up all the families
you know in Santa Clara.
The kids —
Hang the goddem kids. I don't give a shit about kids in school.
You know that. If I could only get my hands on some of that
Bay fill. It's that flat. Shallow and sweet. And that sonova-
bitching salt combine's got it all sewed up. I can't get 'em to

give up a goddem inch. The bastards. Salt shit. I can just
taste it. Boy, they got a goddem city planned out there on top
of those salt marshes, and over the garbage dumps too. Man
if only I could just — hell, fellow, I tell you it's better being
on welfare nowadays. Now we had that dandy sheriff feller.
Captain Something McAllee, down Rio Grande way, and I tell
you he sure knew how to eke out those damned pickers believe
me. Yessirree. He sure did that. Those pickers tried to organize for a strike and McAllee he locked all them leaders up.
All that goddem unionizing and striking and marching to Fort
Worth and for what? March to Dallas, eh? For nothing. Goddem people don't know when they are well off, with us growers
giving them every goddem thing they got, food, wearing, and
keeping them —
    I understand he lied.
Sure he lied. Who? McAllee? Where'd you hear that? That
is another goddem lie. Anybody tells you he lied lies. He,
well, hell, man, tell you what it was. He just wouldn't talk.
You hear how the Mafia don't talk? Well, neither will Sheriff
McAllee. Fights fire with fire. Who say two crimes don't
make a good? Need their heads examined. Hell man, he sure
went around clobbering and busting those goddem strikers on
their heads, they asked for it. They wouldn't work. Anybody
won't work deserves to be clanked on their clobbers. Goddem
pickers, they didn't want no work. Sure he refused to talk.
But he sure got off the hook, I tell you. Sure was great.
    It's all right to lie and clobber people.
Sure. Eh? What? Pickers, Schroeder, not people.
    Look, Turner, what've you got against Mexicans?
Who? Me?
    OK. What else would you do?
OK. You ask. What I got against the goddem Metsicans. I'll
tell you. They got everything going for them. That's what.
We give them, we give them, ah we give them —
    California was once part of Mexico.
Eh? What? Mexico? Well, come on. We won it fair and
square, didn't we? Come on, you going — say, what the hell,
you want to tackle this thing fair or not?
    That's the idea.
Sure. As long as, look, man, the trouble, well, the trouble
is, we don't have enough mom and pop farms any more. OK.
I admit it. Kids grow up in streets. No more little farms
with that rural cow crap. Two people simply can't run any
farm anywhere any more, efficiently. It has got to be run like
any business. What's a farm. It's only dirt, isn't it? You
know it. I know it. Why don't they know it out there?
    They called Captain McAllee a drunkard, a madman, a
    spoor dropper, a filthy liar, a human skunk, a parasite,

an inhuman nasty, indecent brute, a beast on the payroll
of the growers —
You know they are all lies, Schroeder. You know that. He is
an upright American citizen, a Texas Ranger, a mother lover,
he never beats his wife, though he cheats on her now and then.
He is in the top secret pay of some secret official U. S. agency
upholding law and and uh order.

Now, Turner.
I see you aren't answering my direct question. Interesting.
Schroeder, you know I can unload any time I feel like it. There
are forty two greedier bastards ready to take over whenever I
feel like quitting. And colder. And more ruthless. But for
me to give up everything now would be as irresponsible as
Captain McAllee admitting to having committed atrocities over
in Texas. All right, let's say for the sake of argument he has.
I say, so what? He's keeping order, isn't he? Isn't order
more important than law? What? Well, that's just your opinion. Small farms, yeah. Man with a hoe. Come on, fellow.
How else can you produce produce cheaply, and in quantity except by going big? Aren't you going after big game yourself,
man? Hell, you wouldn't be any good if you weren't. You be
generous with your money if you want to, and let me be me.
Fair enough? Oh, your great big heart bleeds for them, for
those ah, for those underprivileged peanut pickers. Why do
you worry? They are happy that way. Ants are ants and sheep
sheep. Let them be. Sobbing sisters. They scream and rant
and pull their hair. Scum is scum.

And dogs howl like howling dogs.
Right again. You're not giving me enough credit, Jim. I insist on being honest. I can't stand the bastards getting something for nothing. That's the worst hypocrisy there is. Something for nothing. They all want handouts, that's what they —
why, when I cheat the IRS, I do it legal.

You say something for nothing.
Right.

What do you do?
Lots of things.

You don't do a goddamn thing, Turner, except sit on your
duff all day and answer the phone while meanwhile all
those thousands of poor miserable human beings out there
in the sweating sun are plucking the fruit and puking their
brains out in the sweating sun, making you richer every
minute, while they worry about getting thru the winter.

OK, Schroeder, but I happen to live in the real, the hard
world, the eat or be turned into shit world. What the hell difference does it make what I call them? The results are what
count. OK, I'm mean. A miser... OK. So? After all it's
my mean miserliness that's nudging your humanity along. I

admit I don't intend it to do that. I just don't give a shit, let's face it. Go ahead. Quote me. I'm not freaking out. The freakybops do that. Now just one more damned minute, Schroeder. Don't preach your lukewarm gospel to me. What in the hell were your ancestors doing twenty thousand years ago? Same as mine. Drawing on goddem cave walls. What did it get them? Brutes, weren't they? Weren't they brute, scum, animal, all the way through? Yet here we are, chum. You. And I. Some up. Some down. I bet their ancestors even slammed mine around.

Your ledgers are out of whack.

Trouble with your romantics is confusing morality with reality. Soft wishes with hard law. Law, lies. Listen, for two hundred I can buy any trained mind to say any goddem thing I want anywhere in the world. That your precious individuality?

Using a bet to prove a point.

The Agricultural Workers Organizing Committee is --

What? The AWOC? You're scared of them?

We'll let the strawberries rot on the ground first.

So the good Senator said.

We'll hold the line.

But the prices go up anyway. What kind of a game are you people playing? I can't see it. When Salinas lettuce went up last year, it wasn't the pickers nor the union that made it go up, Fred. You know that. Prices went up because your fat friends cut harvesting time to four days a week.

That's right.

Doggone lettuce went up, demand stayed up, and the pickers not only earned less money, but they also got all the blame for the price rise. In all the papers. Scared hell out of the public, and it set the workers back another year. Pretty neat trick, all right.

Neat.

What you might call fighting fire with fire.

Right.

Sneaky and dirty and cheating and lying and robbing.

Right again.

You and the Moors and saltpeter and the greedy bastards get everything all sewed up nice and tight, you shut out small operators, then you scream that the unions are coming.

Right-O.

Well, I won't buy your brand of Christianity, Turner.

You're blind.

That's your plate of spaghetti.

You are.

No, you are At least I don't undersell capitalism. I have confidence in capitalism. I don't cheapen it the way you hogs do. Capitalism is the neatest economic system yet

devised by man. It takes care of everything. It has brought
about the greatest good for the greatest number. It really
works. Other systems only bleat. Capitalism feeds everybody, gives everybody work, produces enormous quantities
cheaply of anything anybody wants, encourages productivity,
encourages new inventions, and then on top of all that, it
also liberates the free spirit, permitting a great outpouring
of artistic and creative experimenting.

That's a lot of crap.

But all that you monopolistic bastards want is more, and to
cut us free enterprisers out every chance you get.

I was worried for a minute.

The only thing you really lack is heart.

Morality? Is that it? Come, my dear Schroeder. A moral
sense? Can you eat it? Feed everyone free? There you go
again. Missing every point, reading —

You distribute all the wealth so that most of it is siphoned
off to you and your heirs, and then you're scared shitless
at the families of mothers and abandoned families of poor.
So far all you can come up with is prisons and public welfare and private chains and charitable philanthrophy.

You are hard, yourself. But tell me this. How else are you
going to get them off their duggs? Got any suggestions?

Let them have some fun. Some incentive.

You can't mean that scum, the pickers.

Educate them, Turner. Let them become lawyers. First
thing you know — yeah, lawyers. You know, Turner, you
could even be counted among the great benefactors if you
just gave it chance to work. And it wouldn't cost a thing.

I see what you mean. Hmmm. Pretty soon, now, no, however,
everything's going to mechanize anyhow. And I won't be able
to help your poor slobs out. Hell, all we'll have to do is phone
the bank from the bunk, clear the lines, clear our throats, call
the foreman, give the signal, push the switch, and jump out of
the way. Pour in the jack and the beans talk. The crops do
spring up. No human hands. No human misery. What'll you
do then, Schroeder? Go fishing with me? Plenty of cod — it
is ironic, Schroeder. That machine is going to do you in.
Solve everything for you screwballs. All machined, all planted,
hoed, toed, rowed, weeded, manured, plucked too, and of
course canned and labeled and sold. No more famine. Just give
it away. Not even food stamps. And you, my concerned friend,
are going to have to worry about the suicide rate.

The fact that I'm a businessman doesn't seem to mean a
thing to you. You don't have to steal and cheat and rob —

But who the hell's being hurt, man?

Rob.

I? Rob? I rob? Rob who? Rob what? What rob?

Rob and play dirty and make money cheating. I don't have to. But what's the use? I haven't got a ratty raft of decrepit ragged human beings out there sweating in the fields, burning up, nowhere to piss decently, picking like golden lunatics for peanut butter, just to get my back back double. You are so full of dirty rotten filthy hatred of humankind that you can't see your own image straight. I don't know what to blame for your perverse greed. Not lack of intelligence. You are goddamned smart. Not logic. You are logical. Not sickness. Yeah. You are sick, in a way. You are the final perfect inbred flowering of a modern princely ruler in a modern society. You are Machiavelli in bloom. The great irony, and the great sin is that in your hands lies the power to easily overcome this stupid, shortsighed, inhuman treatment of these poor creatures. And without any real cost to you. That's the rub. It doesn't cost you anything. You just pass it on to the consumer. What's up? Why the hell don't you? That's what baffles me. What the hell's going on? Why do you have to have human beings groping around in such misery like animals to do your pickings? Why can't you let them earn decent pay and work regular hours, like everyone else? Do you rob for sadism?
Somebody's got to do it.
But why does it have to be below a decent level of pay? What the hell am I listening to all this bullshit for. Am I some kind of idiot? Why shouldn't I be making twice my investment and all I can any time I want? Listen, Schroeder. What I want — what I want is for you to get Manuel Gutierrez to join my — Agricultural Workers Orgds for me, as a symbol of a happy picker.
You've got the wrong man, Fred.
Gutierrez?
And me.
No dice, then.
No dice.
OK, Schroeder. You win this time. Let's drink to it.

178

30

With no small satisfaction, pudgy Mr. Quill contemplated his potentially vast domain. He was a true dreamer.

No mere hostel, this, the Western Grande, and he, the Grandee, was the grandest slam in the entire golden west.

Reaching far back into history for rich ideas, this compound of his was being primed for greatness. And to think of it, that he, Quill, was in complete charge of such greatness.

To think of it.

He pictured himself, in his prime years, wearing his expansive cucaracha outfit embroidered in gold, inlaid with gleaming silver threads among the bold, real pearls for buttons, while puffing on a magnificent charro cheroot.

Perhaps Mr. Turner would even let him keep his own magnificent spirited stallion nearby too, in one of the stalls, after kicking out one of the families, to ride to San Jose in every day on.

How, now.... wouldn't that be the day, though?

31

Mr. Quill wasted the better part of the afternoon repairing the damage to No. 16's worthless interior. He found a couple of spare clusters of drawers in The Warehouse which, though splintered and chewed and charred, nevertheless remained somewhat capable of holding some things still.

The rest of it was a matter of cleaning up. Of sending the shredded curtains back out to the dump whence they came. Some sweeping. Some cleanser sprinkled around to give the interior a clean soapy smell. Soon it was presentable enough again, with the energy expended having exactly the opposite effect on his untidy mind. He was livid with fury. He burped neurotically two or three times.

On the morning of the fourth day, after the skies cleared, when another tribe disappeared, stripping their danged cabin of every blessed movable object, Mr. Quill wondered what part of him or his nut would crack first.

Was there no end to the human indignity he had to bear?

He took his full fury out on pretty poor Mrs. Ferguson. After having some cans of creamed oyster stew on the cuff she then thought she could sneak over to the Sureway Supermarket later on, did she, while she thought he wasn't looking, eh, thought he wouldn't see her sneaking back into her cage with a fat bulging sack of fodder for her new boyfriend eh, well let her. As for the others..... Mr. Quill had seen Zeke Jonson staggering about like a giant bird with a broken wing, breaking wind every other step, burdened by one hell of a first class fried drunk on. A congenital alcoholic, indisputable, from his sire or dam. Probably fed on the stuff first in his baby bottle days after mama heard it helped baby sleep fast. Jonson tooled out of that happy cottage every dawn to pick God knew what and did not return to paradise until after sundown. The trick was to separate him from his pay before he stumbled across some bar. The two times Quill trapped him in the dark courtyard late at night, Jonson's eyes were glowing so bright they lit up the compound. Quill couldn't tell whether he was just staggering or shaking his head. This was one case Quill was ready to chuck over to the Welfare. As he well knew from past experiments it was going to be either his skin or his.

Mr. Quill made a short, pungent decision.
He would latch Jonson's chariot to its hitching post.
That night. That very night.
They would be the first to fall. Mr. Quill hadn't pulled this vigilante trick for some time now. But he was going to prove that hitching up was one of modern society's most modern and most effective torts at his command. That wholesome coin.

This here establishment, after all, was no missionary headquarters. No flop house. No charity bazaar. No flea market either. No sir. It was a b c business. Cold turkey. A simple A B B C. A Better Business Combine.

There were, after all, plenty of welfare officers and churches in all the land and around the country set up to take care of the helpless, the shiftless, the nogoods, the indigent, the aged, the senile, the worthless, the castoffs, and the insufficients. The pickers could work.

It was not Mr. Turner's and certainly much less Mr. Quill's responsibility to rectify the blunders created by these simple-minded beings, these mismanagers of their own private previews of hell. There was plenty of land, well, maybe no land. But.... Mr. Quill, at one point, had even worked out a theory whereby he was convinced that prosperity was actually ruining the economy, but he hadn't been able to work the details out in his sluggish head yet. Only a retard or a deliberate sluggard could avoid finding work. Peas were begging to be plucked. Eggs could be laid. Graders were in short supply. Growers were screaming for pickets, migrats, coolidge spudents, they didn't care what the hell level education they had, just so long as they picked and asked no goddem questions, convicts in or out of jails, hell it didn't matter, entire families a la social welfare, men, women en famille, children, anything, as long as they could stumble in, anything. Anybody. They didn't

181

care. They were very democratic when it came to hiring pickers. It was their money they didn't want to be caught dead with. As long as they could pick. Some nutty zoologist from marineland even experimented with simians, apes, and chimps, sending Brazilian stocks zooming up 275 points in one breathtaking day, breaking the previous GE high when Progress Was Their Most Amportant Producto. Lots of agricultural work available all over. True, it didn't pay green. But who cared? Certainly nobody important cared. Because the growers were, er, that is, ah, what, but so what, it was Work, wasn't it? It was good, healthy outdoor work. If they didn't like picnics, the pickers, the migrants, the decrepits, the leftovers, why didn't they go to college, or just go buy a block of marble stocks and carve themselves a statue and sell it as ersatz art? Or better yet, a gravestone and slide under it?

The bell tinkled merrily at The Stores. The screen door opened playfully. Little by little, little Mrs. Pope hopefully wedged her misshapen little elf self inside. Mr. Quill's normally depressed gloom lightened slightly.

"Ah, Mrs. Pope! Well, well, and how are you this fine morning er or say it's afternoon already, isn't it?"

Such a frail young thing she was, wan, pale, always shy. And fatter than the Lord's own avocado around the middle, all set to loose her offshoot anv moment upon an unsuspecting world. And yet another slug, that Charlie Pope, for an ersatz husband. This one was something all right. A big husky blond giant, always grinning. And always grinning stupidly. Quill didn't mind an intelligent grin; it was always the stupid grins that set his few remaining healthy teeth on edge. The thought of it now sent another quiver of pain lobbing through his lower jaw, and that in turn set him thinking of the hated dentist too.

This coward, who never dared talk to anyone's face straight on, always sending this sweet little girl, probably exploiting her from the crying start, while she poor thing had to bear not only her heavy burden in her lopsided belly but on top of it that beast, plus another young child as well. The four-year-old boy was clutching her hand. Two thick streams of mucus oozing down from his nostrils came very close to overturning Mr. Quill's queasy stomach. He very nearly made the mistake of chucking it under its chin.

"Do come on in, I'm sure, Mrs. Pope."

"I'm sure, well, ah, it's nothing, ah —"

He waited for her, forcing more bile back down his gullet.

"Well, you see, ah, Mr. Quill, you see, ah, we're sure ah urg uh I'm sure that is that Chuck you see will surely find ah something real neat. Soon."

"Ah?"

She was so flustered by his echo that she was quite unable either to affirm or deny it.

"Well, don't you worry home child," he said at last, thinking goodly of her, thinking himself God again, thinking to himself how could be possibly be bold enough to bleat 'child' at this luscious, desirable young girl/mother. "But how are you feeling? Isn't there, ah, isn't that ah after all the important priceless purpose in life?" That sounded great.

"Yes," she whispered. Despite her innocence, she really didn't give a shit what anyone else thought either.

"And how is Mrs. Gutierrez?" he asked.

"Yes." Her eyes remained wide open, full of innocence.

Looking past her unkempt blond mop, he could see their snappy blue sedan parked lazily out in front of their shack. That meant the bland blond gland was still hard at it, humped over way in bed. His hunger had probably forced her out to the hunt, to bring him something back alive to eat. A dash of strychnine, perhaps? That would be nice. How about a little rasher of rat liver with cockroach juice. Or a small cooked clot of chicken blood for desert.

"Mr. Quill couldIcouldIcouldIcouldI ah you let meme have a dash of rum I mean a little weeny meeny packet of teeny hut ducks —" The effort it was costing the poor child.

Hot dogs indeed. Hot dogs for breakfast. What about that!! Or was it dog dogs for brunch. With mustard plastered on. Mr. Quill held his forked tongue for a dear moment. Another padlock here? The longer he gave in, the longer these halfbrutes misunderstood his basic benignity and finally ended abusing his incredible patience. A padlock here, then. Tonight.

"— and he's and he's and he's got the got God he's agot this hm appointment today at eleven at that ugh office."

"Do you mean eleven p. m. tonight, Mrs. Pope?"

"At ahhhh ugh eleven an ah not at this employment office yet." She stopped to stare at him, to think of what she was saying, then she got started again. "They told him to come boy come on in for us I mean for sure and he's gone and got ten all ready what for huh."

"Ten what, Mrs. Pope?"

Mr. Quill did not bother to ask this plaintive quivering little jello sack why that giant glut of a slug of her so-called husband had not seen fit to rise off his butt and salaam out of his blessed sack at dawn— he HE had to do it every single blessed day dry or wet rain or shine — and spend those four or five extra valuable hours looking for something useful to make money by. Was there something after all to the ugly rumors of Pope's being a drug addict or an opium pusher? Ah, Quill knew too well too what the answer to that was. He also resented seeing himself put upon, on the defensive, as though it mattered to him what they did. He gave her the warm pack of stale cold dogs and turned his head so as to avoid that teary gratitude of hers.

He continued standing there in the gurgle of bile again, for quite a while. He wondered what part of him would degenerate first. Was there no end to the indignities that had to befall his lot? God, would he have to switch gods again?

Practically out of nut meal, he decided to deliberately run amok that day. In berserk fury, he raised six families who were most in arrears, one day here, three there. At the most propitious moment, when no one was at home, and there - fore least able to prevent or publicize the act, Mr. Quill went forth and lifted whole boxes of their private belongings and in addition securely padlocked their cars and doors for good measure — and Into The Warehouse At Last!!

When — as -- and — if — they wanted their things back, screaming, pleading, threatening, scolding, he was ready to snarl his terms: "I have my hand on this here telephone and I am ready at any moment to call my friends the police. Now you you either pay up or all of you or or get out. Preferably both!"

It was Quivering Quill's finest qualm.

He was finally able to throw his lumpy weight around.

He was truly alive.

32

Drawbridge Courier
September Thirteen

Governor Nolan
Howlin Mad again

SACRAMENTO (UP) — Governor (Howlin Mad) Nolan presented his emotional State of the State Address before embarking upon another ebullient tour of fund and hell raising. After declaring college students persona non grata, he suggested that shutting down the institutions of higher learning would be a good way to quiet some of the uproar.

Labor leaders, he also declared, were incensed when he allowed convicts to help harvest California's huge fruit and vegetable crops. But, the Governor pointed out at the press conference, the union failed to provide sufficient manpower to bring the crops in before they were in danger of rotting. Speaking of union leaders, H.M.N. fired off the following acute observation:

"Somehow they remind me of a
dog, howling with pain, sitting
on a sharp rock and too stupid
to get off."

H. M. N. thereupon ordered his Department of Health & Welfare to find out how many of the State's welfare recipients would be willing to go out and work in the fields to harvest or risk losing their benefits. He also wanted a check on how many dogs the State was feeding free in the pounds. The taxpayers, said the Governor, were mighty sick and tired of paying out charity and getting nothing but the shitty end of the shtick.

*

185

33

Just what was Ramiro Sanchez's serious intent? Was it to
make any overt move for or against alleviating the indirection
of an indifferent civilization?
"I spit on your civilization."
Most assuredly then that was not his intent. Why then didn't
he go back to the land of his forebears, the Aztecs?
"Because this is, was, and will be my land."
For whom then were all these prunes planted?
"Who else? For the very rich."
Why?
"To make themselves richer. Why else?"
Then one was forced to assume he was against both capitalism
and for socialism?
"I hate anything that makes me less of a man."
What about educating the masses?
"I spit on your education."
Education, then, evidently wasn't Ramiro Sanchez's stick.
"I hate all you aristocratic bastards, all you porcine scum,
all you pigs, all you greedy guero Turners."
By gueros he meant only the blond super race? The WASPS?
Well, those who thought they were blond and super and race.
He wanted only to live as man. As human. Not worse than
animals. Nor even the same as animals. Nor did he want

to live like his cousin Manuel. He did not even want to raise his children in convenient accommodations to starvation either, whether of the feudal or the aristocratic or the modern industrial variety.

What did he want then?

He wanted the lovely, lovely Margarita....

Lupe had told him that Rosa had told Margarita that he, Ramiro, being all man, had been fooling around with other women, including that saucy Mrs. Ferguson. Margarita naturally became very upset. But I haven't even been around here, protested Ramiro. How do I defend myself? Well, it's not easy, said Lupe. Do you believe me? Of course I do. Why should Rosa do this to me? She's jealous. Of what? Well, Rosa said you caused Silvestre to break away from her, before the train accident. Ramiro said, who, me? Man, any man can have any woman who will have him. I had nothing to do with Silvestre. Well, there it was. But Rosa would have it that way, and she was paying him, and making him hurt. A vicious woman. Scandal. Revenge. When Rosa was unhappy she moved. It will be up to you, said Lupe, and I think you can do it. I know, in my heart I know Margarita loves you too. On another occasion Rosa deliberately broke up another marriage by flaunting a conquest of hers before the man's wife and when the wife threw the culprit out, Rosa did likewise. Why was Rosa so unhappy? There seemed no end to her bitterness as long as she could find no man of her own. The gossip, the backstabbing, anything to break up budding friendships, lies, lies, lies, just to see others unhappy....

Ramiro knocked on Lupe's door to find out when Manuel was due back. "Hello -- "

A dark form loomed inside the screen door. A girl, not Lupe, said softly, "Come in." It was Margarita. They stood in the semi-darkness. Locked. Looking at each other. Reaching across the centuries. Aztec to Mayan. Reaching in silence. In love. He went in. He bent over and touched Cati's sleeping forehead lightly. "Such a perfect baby," he murmured. "Do you know when Manuel will be back?"

"No. Lupe will soon be here. She will tell you."

Silence.

"I prefer your telling me."

Silence.

"How can I? I do not know."

Another pause. Then --

"Rosa has missed you," she said softly.

"And you?" He knew about Rosa's vicious lies.

Again, a silence.

"May I ask you a very personal question, Margarita?"

187

She did not reply.

"Do not be angry with me, muchacha."

She studied him through the darkness.

"I could not bear it this time. I went away because —"

"You seem to have gotten along pretty well."

"My traveling? Is that what you mean? My going away without saying goodbye? But that only proves, muchacha —"

He waited, and still she did not speak.

"It proves that I have missed you very much, Margarita. And I have come back because — I couldn't bear to say goodbye. Could I ask you a very personal question?"

He knew he could have, but the circumstance forced him to seek out her consent. A pause, relenting; then she said softly, "Perhaps."

"Tell me, Margarita, have you — a novio?"

"Why do you wish to know?"

"Because I must. Have you?"

"You know I haven't."

"I do? Well, a novio is —"

"I know very well what a novio is. Almost engaged."

"Margarita, I wish to declare myself to you."

"But I have never gone out with you."

"Saturday night, then. Done."

"No."

"But why not, muchacha?"

Her large brown eyes opened wide in the half light, studying him, drinking him in. Finally, again, "No."

"Your father? Is that it? Is it Pepe?"

She hesitated.

"You've got to give me a reason." He was getting bolder.

"Ramiro, you have a novia yourself. Do not lie to me."

It was his turn to hesitate. He drew in a deep breath. "Lupe and her big mouth."

"Do not blame Lupe. She never told me anything. It was just a guess. And a pretty good one I see. What is her name? She is pretty?"

He saw the opening, but not the trap. "Si. She is pretty. But not so pretty as you."

"I compliment you. And thank you. You are engaged then."

"Of course not. She probably has another novio by now. We do not write. I have been through with her since —"

"Oh, a pity."

"I tell you I have not written her," he insisted fiercely.

A pause. Then, "Ramiro —"

"Pues."

"There is a dance at the school Saturday night."

"But I am asking you to be my novia."

"I have never asked a boy before. This is the dance where

the girls must ask the boys. "

"What must I do?"

"Nothing. "

"If you say yes. "

"To what?"

"To being my novia. "

"You must be dense, Ramiro. We do not do that here. "

"You mean — ? You girls are like Danny says, all alike. "

"And I suppose your novia still carries a jug of water on top of her head every day. "

"You have a sharp tongue on today. "

"How observant you are. "

"Margarita, I am sorry. I apologize. "

"Do you know what you are, Ramiro?"

"I said I apologize, girl. Please forgive me. "

"You are a prisoner of your own conceit. "

"Believe me, muchacha — "

"But you will soon grow up. "

"I plan to go ask your father's permission. "

She paled. "Whatever for, por el amor de dios?"

"Can you see, can you not see you have won, girl?"

"Won what? A prize? You?"

"Perhaps someone else will take you to the dance. "

"Perhaps. "

A scraping sound outside caused them to stop. Dan ran up to the door, outside. "Margarita, come quick! Papa is looking for you, and he is very, very mad. " He ducked away.

Ramiro grabbed her arm.

"There is Lupe now," she said, pulling away from his grasp.

"How long are you going to do this to me?" he demanded.

"Do what? Ramiro, let me go. "

"Keep me from our kiss. "

"You are crazy!"

"Yes. About you. "

Lupe came in carrying two bags of groceries, trailed by Manuelito and Mariquita. "Oh, thank you, Margarita, gracias. Do you know that Pepe — oh Ramiro, how pleased Manuel will be to see you. "

Ramiro stepped outside, following Margarita. "You are leaving?"

"My papa does not wish to see me with you. "

"He doesn't like me. So what, girl? It is not he I wish to marry. It is you, Margarita. "

She skipped away. She had heard him. She turned. Then she did a beautiful thing. She smiled and waved goodbye to him, beaming, waiting to be sure he saw. He stood there, accepting the full range of love from her heart, and then remained there watching her radiant form flying, wanting to be with her, wanting her with all his heart and soul and all his manhood.

Pepe was another problem.

Ramiro said adios to Lupe, promising to come back for the taco dinner she promised him, as a surprise her Manuel too. He cut out across the compound, pushing past screaming knots of kids, and went down a straight row of plums, taking the short cut to Pepe·s house diagonally across the fat acres. The plums felt good. He wondered what it would be like to own even one goddamn plum tree. His heart sang. He would plant at least one plum for Margarita, and from that they would branch out and raise a whole family of wholesome offspring. He was not prepared for Serafina, catching him in the back yard:

"No, no, Ramiro. You must not. Pepe is too angry."

"Angry? With me?"

"You must not go in."

It was too late.

"So there you are," grunted the tough old bull, standing in his doorway. "You son of a bitch. What do you want here?"

Ramiro held his ground, looking proudly back at his even prouder antagonist. "Pepe, you have no right to yell at me."

"Do not speak to me of rights, you filthy thief," cried Pepe. "I might have not known —"

"Yes? Known what?" Ramiro wanted to see Margarita, to see her eyes again, smiling. But this wasn't the time.

"My power drill is missing," said Pepe. "You were the only one, and the last one to use it."

Eh? What? The day Ramiro repaired the lock on the door — "But what I want your power drill for, man?"

"I want to look."

"To look? Where?"

"In your room."

"No."

"Why not? You hiding someting?"

"No, viejo." The ultimate insult Ramiro clenched to his teeth, real anger rising. He was not about to explain to this stupid old man the important lesson about one's honor, when one was innocent.

"Tell me this, then, desgraciado. What was my Margarita doing alone inside your room?"

Ramiro blanched. What was the matter with this old man? Sure that Margarita had also heard the false charge, he blushed for her. "She was never in my room, alone or —"

"They found all kinds of things in your room when you left."

"Like what? Who found them? That is Mr. Quill's tool room. Those are his tools in there. You know that, Pepe. Come on, what are you trying to do, hombre?" Ramiro was doing his best to keep his selfcontrol.

"Someone put it there on purpose, I suppose. My tires, my drill, my —"

Ramiro blanched again. "I have no way of knowing what are talking about. It is Mr. Quill's tool shed and I say somebody put it there. "

"Tell me another fairy tale. "

"I have nothing to hide, and I do not like your suspicions. "

"No? I suppose not. I wish to have a look nevertheless."

"You come near my hut and I shall break your back, viejo."

"Get away from here, ladron, you thief. Go. Get away and do not prejudice my doorway. " Pepe raised his arm threateningly, pointing across the prune orchard. Both were strong fierce men. Ramiro caught Margarita's fleeting face at the window.

This stupid Pepe had already convicted him.

This stupid, drunken old man.

Ramiro turned away, hurt, angry, and full of sorrow. He trotted off. The run made him feel better. He cooled off. He leaped the lowstone fence dividing the compound from the orchard with an easy leap, hand pressed to the wall. Mr. Quill was unhappy at seeing him. That sludgy flop of an excuse for a man. Mr. Quill had not the slightest idea what Ramiro was asking him about. Sure, he used Ramiro's room as an overflow and for his tools. Ramiro had insisted on having it.

Ramiro now had to start making some new rational moves toward reconnecting him with civilization again. He owed more than his life. He wouldn't blow the world up if he couldn't have his way. He was angry enough to, and now he had tensions that pulled him in opposite directions. Work — or no work. Margarita — or no love. It seemed now that he owed more than his life. A weird circumstance. How could he be so wrong? How could he deny something he had not done? Had it not been for Margarita, he would have gotten himself a trailer. That meant a car. Sure, a car too. He could get one. The motorcycle was fast and easy. And Mexico for the Mexicans. When would all California be his? The stupid Californios spoke with such stupid pride, and all with Anglo-Saxon names. Stupid lout, that Pepe. And Lupe complaining about a few lousy cockroaches. He, Ramiro Sanchez, was making choices every single instant that would affect the whole future of the entire race; I would rather be outlawed, he thought, than be embraced and smothered and mothered by your —

You won't last.

I WON'T?

Chrrrrrrrrrrrrrist —

Ah, you think because Christ failed, then —

Explain how you got the drill.

I never — Listen, I do not beat you because you are old. Explain.

I said I never.
Explain.
And because you are too drunk too boot.
You gypsy, you no good lousy chicano gypsy.
I never —
Listen. You keep way from my daughter, you hear?
Yes. Si. Sure. Ramiro heard all right. He heard her
screams too. He found Margarita huddled, crying in the darkness of the orchard's forest. She was looking for Lupe, and
was lost. He held her sobbing form lightly. I want to take you,
he whispered. I want you to be sure, he said. I want you to be
happy, he added urgently. She continued sobbing uncontrollably.
Lupe took her in, and later she told him why.
Pepe had actually accused her of sleeping with him.Worse,
with being pregnant by him. This gave Ramiro both an anger
and a thrill he couldn't control. But he had to control it. He
had someone else to think about now, beside himself. Pepe
had grabbed her by the hair of her head and had slammed her
against and again against the front door, banging her until she
nearly passed out. His own daughter. Go on, yelling at her,
get out, get to hell out of here, you puta. You prostitute, puta,
the worst possible thing a father could possible call a daughter
of his. Dizzy, her head reeling, hurt, grieving, she ran stumbling, she heard her mother screaming and frightened and
fighting him back: "You brave borracho. Hitting a grown woman. Doesn't that make you feel brave though. Come on, why
don't you hit me, you cabron. Come on, you coward. For
this I raise my children? For this indecency I pick your stupid prunes? Bah—" She spat at him. A sick man, Pepe. Caught
between the old and the new. The ideal and the promise. The
thought — and the desire.
"Bah — " said Pepe back, slamming out of the house.To
the bar, that's good, that's his god,"drown your sorrows in
your beer at the Golden Cork, you unspeakable borracho —"
Lupe took Margarita in with Serafina's approval. But
Margarita was far too mortified even to look at Ramiro's face.
To pay like this for love — !Ramiro understood. He kept away.
He would work. He would work hard. He would back off some
of his cynicism. He also had to avoid Pepe, for the fierce hos-
tility had risen too high for him to respond rationally. He had
never ever wanted to cripple another man and now, for the first
time, he experienced what it felt like to wish another man's
death. How could he? It was so foreign to him. He hated the
rich. But not to kill them. He wanted to be forceful and vigorous, but not violent. How could he come to hate his own kind,
his own people, when there were so many bigger, more hateful,
more despicable enemies all around?
He would simply have to keep out of Pepe's way.

He went out to the prunes, and the cots, and the cherries, and he studied Mr. Quill's running of the Western Grande for Mr. Turner, and he pitied them. Poor against poor. Rich for the rich. The age of the dinosaurs, unfeeling, uncaring, gluttonous appetites, grabbing, stuffing, cramming, taking more more more. And to hell with the rest — they are ants. Human — ants! But Ramiro didn't care. He knew he would do what he could. Deep in his heart he knew he could build a truly new and truly wonderful and truly moral and truly unselfish and truly happy and truly unselfish world with his Margarita. At least he could — once he had the idea — he could try.

No more would he have to or even want to wander.

Ramiro had found home for his restless spirit at last. He had his youth. He had his fierce hunger, and he had his ambition.

He would make California his own.

All he needed was opportunity — and he had that too. Margarita would help him get a better education. Manuel too was working his way out. And soon, this year maybe, Manuel'd get Lupe the washer and drier she wanted to have. Manuel had only his brute strength, too true, but he had it good. The growers were being forced to pay more and more every passing year. Sickness? Even a highly educated man who got sick had to lose some income. The dream was now his: the thing was to proceed, to make the best of it, to make the American system a human system, to grow, to save, to plan, to plant, to buy, to invest. Invest in futures. Send their kids through school. And keep them going to school. Ramiro wanted to have at least a dozen kids with Margarita, all Sanchezes, and soon all California was going to be swamped with Mexican lawyers, Mexican teachers, Mexican jigsaw puzzle makers, Mexican judges, and even a Mexican County Supervisor here and there. And there would still be enough dump plum pickers left over to keep the rich sober and happy — provided they gave honest pay for honest work honestly offered.

Ramiro. Listen. I have these beeg secret.

Lupe. Do not tell me, embustero. Why do you not go to the fortune teller?

Ramiro. How should I tell him? Should I just say, say, gobernador, old man, viejo, could you know that California really belongs to old Mejico?

Governor (Really Howlin Mad) Nolan. How's that again?

Lupe. You are crazy, Ramiro.

Manuel. Well, now. Maybe he's not.

Lupe. Sure he is. Who can fight the rich?

Ramiro. You really want to know?

193

Lupe. I can tell you myself.

Ramiro. What would you do?

Manuel. He is right, corazon. We would do nothing.

Ramiro. OK. I will tell you what I have against the staid Americanos. The incredibly stupid Americanos. They have everything going for them, right? Life, liberty, the pursuit of happiness, right? And you know what they do? They blow the fuse. Over inconsequentials. They worry about house payments and communists and rackets and college uprisings, and they let the racketeers get bigger and fatter and greedier — in order to save a few rotten pennies on the fruit for their table. What I got against the gringos is they don't give a she yit how good they eat provided they eat good.

Manuel. If you don't like it here, they'll tell you you can go back where you can. Or came from.

Ramiro. I am back. This is where I came from. Right here. And here is where I'll stay. I'll starve. I'll take it. I'll be an Indian again. I can still laugh.

Lupe. I wish I could.

Ramiro. The sun looks good. Doesn't the sun look good? Why shouldn't it be good to us, then? The rains look good too. The land is the whole treasure. The land and the sun. The land, the sun, the seeds, the trees, and the rains. That's it. That's everything. The Sun is God and the water and the earth and the fertilizers and the seeds and the pesticides and all of them give off great wealth, and our problems are solved. Why the hell should we starve and turn over our human joy to some miserable psychopathic millionaires just because they got here first and managed to garbage a few solid land titles to their names? Doesn't humanity count for anything? Does the individual inventor invent or, as Einstein said, does the whole human race invent? Share, then, and share alike. Sure. It sounds like utopia. And like a lie. But why should there be misery and war and pestilence and other miseries on the face of the globe when humanity has already solved all of those miseries long ago. ? I'll tell you why — because of greed. Greed is the greatest sin of all. Do you know why they don't make a big issue of it? Because they are the greediest of all themselves. These idiotic millionaires speak of building up these orchards as though they did it all with their own hands. They lie to the end. They hire me and you, Manuel, all of us Mexicans to do it al, to do all the hard work with the earth, with our own land. What a lie. It is only right that the land should revert to us.

Manuel. They will only run you out.

Lupe. Well, I see you have some sense, after all, Manuel. But Ramiro has a dream. I do not know what Margarita thinks. Why do you want to get us into fights, Ramiro, and all that trouble? Why can't you let things be? You'll get stopped or fired or killed or run out. You can't do it all yourself.

Ramiro. That is very true, little sister. Do you want me to stop?

Lupe. No.

Ramiro. I thought not. They certainly do have marvelous jails in Rio Grande City. They even serve the most marvelous frijoles on white platters and they c all it the blue plate special. A kind of joke. They even have a doctor there ready with a band aid when they crack your head open and the blood flows.

Captain McAllee. You're no mmmmminister.

Ramiro. I said doctor.

Priest. God bless you.

Ranger KK. You goddem blackrobe son a bitch if you dont shut chure mouf I'll knock you goddem cross back down you troat you goddem son on a bitch you.

Priest. May God bless you my son.

Ranger KK. Don't call me your fukkin son. That ain't true. Now I dint say that, judge.

Judge. Well, what did you say, son.

Ramiro. He say —

Captain McAllee. Shut up you Metsican basturd. You let ma Ranger talk, heah. Ah nevah tell no lies, yoah honah.

Ranger KK. Yeah, these goddem furriners. All ah say is they goddem better do what ah say cause ah uphold The Law.

Ramiro. Where you say you from, Ranger?

Captain McAllee. Well, we are all here to protext the treatment that us legally consituted amurrican shootin-arn lawabiding lawmen have been abused hereabouts by these heah riffraff who instead a going out and planting the celery stalks decently like they oughta, cause us to get up early and our knuckles all bruised up.

Judge. Personally, I have always felt I can get high with my own body and senses and don't need no drugs or nothing like to go take a trip on. In other words, I don't drink, except to get a little bit high on now or then.

Ramiro. When you going to give us California back?

Captain McAllee. I don't keer bout that so long's you keep outa my Texas range. I swear I have never drawn one single precious drap a blood protecting the rights of the poor downtrodden ranchers, rangers, orchard owners, and celery growers except, of course, where it was absolutely necessary. I just bangbang away with my bb but usually I tries to aim high over their sonsabitching eyes. Somepin must be wrong with my aim, Judge. I never hits 'em. You ever have that trouble, Judge?

Padre. Every time you strike, you strike yourself.

Captain McAllee. I HATE strikes. I truly do.

Ranger KK. Simple assau salt and abba and abba —

Padre. Battery, son.

Judge. I'll just help meself to a nother delicious serving o these here delicious tacos and enchiladas a while.

Ramiro. May all you gringo guero bastards rest in peas.

Captain McAllee. I sure don't get it why the bastard hates us so much, not that I give a good friggin haul.

Ramiro. That's right.

Captain McAllee. What's right?

Ramiro. Aren't we your brothers' tools?

Judge. Boy, I sure pass.

Ramiro. Why do you hate us, Captain?

34

It felt real good. Yessir, it felt real good for once to be throwing his weight around like that. Yessir, sirreeee.

Mr. Quill was finally catching on.

He'd show this scum, this riffraff, these migrating prune rotaters who really was boss around here. Mr. Turner was boss, thass who. Mr. Turner, and his Golden State Prune Pachydermal Packers Assn Combined Inc., was also who.

For the first time in their relationship, Mr. Turner actually complimented Mr. Quill for a good job well done. Unbeknownst to Mr. Quill, Mr. Turner had run a computer and was carefully laying the groundwork for the small one-dollar-fifty-cent raise a week he'd been thinking of giving him, and Mr. Turner did not want it to appear that he was doing it out of simple generosity. Tall, thin, and saturnine, wearing his spats and his regular dark bolue business-striped suit with his orange ascot puffed out before him, Mr. Turner pulled up in front of the compound office in his long, sleek, dark baloo business-striped car. He took a quick look around the compound, wrinkling his long, thin, dark, bland business-striped nose, pressing his lips firmly together in a perverse way, and nodded meaninglessly to himself. Within his office, Mr. Quill stood by meekly at attention while his boss made his usual careful perusal of the stupid ledger before asking his usual incisive questions, while downing his usual royal pint of the Best Imported Scotch Whiskey right in front of Mr. Quill's nasal cavities, and sighing and smacking his lips as he slowly turned to stone.

That was the moment.

Mr. Turner looked up and actually grinned at Mr. Quill.

Mr. Quill was severely shocked by the unexpected smile.

For his second shock, Mr. Quill noticed that all of Mr. Turner's formerly smoke-blackened teeth had either been brightened artificially or replaced. Mr. Turner actually looked friendly. Was he getting ready to present himself to the voters?

It was at that moment that Mr. I. T. T. Turner took advantage of his confusion to tell him of his impending raise.

Mr. Quill nearly passed out, out of gratitude.

Mr. Trueheart Turner, tweaking his ascot, tried making light of it. "Six more crates, eh, Quill? Good man. Great. Just great, Quill. " Back to business. Mr. Turner took a long last heady pull from his joy bottle and then tossed it emptily back on Mr. Quill's cot where he thought the garbage bucket was. Mr. Turner disliked guerillas, but he disliked gratitude in people even more, which was why he was brushing Mr. Q. off. "Well, let's scrounge through them later on, Quill. Worthless, probably. What could there be of any worth? Junk ha ha just like the rest of it. As usual. Now, good man, Q. You are doing just fine. " Then he left, walking straight as a ramrod without even once bending his knees.

Outside, inside the compound, a wicked new brush fire of resentment was a smoldering fiercely among the inmates.

In place of the usual fake smiles and the hypocritical hand waves whenever he waltzed around the compound, Mr. Quill was now getting nothing but hard stares and icy spines. Well, he was showing them. Good he didn't give one good gad dinggg dong any more. Nossir. Not no more. He wasn't running for Senator. If it was a tight fight they wanted, they would get it. If — a good doggone dog fight. To the finish if necessary.

Now that Mr. Turner's polished political say-so in town and all over the prune country was practically all wrapped up, and with his name coming up in the headlines and in short TV commercial bursts as his proud political party's next nominee for Senator — after first, of course, flouting the current incumbent — and there was even talk of getting good old Bagpants as well as even HMN up on the boards once more for a smart hut hut song and soft shoe in memory of their good old stoopover days, when they stoooed over to thank their rich benefactors — and also with Mr. Turner's showing an increased warmth toward him, there just wasn't no telling how high Mr. Quill's feathery fortune might soar. Or, like the sun, rise.

Since everybody in this small world must earn a living, Mr. Quill was dogtired of having to carry more than his share of miseries on his thin round shoulders. He didn't mind some occasional abuse — it was all part of the breaks — like that poor Mrs. Pope, poor angel — but no, no, not even in her case. That sloth she had for a belated husband wasn't even batting out any more. So since their, since they obviously had no use for their good old used car any more, Mr. Quill sincerely chained it up also to their bright green hitching post in the bright golden sunshine along with the others he captured. What a thrill. A real thrill. A real sense of power. It might even run the slug off. Maybe Mrs. Pope would come to him crying for help. Maybe she would ask him if she he he if if if maybe. . . . .

But the blond slug came out slugging. The earliest Mr. Q. had ever seen him shift. "Now just don't you yodel at me like that, Mr. Pope." Mr. Quill calmly cradled the telephone receiver in his catnip mitt like a Luger. "This here things' loaded. There's the bus schedule tacked to the wall. Gawd,go study it. Awghrrrrrrr—" Mr. Quill's feet dangled in the air. "Ro pppppqqrrrrrr," he gurgled. Pope let him down, quivering like jelly. "All right, Pope. Just this one last time. Just this one last time you can have your old car back."

He went out and unlocked the trembling padlock from the shiny bumper and Pope took off like a jet whine's rump with a mighty big rrrrroar.

Mrs. Pope was also in trouble. She was frantic. Mr. Quill told her: "Look here, Mrs. Pope. I'm sorry, but you are going to have to leave your little boy behind here with us in The Warehouse assecurity for your good faith and will in paying us what you owe." He didn't even realize what he was saying any more, that that was tantamount to kidnapping, a federal offense. She rushed away weeping and sobbing. Some of the other delinquent ladies came instantly to her side. One rushed back to her own husband who as it happened happened to be lying on his side resting himself. This splendid fruit tickler shot straight up into the air as though stuck in the behind with a hot pole valut and he rocked out in his unchained car and whooooooshed out into the free air.

High way of life.
What a grand.
A grand feeling.
To be on top for once.
Prunes.
That's what they needed —
To get off their behinds.

Mr. Quill, on top of this world. Ho ho. The Santa Claus of Santa Clara County at last. Swinging from the highest maypole. High as an elephant's eye and all that corn. What whirls and gigs. Never in his life had he ever felt so doggone sure of himself, and without being drunk. He sure was running a tight ship. For once. Captain Q. Q. Quill. A key they wanted eh. A key for their cars. "....the fact that he tried to obtain a key surreptitiously after having been turned down by this office originally, the fact that he cannot replace certain items of equipment and supply because of lack of funds and/or availability...." There. That would show them. He ran back inside his little office for a small slug of wine. Why not. A big slug. Glug glug. They might even give him a ship. Or name a Santa Clara high school after him. Yes. Yessir. Maybe hell, he might even become Mayor of Drawbridge hisself, if Turner turned it down. What a pair they would make ho ho, and at Christmas. At last he knew what it was to be really hated.

That night was an unusually warm and wilted night. An ominous quiet hummed in the monlight. He didn't care. Let them. The women tethered up their stray brats early. Good. The message to Garcia man didn't return, at least not while Quill was still up. He could lift his eyes off the old TV and instanter recognize any car passing by his office window, in or out.

Good.

The quicker Pope came back, the quicker he'd finish him off. Quill fished in four more new sets of prune pickers, really coming in now, dropped them into their slug tanks, and got ready to turn himself in. He checked the blinkers to make sure the outside light was still winking, and checked the empty stalls to make sure they were still empty.

Good.

Now, except for some shrieking of kids and socking of wives, the place was almost dead. After a while the quietus began to get to him, a little. He didn't like it. It seemed eerie, unnatural. But then he didn't have to like it. Neither did he like what they were doing to him, the forty-cent scum. Cars kept humming by the highway. He was finding it difficult to fall asleep. Too many things had happened that day.

All of a sudden, around midnight, a terrific din, sounding like a jangle of trash cans smashing and crashing together, brought him to full alert. A drunk?

He got up. He was wide awake. The stiff whiff of fresh night air felt good. There was no moon. The moon was gone. He stumbled about in the bleak blackness looking for the cause of the noise. A dog? Howling with sharp pain? With a thrill of uncontrollable pleasure he noticed Pope's car had balked in. There it was, in its usual place. Quill galloped to his office and rushed back with a chain and bolted the offensive bumper to its hitching post. He was about to snap the padlock when suddenly waaoooooooooof! he felt himself grabbed from behind by a thick wad of greasy cloth jammed into his mouth.

Horror stricken — unable to make out his tormentors — he saw he was swiftly being, resolutely, determinedly being carried straight back toward the barely visible Hangem Tree, its brackish black branches etched against a barely visible buttermilk sky.

Mr. Turner showed up at dawn.

Quill, drat his hide, hadn't made his usual morning call, nor had he answered the phone.

Mr. Turner took a look around the early morning yard.

Not a sign of Quill anywhere.

Drat him, murmured Turner, not like him at all.

Lupe's sharp, shrill scream sliced the cool morning air into thin shivers as she recoiled in horror from the sight of the fat dumpy potbellied little body dangling from the Hangman's Tree behind her shack.

Turner ran up.

"Black Bart's" sign was tacked not on the straw dummy, but to Quill's chilled pot. Someone rushed to the public phone. A siren flailed the distant air. Trembling with rage, Turner looked at the slowly twirling corpse. Shaking his thin blue fist at the outrageous heavens, he grated, "Drat your scurvy hide, Quill! I'll, I'll, I'll —"

The corpse swayed slightly, now facing him, now turning away, its ratty little teeth exposed from the force of the rope's relentless pull, grinning. Mr. Turner started to run. But the siren and the police and the reporters were already blocking his way, blocking his compound, blocking in the stories reprobating him unjustly. Now he was going to have to kick hell out of Howlin Mad Nolan to try to grab the governor's ship for himself.

But now, right now the main question was, how in hell was he going to find enough new prune pickers right away? Now, smack dab in the middle of the goddem ripest picking season? The plums sure didn't know. All they did was merely keep right on ripening. Relentlessly.

*

ABOUT the AUTHOR

Born in New Jersey, Raymond Barrio is Spanish-American.
He lives in Santa Clara, California, with his Mexican-born
wife, Yolanda S. Ocio de Barrio, and their four young
children. The family is bilingual.

He has lived in California most of his life. A WWII
(European theater) veteran, he attended various colleges
including CCNY, USC, Yale, University of California at
Berkeley, and Art Center College of Design in L.A.

He has taught art at Ventura College
and UC Santa Barbara, now teaches
at West Valley College in Campbell.

He has published numerous articles
in art and travel magazines; his
short fiction has appeared in
various literary magazines.
This is his seventh book.

BY the AUTHOR

The Big Picture. 1967
Experiments in Modern Art. 1968
Selections from Walden. 1968
Prism. 1968
Art:Seen. 1968
The Fisherman's Dwarf. 1968
The Plum Plum Pickers. 1969

71 72 73 74   12 11 10 9 8 7 6 5 4 3 2 1